gotta have it

gotta have it

RENÉE ALEXIS

APHRODISIA

KENSINGTON PUBLISHING CORP.
http://www.kensingtonbooks.com

APHRODISIA books are published by

Kensington Publishing Corp.
850 Third Avenue
New York, NY 10022

All Kensington Titles, Imprints, and Distributed Lines are available at special quantity discounts for bulk purchases for sales promotions, premiums, fund-raising, and educational or institutional use.

Special book excerpts or customized printings can also be created to fit specific needs. For details, write or phone the office of the Kensington special sales manager: Kensington Publishing Corp., 850 Third Avenue, New York, NY 10022, attn: Special Sales Department, Phone: 1-800-221-2647.

Aphrodisia and the A logo are trademarks of Kensington Publishing Corp. Kensington and the K logo Reg. U.S. Pat & TM Off.

ISBN 0-7582-1392-1

First Kensington Trade Paperback Printing: January 2006

10   9   8   7   6   5   4   3   2

Printed in the United States of America

Contents

Acknowledgments

Thanks to: First and foremost, God, for everything he has given me. My family for putting up with me during the crazy writing frenzies. Love you, Mom! D.W., you know who you are and I will always love you, wherever you are. Jason, love always. Fannie, a forever friend. Hilary S., thanks for believing in me and putting up with question after question—all my love, girl! Deatri, thanks for everything. My friends who encouraged me, keep it coming.

Renee

reacquainted

The Kenneth Cole stilettos were damn near killing her, and to make matters worse, her flight to Los Angeles was delayed four hours. Hearing that wonderful tidbit of news didn't exactly make her dance a jig from supreme excitement. Her entire day had been hectic; interviewing prospective *Sports Illustrated* models, many of them with mini brains and maxi mouths, and whenever she made it the hell to L.A., she'd have to do it all again—and attend a business seminar. Nonetheless, that was the life of a successful modeling agency owner. Her midtown office had gorgeous young women practically crawling through the sewer systems to get in. Business was good, but not something she could do here, and thanks to American Airlines, she now had an additional four hours to stew.

Her only thought: *What the hell does someone do in Midway Airport for hours other than read all the tabloids and drink themselves to death in the overly expensive airport bar?* There *was* nothing else to do to the immediate observer, but Ms. Caroline Pierce had just the plan: veg-out at her gate and continue to salivate over what she had seen last night.

As she sat on the excruciatingly hard chairs by Gate 3B, a smile lit up her delicate, medium brown face. Marc Brown had graced her new thirty-five-inch plasma television the night before. He was in a duel to the death with every one of the Minnesota Twins batters and nailed them all. God, she hadn't seen him in years, since her senior year in high school. All she knew was that he'd been the love of her ever-loving life back then, and seeing him last night made the intensity of the memory that much more intolerable. He was beautiful from the bill of his hat to the cleats of his shoes, and the muscles . . . oh, my God! Marc was always stacked, but age and experience seemingly licked him with a magic tongue, because he glistened. Sheesh!

Normally baseball didn't "do it" for her, but there were no vintage Gregory Peck movies on TNT last night, and she needed something to keep her senses alive. The Alize and the mandarin orange salad certainly weren't doing it—Marc did it, yes, yes, yes! Last she remembered, he entered the Cubs organization, married that twit Iisha Burns and moved into a giant castle of a mansion somewhere in Joliet, never to appear before Caroline's eyes again. Many a day she'd thought about him, wondered how he was, and if he could slam in bed the way he'd waxed her in the shower that long-ago night? *My goodness, Marc Brown.*

Caroline's face continued to glow as she thought about the fight on the mound; that's what had made her spill the Alize on her fresh new baby blue carpeting. It was still there that morning. Come to think of it, Alize had been Iisha's drink of choice back in the day at sixteen years old. Seemingly the minute Iisha was weaned from the breast her next move was to the corner liquor store for a bottle of Alize Red Devil. That's exactly what Iisha was back then, a damn red devil, and she had taken Marc into her fiery pit.

Her mind went back to the game. Marc had been accused of hitting a batter; the batter approached the mound and the fists flew in a heated rage. Marc was a fighter and had been since day one of the twelfth grade. Before she knew anything, there was a pile of buff, sweaty, sinfully sexy men tangled up together, throwing punches and ripping away jerseys. In the middle of the chaos was Marc, shirt pulled up his back, stomach muscles heaving in and out, sweat dripping into every single crevice of his body, and delivering punches that surely burned like white fire. Yes, fighting was definitely his thing and he was all man. The bulge in his pants proved that. Sure, there may have been a jockstrap helping that massive tenting, but from experience, she knew it was all Marc and could still feel him invading her body, latching on and climbing deeper into her sunny afternoon over and over again. He lived for a challenge, always had and apparently still did, the way he was being pulled off three men.

Far be it from her to enjoy a fight—she'd always cried when he got into brawls, which was hardly ever because boys only tested his waters knee deep. Having the only boy she'd ever cared about injured or marred would have traumatized her, but Marc always came out smelling like a rose. The same for the mound brawl. Marc had just a small scratch on him and she was thankful, but the idea of seeing him dragged away by his teammates, jersey up to his neck, really did it for her. Everything she remembered licking and rubbing years ago was there, to her delight: perky dark brown nipples, so damn lickable, pecs sweet enough to eat sugar from and an outie of a navel juicy enough to make her lose control. Due to him, baseball was for real her favorite sport now, and kissing Marc seductively with her nectar dripping onto him was her favorite fantasy.

Just thinking of Marc made almost two hours go by. She could imagine people's expressions as they passed her, practically having monstrous orgasms over what seemed to be thin air. She didn't care, though. Marc was embedded in her mind and nothing could cure it but tasting him again, if only for a few seconds. She loved him beyond human reasoning, but thought by now she'd gotten over him. No way, one look into his large hazel eyes and a chance to scope his rich, honey brown skin had turned her into a quivering teenager again, only in a thirty-two-year-old body.

As she licked her parched lips, people started running past

her, women, screaming with crazed looks on their faces while security guards scampered right behind them. Immediately she grabbed her purse in case some terrorist attack was about to go down. Normally, running, screaming people scared the crap out of her, but she followed behind them out of curiosity down the long concourse. She tried to look over the heads of what seemed to be thousands of people populating Gate F19 but could see nothing.

Upon getting closer, she saw the crowd circling a man, pulling at him, clawing him in an orgasmic frenzy. Finally, security made everyone step back and there was ... Marc Brown, trying his best to sign as many autographs as possible. From the square jaw, broad shoulders and deliciously tapered waistline ... nothing had changed other than him getting sexier. How was that possible? In high school he was already a baby version of eye candy, but now, he was the whole candy aisle! Looking at him was like stepping out of a delicious dream; her mouth gaped, eyes widened and everything feminine in her wanted to yell out, *Get over here now, Marc, and take me apart!* He was actually within her reach after all those years of aching for him and there was no way she was going to let him go, Iisha or no Iisha!

The crowd stayed forever, but no matter how long it took, she knew she'd wait there for him. Caroline just stared, remembering how he'd never failed to treat her like a lady no matter what she looked like back then; the boy who rocked her world the moment she first laid eyes on him. ...

Marc Brown was not a geek in school who wore floods with street shoes and pencil holders on his chest pocket. No, Marc was born fly, had his act together since kindergarten, where the girls probably fought for his attention even then. Caroline was one of them. School had only been in session for one week when she first saw him. It was early Monday morning and English Lit was boring the hell out of her, though she was good with the subject. It was just too early in the morning to have to concentrate on Shakespeare's *Much Ado About Nothing*. Math and science were her true loves, but she was well rounded, and all the kids knew that. That was how they got Caroline to do their homework for them, and she did it because she wanted to fit in.

The way she looked, she assumed she'd have to do damn near anything to even be an associate friend. But it hadn't worked in ninth, tenth, or eleventh grade at Valley View. What made her think it would happen in her senior year? Hope, prayers, and the need for a new start. Despite how much she looked like a boy with barely-there tits, in-between hair length and a face that even makeup couldn't help, she always had hope for new and better things for herself. It was a new year at Valley View and although she knew she'd have to probably do someone's Shakespeare homework, she felt good about the semester.

The morning in question, Caroline actually had the gall to try some of her older sister's makeup. She didn't know why she had that inner feeling to look better that day than any other. All she knew was that something was changing with her. She smeared the powdery pink blush across her light, ashy-brown cheek and smiled into the mirror. It looked good, so she did the other side. Once satisfied with how she looked, she picked up the MAC Peachy Delight lip gloss and applied it. It even tasted like fresh fruit. That was the main reason she liked it. Her hair still looked like she'd slept with a jackhammer so she ran a comb through it, slid in a few crystal butterfly barrettes, and called it a day. Her clothes—well, she knew it took more than a day to turn a frog into a princess. The worn jeans and vintage Jim Morrison T-shirt remained.

That was another thing about her; she was the only African American teenager, to her knowledge, to like The Doors. To her, they were cool. All the other chicks were rockin' around the clock, with whoever was climbing the stage to stardom, and of course, there was Mr. Timeless, Prince. Though "International Lover" was old, the teens had rediscovered the part where he sexed-down a microphone. It even rattled her hormones on an occasion or two.

Caroline took one final look at her persona, grabbed her books and headed through the door, hoping her mother would not be around to see the awesome transformation of her child. She waved good-bye to her mother and ducked to the front door; then it happened: "Caroline? Come in here a minute."

Damn, double damn! "I'll be late for school."

"Just get in here. This won't take too much of your day away from you."

Caroline slowly poked half of her face into the kitchen, hoping her makeup couldn't be seen. "Yes, mother."

"You know the Honda is down and I can't leave the house until your father—wait a second. Step in here and let me see you."

The jig was up and the floor was open to all commentary. "I'm going to be late."

Her mother eyed the fusion of pink and ashy brown and delivered a half smile between cigarette puffs. "Now I know why you took an awfully long time in the bathroom this morning. Normally it's an in-and-out mission with you; barely having time to brush your teeth. Come on, get in here."

The last thing she wanted to do was step into a smoke and coffee-smelling kitchen and have her *own mother* poke fun at her sudden desire to look like a fashion queen. Those kinds of things happened in that house. Though everyone loved her dearly, they were used to her being constant, the same thing over and over, figuring she wouldn't be Caroline if she changed one iota.

Despite the ridicule she knew she'd get, she stepped into the kitchen. Her mother was sitting next to an overly loud tiny television with Maury's face all over the screen. Mrs. Pierce was puffing the stinkiest shit in all America, a menthol Camel. "Yes, mother?"

Mrs. Pierce's eyes narrowed. "Is that Carla's makeup I see on you?"

"She said I could use it."

Her mother smiled and shook her head in agreement. "I'm glad. It's about time you start doing girl things instead of doing everyone's homework to be liked. Your brother Casey told me last night. What's been going on for the last two years? No more of that, Caroline and I mean it. You have enough to do."

"But mom, I—"

Mrs. Pierce's brow raised. "Do I need to contact parents? I *can* get numbers."

"No, mother. Is that what you wanted to talk to me about?"

"Yes, mostly." She tossed a five Caroline's way. "On the way home, stop at Morrow's Market and get some bread."

A smile curved her sparkling pink lips. "Can I keep the change?"

"Yeah, buy a tube of Cover Girl for yourself. You look pretty today."

"I do?"

"You're always pretty to me because you're Momma's baby. I hate those clothes, though. Let's work on that." Mrs. Pierce's eyes zeroed in on the Jim Morrison shirt. "What the hell makes a black girl like a dead, crazy-ass rock star?"

"He was cute, mom, and he was a genius."

Mrs. Pierce took a long drag from her cancer stick, and slowly rolled the smoke from her mouth. "Yeah, being cute and ingenious got him far, didn't it? HE'S DEAD!"

"Whatever. I've got to go."

The moment Caroline stepped foot in school, the hoochies took notice and laughed like crazy. As she continued down the bright blue-and-white colored halls, everyone stopped and stared, pointing while whispering. Caroline didn't care, she simply chalked it up to them being bitches from hell with nothing else in life to do. That was the case until Iisha Burns, the top hoochie, stopped kissing whatever jock was lip-locked to her, and took notice of the scene.

Iisha, who dogged everyone not in her clique, stepped into sack-chaser mode. She approached Caroline with her hand on her hip, her short white-and-blue cheerleader outfit and overly done up plastic face. "Umm! Who the hell you thank you is suddenly, *me*? Like that shit will ever happen!" At that, she broke out in hysterics. That was everyone else's cue to laugh because no one moved until Iisha Burns said so. She owned the school and everyone in it other than Caroline, who she wasn't interested in purchasing.

Caroline stood there feeling rather sorry for herself as the clique of hoochies took off for class. Since ninth grade, she'd had a dislike for Iisha. She couldn't see what the boys saw in Iisha; she was bony, arrogant and always looked like she was constipated. Maybe the boys liked the way her lips poked out in a wanna-be-pretty look, but as far as Caroline was concerned, at any time, Iisha would become mayor of Hoochie-ville.

With only minutes to go before the bell rang, she hustled to English Lit, where she knew she'd have to endure more of Iisha's abuse. She was okay with that, though, because the day seemed special for some reason.

Halfway through the class, the door opened and in stepped the prettiest boy she'd ever seen. One look at him made her realize why she'd had a premonition to doll up a bit. The class became quiet. Even Iisha stopped running her mouth long enough to see the new student. All of a sudden, she had a dreamy, faraway look on her arrogant face. When the teacher announced him as Marc Brown, Caroline smiled from ear to ear. He was known around the city as the hottest prospect in minor league baseball. After graduation, Marc would be on his way to the Cubs farm system and Valley View was the launching pad.

Iisha's eyes followed him clear across the room as he was escorted to a seat near Caroline. After smiling, trying to get Marc's attention, she threw Caroline an expression that would have melted an iceberg. Not that Caroline cared. What got her attention was Marc smiling her way. Boys normally didn't smile at Caroline because they were too busy asking her if she was someone's lab experiment. Those miserable memories vanished the minute Marc's dazzling eyes met hers.

While the teacher was deep into Shakespeare, Marc passed her a note. *"As you know, I'm new here. Can you show me around later?"*

Caroline quickly read the note and bobbed her head like an excited puppy dog. Throughout class, she'd cop stares at him, imagining he was kissing her, making her feel like a real teenager for once, wondering how his bare skin would feel against hers. He looked so good in his tight jeans and Lake Shore High team jacket, good enough to eat up and lick like a lollypop. Just how to do that, she wasn't sure. Her only knowledge of the male anatomy came from her father's medical books that she and her sister used to salivate over, but only when it came to the genital areas. Since then, her sister Carla was making moves on real men over at Illinois State.

Marc and Caroline decided to meet for lunch so she could show him the ropes of Valley View High. At twelve on the dot, Caroline saw Marc sitting in the cafeteria at a table by himself and smiled almost uncontrollably. She missed him already since they didn't have second and third hour together.

As she approached the table, Iisha and her damn friends rushed in, almost pushing Caroline into a trash can, and heading in Marc's direction. Knowing Marc saw the action, she assumed he'd think her a wuss for not fighting back. Caroline slowly left the cafeteria as Iisha and her clones took over Marc's mind and probably his body. *Bloodsuckers usually do that, you know?* On her way back out, she cursed Iisha under her breath, hoping Iisha would roll her eyes one time too many and they'd stick in place. *Yeah, that'd be really sexy to the boys, wouldn't it?* The thought of it made her happy as she sat alone at an outdoor picnic table to eat her lunch. . . .

The autograph seekers around Marc managed to dwindle to only a few people. Caroline could really see him now, so sexy, so hot. But would he feel the same about her? That's what concerned her; time had separated them, and maybe by now he'd only see her as someone from his past, not a woman who'd totally transformed from that shy little nerd he had to pull from her shell. Knowing it was a possibility Marc would never really be in her life again, she thought of the invitation she'd received years ago to his wedding. What on earth did he or any boy see in Iisha? Was it that Iisha readily gave it up? Could be, and in that case, what would have possessed her to wear a white wedding gown? She'd screwed all of Peoria by then. Caroline remembered her very thoughts as she'd watched Iisha walk down the aisle. *Why didn't she wear rolling flames with red pumps like other devils do?* She half expected Iisha to hold up a fist when the minister asked if anyone objected to the union.

Just why was Iisha still a major thorn in her ass after more than a decade of hardly having to think of her? Life was like that, but Caroline knew she was the one who was supposed to be with Marc . . . they were meant to be together.

In school, she used to study him much the same way she was doing while he signed autographs. Others at Valley View were studying French, English, Calculus, but she was studying Biology—his.

Caroline regained her composure in time to see Marc smiling and approaching her. He'd recognized her, smiling as though he was happy to see her. Then her nerves kicked into gear and fear tingled through her body, but not fear of him—fear of not feeling worthy of him.

She wanted to move to him, meet him halfway but her feet

wouldn't budge. She was too nervous to move, though that hadn't stopped her from smiling at him, wanting him near her. As he got closer, she saw remnants of his fight: a small cut across his cheek, a bruise on his chin; they looked so super-sexy that she couldn't help herself and reached out to him.

Marc stopped dead in front of her, taking her delicate hand in his. "Damn, Caroline Pierce! How have you been? Where have you been?"

"My God! I thought that was you, Marc."

He quickly dropped his luggage and they embraced one another. Feeling Marc Brown in her arms again almost gave her another orgasm, one she hadn't had since her last boy-friend a year ago. No matter who she'd dated within those twelve years, there was no one like Marc. He was the only man who truly felt good in her arms.

Her body pressed into his, feeling him return as much emo-tion if not more. Her voice lit up with glee as she answered his question. "Ummm, I'm fine, Marc, just fine." She could feel her own voice vibrate against his warm neck. He felt so damn good, and he was bigger than he used to be; taller, thicker. Damn, seeing him in the raw again would be too much for her nerves but she was willing to risk it.

Stepping back to take a good gander at him was a must, but before she could truly see him, he planted the sweetest kiss upon her lips, tasting her fully, as if they'd made love just a few minutes ago.

For Marc, feeling his best friend within his arms again made him instantly hard. He couldn't believe he was looking at her again, feeling her body against his again. Twelve years was a damn long time not to feel perfection. His hands moved up and down her silk business suit, his lips moved to her neck. He didn't care where they were or who was watch-ing them. After tenderly nuzzling her neck, he faced her, tak-ing in all the beauty that adorned her. She was magnificent, had grown lovelier with time. Caroline Pierce had to be the only woman who could make him speechless. As he looked at her, his words slowed. "I . . . I can't believe this is you. Where have you been, girl? I tried to find you a few times."

"I've been here, Marc. I've been here since graduating from Joliet University. I own Maxim's Modeling Agency here in Chicago. In fact, I'm off to L.A to interview prospective *Sports Illustrated* models."

"A modeling agency? *Sports Illustrated* models? Are you one of them?"

She beamed at him. "I'll never look that good."

"The hell you say. Look at you, a successful business owner, beautiful as all get out. I knew you were smart, Caroline; smart and beautiful."

"You really think that?"

"I always have. You know that, Caroline."

"Yet you married Iisha and not me."

He rubbed his chin and delivered a little laugh. "Let's not get into Iisha. She's a totally different story."

"You two have been married about eleven years now, right?"

He retrieved his carry-on from the ground and slung it over his shoulder. "Actually, Iisha and I have been divorced for three years."

A terrible amount of glee spread across her face, though she tried hiding it from him. "I'm . . . I'm sorry to hear that."

"I'm not. Those were the longest eight years I ever spent anywhere."

"Well, it's over now and you can live your life." *Good! Iisha was never the type to satisfy anything other than her own lust for a man's ATM card, and with Marc, she had access to plenty of dead presidents.*

"I tried finding you, Caroline, but every time I got the chance I was called out of town." He looked at his watch. "Can we finish our talk after I return from baggage claim?"

"I can go with you."

"No, that's a long way and I'd hate for you to be stressed-out walking in those heels—which, by the way, look so incredible on you."

"Wear a pair of these puppies and you'll sing another tune."

"Nonetheless, you look sensational. Tell you what, let me get my bag, toss it in the trunk, then we can get reacquainted all over again, maybe get a drink. What time does your flight leave?"

"Actually, the plane is very late. Mechanical problems."

"Good for me. I have more time to spend talking to you. You want to grab a drink or something?"

"Funny you should say that. When I heard the commotion at your gate, I was thinking about you, not expecting to see you enter Midway Airport."

"I usually come in with the team, but I made a side trip to Cincinnati to see a sick friend."

"Will he be okay?"

He smiled. "Isn't it just like you to be concerned about someone you don't even know. He'll be fine, it was a minor auto accident." He pointed to a chair. "Give me ten minutes and I promise, I'll be right back here, to stay, dream a little about you and try my best to make it come true."

"It already has, Marc. Just seeing you again is worth a flight delay."

He kissed her forehead, feeling her warmth, the smoothness of her skin, feeling his pants tent on contact with her. "Umm, if I don't get going now, my luggage may be loaded onto another flight. But after seeing you again, I don't actually give a good damn about anything else."

"Always one with words, flattering a skinny, ashy brown girl to death. Go, get your luggage and come back to me."

"That's a damn promise."

Caroline watched Marc walk off, seeing how he filled out his slacks, how juicy his butt was and how she still ached for him as though she were still that inexperienced eighteen-year-old girl. As he disappeared from her sight, she thought about how she really got to know the famous Marc Brown one night after the big game. It had been a night to remember forever. . . .

It was a late spring evening and Valley View had just defeated Harrington High. Marc was usually the last one out of the locker room because he was the star pitcher. He tossed balls that literally had flames behind them. He was the school's everything, winning practically all of his games. The local press would always keep him a little longer for interviews. That night he was really late returning to the locker room because it was the citywide championship.

And there was Caroline, the no-big-deal girl. However, in her own way, she was just as popular as he was. Her job was being the best team mascot the Vipers had ever had. And since her nickname was already nerd, wearing a big snake head and rattler of a tail didn't help her climb the social scale. But Caroline was good at her job, getting the crowd excited by shaking her rattler and prancing around the field, all for the sake of the team. What she really wanted to do was shake her stuff for Marc, so he could see her other side—the side that was just as attractive as her ability to solve logarithms, at least in *her* mind.

The night of the big game was also her birthday. All she wanted to do was go home and celebrate, since her mother had made her favorite cake—vanilla with strawberry filling and frosting. After returning to the girls' locker room to return the viper outfit and collect her book bag, she found a note on her locker: *"If you wanna take your book bag home, you'll find it in the boys' locker room. Besides, don't all dudes use the boy's locker room?"* Christ! Caroline knew she wasn't the epitome of teenaged beauty, but she didn't think she looked like a boy! She knew the note was some of Iisha's antics, either that or she'd had one of the other hoochies do it for her.

Nonetheless, she trotted over to the other side of the hall to retrieve her belongings. As she walked inside, she thought she heard a shower still running. Everyone was supposed to be gone, but she investigated. As she approached the shower stalls, she heard throaty sounds, like someone was making love in there. *What the heck?* She approached the last stall and saw Marc inside with the stiffest erection she'd ever seen. At first, she was taken aback, never having seen a real one before other than her baby cousin, Jack—nothing really to look at there.

As she continued to stare at Marc getting off, the sight of it started to excite the hell out of her. And the fact that it was Marc made it that much better. She'd always envisioned how his would look. She'd cop looks at it pressing against his jeans, his baseball pants; any time she could spy looks at him and any part of his anatomy, she gladly did it. It was sexier now because he was sudsy, water spraying against his smooth, toned body, and the expression on his face was so intense, like he was enjoying the hell out of it. She sure was.

Before she realized anything, her lips were trembling, wanting to scream out, reach for it and rub that incredible erection against her feverish hands, lengthening him that much more. Her purse fell to the floor with a thick thud. She watched as Marc jumped, releasing his oversized phallus. The expression on her face alerted him that she was enjoying the show.

He smiled at her and claimed the erection again, taking it one step further by stroking it for her benefit. Her eyes widened when he massaged his scrotum. Damn, it looked so good, but what the hell did she know about sex? She knew which hole the delicious thing fit into—but not much else. Her father's medical book was a gross misrepresentation. The only thing missing on Marc was the plastic film that showed the inner workings of the male genitalia. Marc's was better, way better, but it took her by surprise, not expecting to see her friend in such a compromising position. Automatically, she lowered her head, gave a barely audible "Sorry," and tried running from the sight of Marc's fully engorged sex.

Not that any part of Marc was scary, because it wasn't. He

was straight up and beautiful—and she meant that literally. But she was shy and didn't know what to do. When she looked back, Marc was running after her. Everything was moving on him and it looked so great, yet she kept running. He caught up and grabbed her arm. "Hey, don't run, Caroline. That's what boys do sometimes when they think of girls. I was thinking about you."

Even his sweet words couldn't stop her from shivering within his grasp. That brought on a flood of tears, as the water from his body saturated her. Slowly and methodically, he led her back to the shower stall. Though he was naked with a stiff cock pressing against her stomach, his voice calmed her—the way it always did. "Please don't run. I won't hurt you." Then he smiled. "You know I like you, Caroline. The whole school knows it."

Her voice quivered. "Me? You've always liked me the way you like other girls?"

"Yeah. I liked you the minute Ms. McGreggor sat me next to you in class that first day. I liked you more the first time you let me slow dance with you in your basement. The way your body felt next to mine made me want you really bad, Caroline. I knew you'd never give it to me, so I didn't ask . . . but I'm asking now."

She looked down at the fabulous erection throbbing against her. It was scandalous, thick, long and hard and all she wanted to do was touch it, taste it, feel it. Her core became so wet just looking at it, but she was confused, wondering what the deal really was. *Was he part of the book bag joke? No, Marc would never do that to me.* He was simply trying to make her feel good since others always made her feel wrong about herself. No matter what, his actions brought mixed emotions.

His voice brought her mind and body back to reality. "I know what you're thinking, that I've lost my mind, but I haven't. Compared to you, I'm a dumb jock, but I've always been crazy about you. You know that."

His words made her relax. Marc *was* always kind to her, made her feel real and that was the major reason for her attraction to him. And yes, he was a bona-fide stud muffin that any girl who wanted sex would cream over, like she was about to do.

Marc took her hand and led her into the shower. The steamy water wet her clothes, making them cling to her. When his tongue entered and coiled around inside her thirsty mouth, she couldn't believe that anyone could taste so good. Marc's lips were beyond heaven, beyond human reasoning.

He peeled away her wet jeans and panties, tossing them on the bench. Seconds later, she felt his warm, wet fingers parting her thighs, diving into her moistness. She was his new toy and he explored her depths way beyond her imagination. His talented fingers felt so incredible within her mellow purity. He found a place within her that she didn't know existed, and he strummed her delicate clit until it literally vibrated. Her slow moan reflected his precise movements.

Her body melted into his as tears of joy stained her face. She'd never felt anything that arousing, didn't know a feeling that sensational could be real. She'd hoped, prayed something that magical existed but wasn't sure until Marc's fingers proved her point. Within seconds, Marc's tongue and fingers were performing double duty on her, and she let him, she let him. He pressed her sex flush against his as he entered a second finger into her. Her body tensed at first, but his warm breath against her ear soothed everything. "Does this feel good?"

Her arms tightened around his slick shoulders, her soft voice now more breathy against his neck. "Marc . . . Marc! God, yes. What are you doing to me?"

"I'm making you feel wonderful for your birthday. I couldn't wait until May fifth got here, Caroline."

"You remembered my birthday?"

"The minute you told me, I made a mental note."

Her eyes met his again. "Did you like the gift I gave you last month on your birthday?"

"Sure, the headphones were cool, but Caroline, this is the gift. I've wanted you so badly that I could barely walk around you at times." He kissed her again with more power, more steam, more tenacity, feeling as though he'd never let her go. His fingers continued to slide in and out of her; his sex about to burst from want of her inner warmth. He broke the kiss. "Caroline, please, let me do it to you. Let me slide inside and rock in and out until this pressure is gone. I want to know what it's like to feel you constricting around me."

She barely pulled away, staring into his caramel eyes. "Marc? Why?"

"Why do I want to be inside you?"

"No, why me at all? I'm a nerd. Everyone says that."

"You're not a nerd, you're a beautiful girl that made me hot the first time I saw you. I just could never understand why you didn't meet me for lunch that first day."

"What? You didn't see Iisha shove me out of the lunch-room?"

"Had I seen that, I'd have kicked her ass that day. I'm really sorry she did that."

Caroline managed a small smile. "Wouldn't have looked good on your first day at a new school to be in a fight with a girl."

"I'd have done it, though. Anything for you, Caroline, is worth getting in trouble for."

"You're the sweetest thing, but that still didn't answer my question. Why do you like me?"

"Because . . . I'm not supposed to. You're forbidden. I'm the jock and jocks are supposed to like the popular girls, right?"

"Right. Does Iisha know you're here?"

"Fuck Iisha. I'm here with you because this is the only chance I'll be able to steal with you." He kissed her again, rocking his fingers in and out of her with fiery speed. Her breath quickened. Her mind felt crazy, not being able to fix on anything other than the pleasure Marc was giving her, and her heart raced so fast that she thought it would pump right through her chest. Then that sudden quivering rush bombarded her, making her cry out for him in squeals. From that point on, she knew what girls were talking about when mentioning the "magnificent dreamy-creamy." When it calmed, she could still feel her body twitching from him and she wanted more, needed more.

Marc took her hand and placed it on this throbbing shaft. His hand rocked hers up and down, making her feel its veins, the rig of its tip, the smoothness of it. His voice shook as she took it upon herself to continue the assault. His back leaned against the tile and watched her explore his precious tool for the first time. As her fingers rubbed him, he took her face into his hands. "Take it, Caroline. Taste it."

Without consideration of how she'd feel about herself later, she bent and faced that perfect tip. Without having had one lesson, she took him between her lips, tasting the saltiness of his skin. From that point on, it was second nature. Her mouth coveted him, stroking him in and out, looking up and into eyes that were almost shut from pure passion. Caroline's rhythm quickened on him, relishing him, fitting him almost completely into her eager mouth.

Marc reached on the soap dish for one of the strawberry condoms he'd bought from his friend Larry earlier that day. He took her hand and brought her face to face with him again. He slowly unfolded her tight fist and placed the condom within it. "Put it on me."

"Is it time?"

"It's been time, Caroline."

Without hesitation, she unwrapped the foiled item, rolled it onto his feverish shaft and stood to him again. "How do we do it? I've never done this before."

Without words, he sank to the floor of the shower as the water trickled down upon him. He parted Caroline's legs and slowly helped her lower to him. The moment his tip touched her liquid, he wanted to cum, but held off.

For Caroline, that magnetic tip electrified her and she sank onto it as Marc massaged and stroked her nipples. The more he pressed into her, the wider her thighs parted for him. The feeling was unimaginable; hurting a little at first like her mother said it would. As she relaxed to his size and slowly took him into her, the more she wanted him. She smiled from sheer eroticism once Marc's inches totally invaded her. Her hips automatically rocked to his, slowly at first, then faster and faster.

Her only thought, *What have I been missing?* Looking into Marc's perfect face as he screwed her intensely brought on her second orgasm, one that just about exploded her insides. Then and only then did she know what the girls talked about; she'd finally had one, and Marc Brown gave it to her. What she'd done to herself on many an occasion hardly compared to what Marc did to her. Having Marc in her body was top-secret information that any dame at Valley View would have paid dearly for. She braced her hands against the walls as she rode up and down on him. Finally, she saw that intense expression on his face as he bucked and slammed deeper into her. Before it was all said and done, Marc filled that condom up, and kissed her wildly, erratically, completely.

When they broke the kiss, he looked into Caroline's flushed face. "I knew you had to be fantastic. Was it good for you?"

"It was . . . I don't know what it was, other than way beyond what I thought it would be."

"Then happy birthday, baby."

They kissed again. Her only worry after that was explaining to her parents why her clothes were wet and why she was late to her own party. She wasn't late to her party, Marc gave her one that would last a lifetime. Minutes later, they heard the door open. Marc uttered under his breath, "Please don't let that be Coach Porter."

"He didn't leave for the evening?"

"He always leaves after me. Be quiet and let's get dressed as quickly as possible."

Their timing was poor and so was Coach Porter's. He took one look at Marc wearing nothing but wet underwear and socks and Caroline in just panties and a towel wrapped around her. His eyes widened to the sight of them standing before a drippy shower. "What? What the heck is going on in here, Marc?"

"I . . . I—uh . . ."

"Speak up, boy. What is Caroline Pierce doing in here with you wearing only a towel?" His eyes narrowed, sniffed the sex-fragrant air then smiled a cocky smile. "I know what's been going on. You two get dressed and meet me in my office." Before he left, he looked at Caroline, then to Marc with a surprised look on his face. "Damn kids! Hurry up."

Everything on Caroline started shaking; tears rolled down her cheeks. "My parents are going to kill me."

"No, they won't. We'll probably just get some hand slaps, a two day suspension and queer looks from that fart for the rest of our lives."

"Why did he look at us like that? It was like he didn't expect you to be with me."

"Fuck him. Did you like it?"

"I loved it."

"Wanna do it again?"

"Yeah, but not here."

"I'll find a place for us."

That never happened because the next week he was back to doing what everyone in school expected him to do, dating Iisha Burns. However, he made sure no one did another damn thing to Caroline. Funny thing, he had to beat asses every day to accomplish that. Hooray for him! But that was then. . . .

Marc reentered Midway and sneaked up on her, kissing her neck from behind. The delicate tongue lick startled her and she quickly turned to him. "Marc, you scared the heck out of me."

"I saw that delicious look on your face. What were you thinking about?"

"I don't think you want to know that."

His eyes narrowed seductively. "Now I really want to know. That smile on your face is killing this busting zipper."

She had to look, and yes, there was definitely something there. "Well, if you must know, I was thinking about what we did in the locker room so many years ago."

"You still remember that?"

"How could I not, Marc? I feel like I became a person that day."

"You were one way before that, sugar." He took her hand. "Come on, let's get that drink. I want as much time with you as possible before L.A. kidnaps you." They walked the long corridor together. He opened the door to the pub, escorting her inside.

Immediately the waitress walked over smiling. "Mr. Brown! Back in town for a while?"

"All Star break. Too tired to participate this year despite my votes."

"What can I get for you?" The waitress smiled into his face.

"A martini."

"And for the lady?"

Caroline smiled up at the overly-infatuated-with-Marc hostess. "I'll have a Blue Crush."

After the order was jotted down and they were again alone, Marc gave her a look of surprise. "Do you know what's in a Blue Crush?"

"Sure, I make them at home sometimes, when someone's there to share one with me."

"Is there anyone at home you *share* things with?"

She knew what he was getting at and was glad to set his mind free. "Not lately. I date now and then. Usually I go straight home and fix plasma televisions."

"Plasma televisions?"

"I bought a new one and the installation wasn't handled right by cable so I had to do it. That's what I was doing last night when I saw you on TV. The only thing my television would broadcast was the ballgame. I couldn't believe I was actually watching you." She touched the few scratches on his face and jaw. "What did those terrible men do to you?"

"Not as much as what I did to them."

"I know. I saw you slugging it out. You're still a hell of a fighter, aren't you?"

"Only when I have to be."

"It was exciting, actually. Watching you is always so exciting. I haven't seen you in so long, Marc, not since your wedding."

"Same here. I thought about you all the time. We went our separate ways; me going to the Cubs organization and toting Iisha and the baby with me, and you to Joliet U."

"The baby?"

"She and I have a son. Winston was born eight months after we graduated from Valley View."

"I know he's a dreamboat like his father."

"Thanks, but he looks like Iisha."

Damn! At least I hope he has better hair and no constant look of constipation! "Like Iisha, huh? I'd love to see him."

"You will. I didn't know you watched baseball."

"Normally I don't. I couldn't get the channels to change on the TV so I watched you beat the hell out of the Twins. Turns out there were no batteries in the remote."

"That game wasn't my finest moment."

"You were great, winning fourteen to five. You showed off your prowess with that poor shortstop. It was, well. . . stimulating watching the aggressive side of you."

He sipped the drink placed before him. "Stimulating, huh? Too bad there aren't any showers around here."

"I'm glad you remember that as well as I do."

"I'll never forget it. Best damn time of my life, and you're even more beautiful now than when we made love."

"I was a wimp back then—no breasts, could hardly comb my hair."

"You weren't a wimp, you just didn't know how to bring out your inner beauty. I always saw it, though."

"I've changed a bit. The breasts are bigger, they're now a whopping 34B."

"Yummm!"

His response excited her, yet she felt like withdrawing. Immediately she felt she had to get the attention from herself and back to something safer—him. "Why aren't you with the Blue Jays anymore?"

"The Sox gave me a bigger deal. Besides, I wanted to be near my parents, because they're getting older. I bought a place on Lake Shore Drive."

"Those aren't *places,* those are mansions. Really, you own one of those?"

"Sure do. Maybe I can show it to you one night."

It was the word *night* that propelled her brain to the stars. Night meant sex to her and having it with him again was definitely on the menu, after she got back from L.A. She couldn't believe looking at him could bring back memories of falling in love with him that night.

"Caroline? Where did you go?"

"What?"

"You zoned out on me. What was on your mind?"

"I was just remembering how much I was in love with you back then."

"I could make that happen again. We did have a lot of fun, didn't we?"

"You were the best thing that could have happened to me at Valley View."

He moved in closer to her, taking her hand into his. "I wish we could do those kid things again. Slow dancing in your basement, sneaking out to the movies."

"That would be fun." She could feel the power in those hands, realizing exactly how he could throw smokers into the mitt of his catcher with a velocity of 98 miles per hour. He was strong, seductive and taking her mind on a journey she'd dreamed of many times. His voice brought her back.

"Do you really have to be on that plane today? I have a nice, big shower in my bedroom; one big enough to play in all day and night if you so desire."

Being tempted into his bedroom was so easy, but she had a commitment to the L.A. models, attorneys and the small business presentations. She withdrew her hand. "I can't cancel. However, I don't have to be there until tomorrow afternoon. I always get in early so I can settle in. Those meetings usually wear me out."

"I'd rather wear you out." He pulled a credit card from his wallet. "Let me book another flight for tomorrow morning."

"I really shouldn't."

"You really should. I need to be with you, Caroline. Eight years of being married never stopped me from thinking about how good we would have been together. Please, come home with me; let me show you how a queen should be treated. I'll give you everything you want and need." He kissed her hand, seductively licking between her fingers.

His advances made her forget she was in a crowded little bar with people also waiting for a four-hours-late plane. They were not her concern. What concerned Caroline Pierce were her panties, now sopping wet from her own thick moisture. She could feel her core swelling, and sliding every inch of Marc Brown into that throbbing flesh was the only remedy.

Again, she withdrew her hand, but a smile was on her face as she spoke. "Can you imagine what Iisha would be thinking if she saw us here together? I remember sitting with you at lunch one day. She and her hood-rats walked by and laughed at me. I remember her very words to you, *What are you doing having lunch with that miniature Clydesdale? She should be running in the Preakness.*

"Yeah, I remember that, and I trashed her after lunch about it."

"That was Iisha for you."

"If she'd had any sense, she would have known a Clydesdale is not a race horse. It's too big. You know for damn sure she couldn't spell it. I was just surprised that she knew what the Preakness was. Of course, with her, hearing stupid things was customary. We were in history one day and Mr. Franks asked the class what the Tai Ping Rebellion was. That dummy actually raised her hand and said it was when secretaries rebelled against having too much work to do. Mr. Franks embarrassed the hell out of her and told her it wasn't the 'typing rebellion.' The class dogged her the entire day about that."

"You're kidding. Was she that dense?"

He finished his drink. "I only wish I'd been smarter back then with her. I don't regret having our son, but I could have done better."

Marc moved in next to her, lacing his hand up and down the silkiness of her skirt. "Please, Caroline. I really want to be with you now that you're not in my imagination." The tablecloth kept anyone from seeing him slide his hand under her skirt and stroke her smooth upper thighs just above her garter. "You're right here with me, and you smell so damn good." He kissed her earlobe. "Come home with me. I won't force anything on you. We can do whatever you want to do."

The way he was making her feel, she'd have clearly jumped into a pool of stingrays with him. "What . . . what about my ticket?"

He placed the credit card in her hand. "Let's get it changed, and if nothing's available, I'll let you go, or drive you there myself. Please! I want to make love to you so badly that I can taste you. I can still feel your breasts in my hands, your tongue winding around mine. Your flavor is still on my fingers and I'm just shy of sucking them to regain that sensuous aroma."

"Marc . . ." No one alive or dead ever said that to her and in the way he said it. Marc had a way with words and sex, and if his tactics developed the way his body had over the years, she'd never leave Lake Shore Drive. Her life would be spent within his world.

She didn't know if it was her mind playing games with her or if Marc's fingers really found her spot. Without thinking, her hand lowered, landing on top of his and from that point on her hand guided his movements. Her thick moisture saturated both her hand and his as his fingers swirled around her clit, stroking it with smooth, precise caresses. He inched deeper inside, filling her. She could hear her own moisture mixing with his movements and the sound alone made her quiver and constrict around him. "Marc, Marc . . . please . . ."

His voice tickled her ears. "Come home with me, Caroline. Take me out of this misery."

The erection busting his pants apart beckoned her, and her hand gripped the clothed swelling, working it, manipulating it until he could barely stand the pressure. Their mouths met with steam and passion, exchanging kisses like lovers who'd been separated from each other for way too long. His mouth temporarily broke free from hers, trailing across to her earlobe then down her neck. His breathy voice purred. "Let's buy your ticket. You're not getting on that late plane."

Without any hesitation, Caroline followed her captor through the bar, leaving a half-finished Blue Crush on the table. Hand in hand, they approached the American Airlines ticket agent and made the exchange with ease.

With a new departure date the following morning, Caroline happily skipped out of Midway Airport with Marc Brown by her side. They reached his Porsche and she stared in wonder. "You see, this is what money does for you. It gets you shit like this."

"My shit is your shit now, so anytime you want it, it's yours."

She smoothed her hand along the jet black auto. "No, what I really want is the man driving it. That's all I've ever wanted, Marc."

"Then your life is made because there's no way in fucking hell you're getting rid of me." He unlocked the door and helped her inside. Her skirt slid up her leg as she entered the vehicle and Marc's tongue practically wagged out of control. *Lord, get me and that girl home fast before I explode!*

The tour along Lake Shore Drive was amazing. She'd seen it many times, but never from Marc's window. It was a beautiful, sunny day, a more perfect one hadn't been created, and what made it *absolutely* perfect was that she was spending it in Marc's arms. The minute they entered his mansion, she knew she'd wrap herself around him so tightly that they'd make the first human rubberband. She could actually feel Marc sliding that hulking thick meat into her and shattering what was left of her sanity. That was what she needed. No man in her past left an impression upon her the way he had with one evening in a shower. From that point on in her life, wherever she moved to, she would make sure the shower was on jam!

Marc took her mind from her bathroom orgasm. "Hey, pretty girl. Whatcha thinkin' about?"

The side of her dainty little mouth perked up. "I don't think you want to know that."

"Now I really want to know."

Her hand stroked his inner thigh. "Well, I was thinking about showers." She faced him boldly. "And I don't mean rain showers."

"Girl, I like the sound of that. So tell me, what were we doing in the shower?"

"I didn't get into it that deeply, but there's something about showers that turns me out!" Her hand moved from his leg, to his groin, on to his stomach and caressed his chest. He was still so soft, baby flesh, like she remembered from years ago. "You still feel so good."

"I think it's that aftershave I advertise."

"My girlfriend saw that commercial. Sexy, sexy as can be."

"So, finish that shower thing you went off on."

"I was just wondering how it would be making love to you in your shower. I'm sure you have many."

"I have four, and I plan to christen you in all of them."

Her hand moved back to his erection, stroking it, making the linen pants cause friction against it. She loved the way his eyes rolled at her attentions; how his muscles tensed, how much heat was under those pants. But heat wasn't exactly the only thing she wanted from him; she wanted fire, steam, white-hot lava and she wanted it dripping slowly and thickly down his shaft. She tugged at his zipper, then eyed him. "May I?"

"God! Yes."

There was no one on the tree-lined street but them and his Porsche, so he pulled to the side of the road. "Why wait for the shower when we can get wet right here?"

"Ummm, I like how you talk, Mr. Marc Brown, king of the Sox bullpen."

"I want to be your king, your every-damn-thing, pretty girl!"

With his hand covering hers, they slid his zipper down. Before the zipper was at half-mast, his tight, seething erection was trying to bust past all that was in its way. To tease Marc into exquisite hardness, her tongue darted at the clothed tip, rubbing wetly against the softness of the Hanes briefs. Marc was ready to go into spasms just from the friction of under-wear and her mouth. The pièce de resistance came when she totally took the covered shaft into her mouth, sucking the damp material, making it cling against his rod.

Watching Caroline dine on him made his breathing quicken, his stomach heaved in and out. Her other hand raised his shirt, stroked soft thick flesh and muscles—taming his breath-ing. His words worked on her as she worked on him. "Damn, this is so fucking good, Caroline. Don't stop . . . don't stop." He reached down and delivered his shaft from the wet mate-rial while reclining the bucket seat.

Exposed to her hungry eyes was a shaft so beautiful and cinnamon brown that she almost came. Her fingers glided up and down the thick, rigid erection as it continued to pulsate. The sight of it took her breath away. It'd been so long since her beloved Marc was in her arms; she'd long ago gotten used to knowing she'd never mix with him again, never feel any real love from him. But as she stroked his molten flesh, she knew this was real, Marc was real, and her dreams were about to come true again.

He beckoned her. "Take it, darling."

More than just words, it was action. Caroline's mouth started at his tip, feasting on it, tenderizing it before she dove in for the rest. Marc stroked it up and down for her satisfaction, and his, as her mouth sank deeper and deeper onto it. His thick veins tickled her inner cheeks and throat and she smiled over the fact that he was still way different from what she remembered in her dad's medical book. He was an awakening, then and now.

Marc's hips pumped to her rhythm, forcing the shaft deep within her mouth. She was taking it, taking it all but found her comfort zone at the plump, rounded tip. She sipped him, as though he were a fine wine and watched as he erupted from her hand action. He slumped in the seat, staring at his glorious princess. "You are so incredible, Caroline. How'd you learn to do that?"

"I had a good teacher—you. You made me want to be good at it."

"But we only did it once."

"Good teachers need only teach a lesson once."

He kissed her in a long, sucking motion, getting his fill of her before pulling away. "Sit on me. Let me feel what it's like again to be with you. You were so good."

"I was a virgin."

"That meant you were a natural. Come on, sit on me."

"No, when I have you, I want all of you exposed to me. I

like to take all I can get." She stroked his still-hard member. "How long will it be before we're at your house?"

"Minutes. I swear."

As they drove along, they saw a Taco Bell and he smiled. "Let's pull in and get some of these the way we used to on Saturdays after a movie. Remember?"

"I sure do. Those were the Saturdays Iisha was at the beauty parlor getting her fake hair done."

"That's for damn sure. So, you want some tacos, for old times sake?"

"I want whatever you can give me."

"You want a lot."

Twenty minutes later, they drove onto Marc's winding driveway. She looked at the looming house with a lake backdrop. "This place is yours?"

"Sure is."

"I've passed it so many times but never knew it was yours."

"I've thrown a lot of pitches to get this baby."

He helped her out and the two of them, holding the tacos, walked the winding staircase to sexual nirvana. As she scoped the mansion, she realized just how well Marc had done for himself. Beating up on Indians, Tigers, Rangers, Angels, and anything else in major league baseball afforded him many a luxury. She held tightly to his arm. "This place is magnificent. I bet your son really loves it."

"So does Iisha."

Concern clouded Caroline's mind, wondering if Iisha was a permanent fixture around there. "Is . . . is Iisha around a lot?"

"She tries to be, but I meet her at the gate when she brings Winston over. She's the kind that lives in the lap of luxury. Yet when I tried giving it to her, she took advantage of it and ran through a right smart amount of my money. She didn't even buy for Winston, it was frivolous stuff. Not one charity was donated to, and I specifically asked her to donate to children's organizations, cancer foundations, anything I thought was beneficial. I wanted to give back to society, but when I got my quarterly statements, I saw nothing indicating donations. Oops, sorry, there were some—a house for her mother and sister, Asia."

"Asia! I remember her. She was right behind us in school."

"Yeah, and she was a junior hoochie. I was so blind back then, Caroline. I had love right in my face with you, but was too blind to see."

She stopped him at the front door and planted a gentle kiss on his full lips. "You have it now, and that's what matters, Marc."

"Do I have it?"

"If you want it."

His arms tightened around her. "I definitely want it, Ms. Caroline Pierce. And it's time for me to stop playing around in the love department. Will you be with me? I mean really be with me; a girlfriend . . . maybe more."

Her only response was to lay-in on his lips again, smothering him with tiny nibbles, gently sucking his bottom lip until the bulge in his pants separated them. Caroline stared back into his sparkling eyes. "Does that answer your question?"

"That was a great answer."

"Good. Let's get the suitcases from the trunk, take those tacos into the kitchen, then . . . you can show me those bathrooms."

"I can do more than show you. And about the suitcases, I don't think you'll need yours tonight."

"Since I'll be heading out early tomorrow?"

"No, since you'll be naked all night long."

She rubbed her nose against his. "I like the sound of that, boy."

"This time, there'll be no coach to make us get dressed and go home."

"That was positively embarrassing. I know everyone figured me to be the last one you'd get caught in a shower with. Even Coach Porter stared you down in disbelief over that one."

"He should see us now."

They entered the large living room that housed antique-ish furniture, a large crystal chandelier, plush carpeting, wood paneling and a large-screen television tucked against the front wall. The room was bright and cheery, and the view from the back window was a captivating scene of Lake Michigan. He walked to the middle of the floor and spread his arms. "Well, this is home sweet home. You like it?"

She stopped in her tracks, mesmerized by the beauty of the place. "It's . . . it's gorgeous. I've never been in a house this large."

"You want a grand tour?"

"Yeah, let's start with the first bathroom."

"I like the sound of that, Ms. Caroline. How about we work our way up, build our anticipation, then explode on one another at the exact perfect moment?"

"And when would that be?"

"The minute you see my bedroom."

"Ummm, a room I've wanted to see since I turned eighteen."

The tour started with the large kitchen and dining room. Imported marble floors spanned the length of the room and the latest appliances were there for his convenience. Continuing their way around the first level, they stopped briefly at the entertainment room equipped with pool table, video games and another large television. Finally, they reached the bathroom on the lower level, and he pulled her inside. "This is the first one. We'll start here and work our way up. Sound like a plan?"

"An excellent one." She stepped into the spacious bathroom that contained a sea-blue-and-white tiled shower with double doors, a large sink and dressing area. "Wow, this is bigger than the main one in my parents' house."

"This is only a partial bathroom. I have bigger ones up-stairs."

"Umm, I know you do, but I like this one for starters."

"You're about to like it a lot more." He hoisted her on top of the sink, spread her legs and nestled between them. His mouth engulfed hers, tickling her lips, her throat, nipping at her tongue while he slowly removed her blouse. When he got to the lacy camisole, he stopped, pulled away from her wait-ing mouth and sucked perky nipples through the sheer fabric. The feel of her high breasts against his tongue and lips made him feverish, yet he didn't remove the camisole. Instead, he lifted her from the sink.

"Why have you stopped?"

"Because we have other bathrooms to explore. When we get to the second one, you get to take something off of me."

Quickly they ascended the staircase and he whisked her into yet a bigger bathroom. She stared in wonder at the large cream-and-black tiled full bathroom. He leaned her against the cool tile and kissed her briefly. "It's your turn. Take my shirt off."

She was beginning to really like that game, and her fingers, without haste, undid the buttons on his silk shirt. Heat emit-ted from it; shadows of his darkly hued nipples peeked from under thin fabric. Once spreading the shirt apart, she saw all the wonders that awaited her since their night of passion years ago. Her hands stroked his rugged pecs, contours, rip-pled stomach. Antsy fingers moved down his torso, circling his navel, poking it playfully with the tip of her fingernail. His stomach heaved up and down, exciting her so much that all she could do was lick his nipples in slow, even strokes, leaving wet lines across his hot skin. Mouthwatering.

Marc brought her face to his. "There are more bathrooms. The next one is down the hall, and again, I get to remove something from you. Are you up for it, because I know I am?"

He definitely was up for it as she stroked the stiff phallus inside his pants. She took in a deep breath, swallowing hard. "Come on, where's that other bathroom?"

Hand in hand again, they walked to the end of the hallway and entered, of all things, a bathroom decorated with *The Incredibles* cartoon characters.

"Winston's?"

"Yeah, but he's not here."

"Cool." She pushed him against the wall. "This is better than strip Monopoly."

"I wouldn't know. I'm always naked before the game starts." He tugged on the zipper of her skirt and watched it fall to the ground along with her half-slip. Looking at Caroline wearing nothing but a camisole and lace panties twisted him into a million knots, and he ached for release.

Caroline, being almost completely exposed to the one man she'd lived a million lives with in her mind, was beyond release. The idea of him sent her into orbit and she pulled him closer into her, whispering into his ear, "Take them off."

"You first; this jockstrap is ready to combust on impact."

Willing to accommodate Marc to the max, she unzipped the zipper, feeling his erection rubbing against her warm hands. Reaching into Marc's pants was a fantasy she'd had since the first day she'd met him. There was just something so exciting about reaching into a man's pants, rubbing a warm erection and toying with an oozing tip. She could barely contain her words as she stroked the tight jockstrap. Her legs became weak, her mind turned into jelly and her body, nothing but his playground. Her sex throbbed from touching him and to relay what she was feeling, she placed his hand on the cotton lining of her panties. "Feel this, Marc. This is all for you. Destroy it, destroy me until there's nothing left."

His lips trembled against her ear. "No way. When I get it, I take care of it, pamper, feed it well because I want it around forever." Without another word, he pulled the panties aside and slipped two strong fingers into her.

Once making contact with her wet folds, he let out a soulful sigh that took her by surprise. "Marc, are you okay?"

"Just great, baby, just great. Umm, you feel so fucking good. I've ached for this moment with you practically since my honeymoon with Iisha. I was so stupid."

"Don't say it. You weren't stupid, just young and following a crowd."

"And you forgive me?"

She rocked his fingers slowly in and out of her, her voice lowering to a seductive whisper. "Does this answer you?"

"Let's go to the next bathroom and answer more questions." He took the petite joy of his life into his arms and carried her up the final flight.

The bathroom they entered was off his bedroom. It was a large room with a king-sized bed in the middle of a sunken floor. There were tiger-striped curtains and matching bed sheets. Caroline smiled. "I thought you liked beating tigers, not sleeping with them."

"I don't have to wrestle with these tigers. However, the Tigers in Detroit's Comerica Park, they can be something to reckon with at times."

He placed her upon the soft dark brown carpeting. "Wanna see the master bathroom?"

"As long as my master is with me."

More brown and beige stripes met her as she walked into a bathroom almost the size of his living room. The spaciousness of the room took her by surprise. "Marc . . . it's incredible." Her eyes moved from the large shower, to the tub, then to the Jacuzzi. There were tropical plants cascading from the ceiling down to the floor, and the big picture window gave her an even better view of the lake as the sun made its slow descent. She walked to the oversized window, barely touching the glass. "I can't believe how enchanting everything is."

He moved in behind her, pressing his engorged penis against her back. "Not as enchanting as you are. Turn around, darling. I have something to show you."

She turned to watch him slowly stroke the length of a massive erection, making it so rigid that it stood in place. There was no wavering, no gentle bounce due to mass. No, just Marc wanting Caroline so badly he could explode.

Watching him get harder and harder controlled her. How many times had she imagined Marc Brown doing that for her benefit? Many times, but Iisha had always popped up in her daydream like a computer virus or something. She wasn't there that night, and wouldn't be again. As Marc fondled his scrotum, she practically sank to her knees, wanting to feel him between her lips, soothing her throat, but her strongest urge was to feel him entering her body, pressing and forcing every inch of him inside her.

She tried sinking to her knees to accommodate him, but he stopped her. "Not yet. Let me strip away what's left on you, and I want you to do the same for me. Will you let me?"

"Don't talk, Marc, just strip me and spread me like jam on bread."

"That's not what I want. Let me make love to you. Let me swim in your ocean again. I wanna drown in it, sip it, let my canoe paddle away inside of it."

She brought his face back to hers, kissing him like she'd never kissed a man before. "Let me hold you, for a while longer before that happens."

Barely clothed, they embraced, sinking into one another and closing the gap on all those years they were apart. Marc stepped back, removed the camisole straps from her shoulders, exposing her breasts. The taut, soft swells invigorated him as he stroked them. The pad of his thumb moved across her tight nipples, making her back arch toward him. Her panties made their departure next and Marc marveled at his naked queen. "My God, Caroline, what the hell have I been missing?"

She tugged at his pants and jockstrap, helping them both fall to the floor. "Step out of those before I go crazy, Marc."

"Anything baby wants, baby gets."

They stood before one another, marveling at every single detail they'd wished upon for so long. He kissed her, then pointed, his voice barely audible. "The . . . the shower or Jacuzzi?"

"I've never done it in a Jacuzzi before. Let's go for it."

"Wise choice."

Watching Marc walk to the middle of the Jacuzzi with nothing on almost made her die from rapture. His tight buns looked so smooth and unblemished. His muscular back and shoulders made her juices drip; the way his erection bounced a bit as he walked made her immediately trail behind him.

They stood in the middle of the Jacuzzi kissing as jets of water pounded their ankles. Once the water reached his shins and her knees, he sat down, lowering her slowly onto his shaft. He played at her opening, teased it, letting its rigid veins touch her outer skin. He pressed her breasts together, his lips ferociously sucking both of her nipples at the same time, feeding on her as she rocked him.

As the water covered his belly, he looked into her loving eyes. "I can't take it any longer. I need to know what it's like to be inside of you again." There was a condom in light purple wrapping resting against a scented candle. It had been there since his last night with Iisha, forgotten. He tore it open and handed it to her. "You do it."

As if being commanded, she took the condom and rolled it onto him. It fit over his tight rod like a latex glove and she smiled in satisfaction over her accomplishment. "It's time, baby. It's time to skyrocket my ass to the moon and back."

"Then do it. Sink onto it, feel it as it spreads you apart."

Those words were like diamonds to her, and she lowered herself onto it, inch by thick, wonderful inch. She felt him climb into her sugar and latch on, bucking inside her like a wild bronco. His moaning voice was so sweet, and she ate up every word.

"Rock it, girl. Take it, take it all. . . ."

Over and over again, his words burned within her mind,

making her clench him harder, deeper. She never knew words could take her to the point of insanity; then again, she knew it had to be the man saying them. Marc could have gotten away with anything that night and all she'd have done was tell him to do it again—more, more of everything he dished to her. All she could do was stare down at him as he melted her down in wild spasms. It was unbelievable watching him do that to her, squeeze his life force into her hot opening and pull it apart.

Their bodies rocked against one another, bouncing out of control, kissing, touching, scratching . . . and wet from head to toe. Their frantic splashes wet the cinnamon brown tile. They didn't care; all they cared about was climaxing to the stars and drifting back to earth on a cloud, their cloud.

Marc jerked in raging fashion and spilled into her, busting the condom and spraying the rest against her chest and stomach. He quickly rolled on another he grabbed from a drawer and moved back into her, ready to give her more, make her come in ways she probably never dreamed of.

His thick stream was too enticing not to be massaged into her skin. Smelling his aroma, feeling his potency against her fingers caused a wildness to erupt within her. Her eyes rolled, and she screamed, "Harder, Marc, harder, harder . . ."

He worked his body into hers, pounding away inside, shattering his sanity and hers with wild thrusts, slamming into her opening. The Jacuzzi constricted his movements and his only recourse was to stand, taking Caroline into his arms while still joined and laying her back against the wet tile to give him the latitude he needed to totally nail her. Their bodies rubbed, slammed and bounced against one another's until they were halfway across the bathroom floor.

Their writhing landed them against the shower door that Marc immediately opened. He lifted her inside and turned on the jets. The drenching water spraying against their bodies made them explode in unison . . . and then collapse in each other's arms.

Marc stared into her beautiful flushed face, barely able to speak but managing nonetheless to attend to his lover. "Did I give you everything you wanted, everything you needed?"

Words were caught in her throat. Caroline didn't know how to respond after the only man she'd ever loved made wild, wicked, love to her. "I can't believe a man can make my body feel so fine. How . . . when . . . did you learn to please a woman like that?"

"The night I first made love to you. Sure, I'd done it with Iisha, but it wasn't the same. You were good, tender, natural, where she was already a pro from years spreading it around. You were a treat, Caroline, a breath of fresh air. And when you made me come, it was like fireworks inside my head; there was smoke behind my eyes, fire fueling my rocket."

Her face radiated. "Really?"

"I'm serious. What can I say? It was special with you, mechanical with Iisha."

She nibbled his ears, his neck, his collarbone and relaxed within his arms, letting the hot jets relax her tight muscles.

The bag from Taco Bell still rested on his kitchen table, and after drying every single inch of her with a thick, plush White Sox towel, he ran down in the nude to retrieve it.

While he was gone, Caroline laid back against the carpeting and watched the roaring fireplace in front of his bed flicker, slowly burning the embers. Watching the red glow reminded her of how he'd made her burn every single day of her life after meeting him. Now, for sure, she knew what real love was. She thought she'd been in love with Dan a year ago, and before him, Mike. Those relationships had been nothing but a backdrop for the really big romance, and the entire time, she had somehow known Marc Brown was the one. She smiled in contentment of finally having her dream come true.

Marc returned minutes later with nuked tacos, wine and something wrapped in a cloth napkin that he refused to unveil until the perfect moment. They ate their tacos, drank their wine as they talked over old times, new ones to come and how their evening was so totally orgasmic.

Marc ate his last taco and took her hand into his. The most sincere look crossed his face as he kissed her hand. "I have always loved you, Caroline."

"I wish you'd have told me. It would have made me feel better about being a geek."

"Nerd. Geek. You keep calling yourself names but you were never that. Maybe you didn't know how to use makeup or dress like the other girls . . ." He stopped, laughed a bit. "Come to think of it, Iisha and her clones couldn't apply makeup either. Now that I think about it, she did kind of look like a clown. But you know the really sad part, I was so busy getting the coochie that I could barely see."

"That's how boys are at that age. They can't see straight."

"I can see straight now, and now that I have you, I'll never let you go."

"You may want to think about that. I am still a geek. I still watch episodes of *Welcome Back Kotter* on TV Land."

"So do I."

"You're the one who got me hooked on sitcoms. By the way, I still have that Jim Morrison T-shirt."

"You do?"

"It's a little small on me now that I have boobs."

His brows scrunched. "I'd love to see it on you. Wet. See how it exposes you."

"One day when I dig it up from the old boxes I'll let you have a ball." She eyed the napkin-covered bundle lying on the carpeting. "So, what else did you bring up here?"

He patted it. "This ole thing?"

"Come on, spill the beans."

"It'll make you laugh, I swear!"

"What is it, Marc? Don't torture me. . . . well, maybe you can do that again later, but what did you bring up here?"

"Something that will remind you of school."

"I'm not sure I want to see that."

"I'm certain you will." He slowly uncovered the bundle, picked the item up with his thumb and forefinger, and dangled it in front of Caroline.

All she could do was stare in wonder before asking, "What the *hellll* is that?"

"Something I found in one of the bathrooms shortly after Iisha and I were divorced. It's one of those fake hair extensions. Gross, huh?"

Caroline slid her fingers through the loose strands while laughing. "As I live and breathe. How many times did I want to snatch one of those things from her arrogant head? A lot of times, Marc, especially after she called me some barnyard animal."

He dropped it back onto the napkin, as though further exposure to his skin would make him radioactive. "She actually accused me of taking it from her. I think she did that because of the divorce."

"You said you divorced her."

"Right."

"Well then, I can't blame her for being mad at you. I'd be mad too if you wanted to divorce me."

"That'll never happen, baby-girl. If I ever get the chance to put a ring on your finger, I'll burn the city down to keep you."

Nothing but love for him filled her. His words were so potent Caroline could barely respond. She was so nervous all of a sudden and didn't know what to do with herself. Instead of letting Marc know how overwhelmed she was, she retrieved the fake hair. "Has she learned how to comb her own hair in a normal way yet?"

"No, but I do have some news. We parted on decent terms and I agreed to finance her new beauty parlor. She can do a really good job on other heads but not her own. I've actually seen some of her work and it's great."

"Really?"

"Yeah, believe it or not. She wants to do some work with a consultant to help her get some ideas."

Suddenly, she cut into Marc's words. "What . . . does Iisha look like now? I mean, is she older looking, as in looking old for her age?"

"No. She pretty much looks the same."

Whu! "Good."

"Why?"

"Just wondering. I haven't seen her in years. I have a friend with a consulting agency. Maybe I can hook the two up."

He moved in closer to her, stroking her inner thighs. "Well, if you want to talk to Iisha about that, why not come with me to pick up Winston in a few days?"

Fear rose in her; that same fear she got back in ninth grade when Iisha would beat her up on the way home. That was before her "Marc in shining armor" appeared on the scene, protecting her from harm in a single bound! "I . . . I, uh . . . maybe."

"Don't be scared of Iisha. She's actually a very lonely, scared person who has nothing going for her other than that shop."

"I hope it works for her."

"It will."

There was still something about the idea of Iisha that got to her. After all those years, Caroline had hoped nothing would turn her into that scared child with the Jim Morrison shirt that read, *"I am the lizard king . . . I can do—anything!"* She wanted to be as strong as those words across her chest but never was, and still wasn't . . . she thought.

Hearing Marc's sweet voice assured her she wasn't alone in the world, and that he would let nothing harm her. He kissed her cheek, worked his way to her warm lips, engulfing her heat, then slowly pulled away. "You know that a big, juicy bed over there is calling for us."

That relaxed her, and she automatically jumped back into

Marc mode, teasing, "Really? Is that a bed over there? Golly gee, what ever would we do on that thing?"

"I don't exactly know, but we can explore."

"Sure, if you don't mind sleeping with a woman who has the taste and smell of guacamole and cilantro on her breath."

"I love those things, but I love you more." At that, he swooped her into his arms, carried her to that big ole sunken bed and ravaged her until they both practically drowned in their sea of love.

The shining sun peeked through the thick brown blinds, a radiant type of sunshine that promised everything good and natural. She looked up at the ceiling, realizing it wasn't the one in her own bedroom. Then she looked over at Marc. His precious body laid so close to her own that she felt they were one. It was incredible looking over and seeing that famous White Sox pitcher instead of the empty pillow on the other side of her bed. She listened to his calm breathing, so different from the night before. His heavy breathing and groaning had excited her so much as he slammed himself into her over and over again. Now he was quiet, truly resting, truly satisfied. Whether he was screaming out her name in orgasmic bliss or sleeping quietly next to her she was at peace—and she knew, for once, that her love life was headed in the right direction.

The alarm clock startled her from her precious daydream. Marc stirred to the sound of the O'Jays "Love Train" blaring from the clock radio he lovingly set before they went to sleep.

Marc rolled over, immediately taking her back into his arms. "Did the clock scare you?"

"I was awake already."

"This early?" He looked at the flashing numbers on the clock, reading 5:30 a.m. "What awakened you?"

"Thoughts of you."

"Wow! That must make me a pretty powerful dude."

"Indeed."

"Then plant one on me. Give me one deep and long, deep enough to bury me."

"With morning breath?"

"Baby, everything about you smells as sweet as a rose. Come on, plant it."

He took her into his arms and latched on for dear life. Feeling Caroline's warm body circling his stimulated him to the point that he had to have more. "Let me do it again, girl."

"We don't have time. I have to be on the plane at 8:50."

"That gives us an hour to dance a jig; get what I'm saying?"

"All too well. We practically moved the mattress from the bed."

"Let's complete the mission."

The minute Marc entered her body with long, rugged strokes, in and out, up and down, under her, above her, to her side, he could barely contain himself and let loose on contact. No woman had ever made Marc Brown come that hard and fast. It took a special woman to take him there, and her name was Caroline Pierce, his dark, mysterious empress.

Once they climaxed for what seemed to be the eightieth time, they both looked at the clock and scurried to get dressed. Caroline was glad she made him get her suitcase from the trunk because she had exactly one hour to dress, look human again and be at Midway before the plane took off without her.

Marc waited at the gate with her. Naturally, they called the first-class passengers first, then her section—the slightly less than perfect group. As she held his hand, she noticed how cute he looked wearing jogging pants, a White Sox T-shirt and his running shoes. He had to dress in a hurry but he looked so damn cute in an unkempt state, almost as cute as being dressed to kill. Well, he'd just about managed to kill her last night, and the thought of it would keep her mind occupied the entire trip to Los Angeles. She was thankful for that because it would be a long flight.

Just before her row was called, he kissed her one last time and walked her to the plane entrance. "I'm really gonna miss you, Ms. Caroline, damsel of my fucking dreams. When is your return flight?"

"In two days, so you won't have too long to wait."

"Long enough. Will you miss me?"

"I already do, pretty boy."

He nuzzled against the crook of her neck. "I love the sound of that. Think of me, but enjoy the seminar. Sign up a few pretty models who wish they looked as great as you do."

"You're too kind, but paying attention will be hard. I'd rather think of you."

She kissed him one more time before boarding, walking practically backwards to keep her eyes on Marc until the stewardess instructed her to watch her step.

Once Caroline was out of view, he walked to the large window to see the plane take off. A half hour later, Caroline's plane taxied and disappeared into the clouds. He couldn't believe he'd miss her the way he knew he was going to. The only thing left to do was return to his house and to try to relax, but he knew he'd only lie down on the bedsheet they made love on and keep her scent fresh in his mind until she returned to him.

The plane taxied into the airport and the bumpy landing awakened her. She'd been dreaming about her Prince Charming, wondering if he'd been an actual dream or if her whirlwind romance was a true story. Either way, she liked the fact that it occupied her mind. The flight movie, *Missing In Action*, hadn't interested her. The only action she missed was Marc's.

Once arriving at the Marriott L.A. Southwest, the breathtaking scenery took her away. It was the perfect hotel to visit with a lover. The cascading trees around the property and the lake at the outer side was like a fantasy.

She tipped the driver heavily for taking her on an unexpected guided tour of the area and helping her with her bags. The inside of the hotel was marvelous and she planned on taking another tour of it once she was situated. She was still a few hours early for her seminar and decided to make a quick call to Marc to let him know she was okay, and on the agenda. It only rang twice before he picked it up. His hurried voice made her smile, knowing he'd waited by the phone like he said he would. His sexy voice really cheered her up. "Caroline?"

"It's me, baby. I just made it in twenty minutes ago."

"How was the trip?"

"Good. It would have been better if you'd been with me."

"One day, baby. One day we both will have everything we want."

"I have what I really want in life, Marc—you."

"Same here, now that you're back in my life. What time does your seminar start?"

"Four this afternoon. That gives me time to shower and take a much needed nap. You really wore me out last night with those powerful moves of yours. It was absolutely mind-blowing, Marc."

"I aim to please, and I aim pretty damn well. It was what I always knew it would be. You go on now, take your shower and rest. I'll call you tonight and check on you. Rest well, baby."

"Only when in your arms."

"Soon, real soon."

No one ever called anywhere to check on her besides her overprotective parents and her brother Casey. It was actually refreshing to have a lover concerned for her, and she couldn't wait to get back to him. Once unpacking her business suit and hanging it up, she took a shower, imagining Marc was in it with her, reliving all those fantasies they'd dreamt about and the new ones they created.

The loofa sponge soaped her body, but her mind was constantly on the mind massage Marc had given her. He'd always been a sweet fellow but maturity and time made him a dream come true. As the sponge glided across her skin, all she could see was Marc massaging her in that giant shower off his bedroom. It was incredible, exasperating; her body still tingled from his touch. Her fingers manipulated the still swollen outer regions of her sex, and her mind danced with visions of him moving his long, thick fingers in and out. The water drenching her skin reminded her of how hot and powerful they both were while ravaging one another.

Marc was the only man who could take her on sexual vision quests. She needed a patient lover—one that took his time and introduced her to her own body and showed her what to do in order to get total satisfaction—and a passionate one. Marc was both.

Realizing she was letting her mind run away with her, she quickly turned off the shower jets, though hating to do so as if Marc was somehow in there with her, and quickly dried off in one of the thick hotel towels. Even the way she dried herself took her back to Marc; the way he had slowly toweled each and every part of her . . . concentrating specifically on her still wet folds—wet from him, not the water. The way Marc wrapped the thinnest part of the towel around his finger and inserted it into her made her crumble for him then and now when she thought on it.

Knowing she was totally wasted and incapable of rational thought, she decided to take a catnap and truly dream about him. As she looked at the clock, she felt totally thankful that she had almost two hours to lay on that bed and wallow in fantasies of Marc.

Forty minutes before the start of the seminar, Caroline jumped from the bed, quickly applied her makeup, fixed her hair in a cute under-curl bob and smiled into the mirror. She remembered doing that the day she met Marc, although she did take a bit of ridicule for it. Back then all Caroline saw in that mirror was an eager girl who did everyone's homework, in hopes of becoming popular . . . that never happened. A minute ago when she stared into the mirror, the face was the same, only older, prettier. She'd matured, become confident, realized she had a smart head on her shoulders. What pleased her most about herself was that she actually didn't give a good damn about being popular anymore.

She was happy about who she was. The fact that she'd been in Marc's arms last night and more than likely would be again was icing on the cake. With that thought in mind, she slipped into her cream and pink dress with matching cream blazer, slid into three inch pumps that made her see over everyone, and set out to conquer the rest of the damn world.

The awards half of the seminar took place the following evening in a large conference room. It was filled to capacity with other marketing executives, consultants and small business owners expecting to get acknowledged for their business efforts. Caroline was expecting the same thing. After all, she worked her butt off to make her firm run as smoothly and effectively as humanly possible. She had good staff working with her, business-minded people whose mission in life also was to get ahead. She'd prepared her speech before meeting Marc but had taken last night, since she wasn't in his arms, to tighten everything and make sure it read smoothly. In other words, she was prepared. After having a long day with top models breathing down her back, she was ready to go to her room, tighten her speech and veg out with a glass of Purple Passion sent up from the bar and a shrimp salad. As she looked through the large window overlooking the lovely sight of L.A.'s skyline, she hungered for Marc, his feel, his touch, but she would have to wait for that.

*   *   *

The other speeches were enlightening, and her speech to the head of the Chicago Small Business Commission was wonderfully executed. Her grace, style and sense of humor lit the room. Yes, Caroline Pierce was a natural. The fact that everyone approached her for her business card at the end of the seminar proved only to boost her confidence in herself and her business tactics. Yet, beyond all the glitz and glamour, professionally speaking, what she truly yearned to be good at was being a wife to a certain delicious baseball player. Still, having a business booming with more clients wouldn't hurt either.

She wasn't exactly sure, but she thought she was in the running for an enterprise grant and an award for the fastest growing business in the Chicago area. With all that on her mind, she tried her best to act as cool and calm as possible because there were some really big sharks in her line of work; sharks known to swallow a sea of smaller businesses. The fact that Marc was in her life again helped keep her on an even keel.

By nine that evening, Caroline left with the rest of the dispersing crowd and walked to the bank of elevators with a grant check in hand and a silver and crystal rosebud honoring her new venture. She'd won! She'd won everything there that she set out to achieve. Her hands were full of goodies and her stomach was full of shrimp and lobster. All she needed to top off her night was another wonderful dream of Marc Brown.

As she approached the bank of elevators with a new associate next to her, a voice called to her. She looked around and saw the reservation clerk swiftly approaching her. "Ms. Pierce, just one moment." He stood before her, smiling from ear to ear and practically out of breath from running.

Caroline looked into the face of the euphoric manager. "Can I help you?"

"Your husband Marc told me to deliver a message."

The *husband* part took her off guard, but before she could respond, the frantic man handed her the message. *"Don't bother bringing up any champagne. I have plenty for us. All my love, baby-girl. Marc."*

Her eyes met back with the man still standing before her. "When did he . . ."

"He actually gave me an autograph. I've wanted Marc Brown's autograph for years." His eyes danced again. "Funny thing, I never knew you were his wife."

"Yeah . . . neither did I."

"Pardon?"

"Oh, nothing, just thinking out loud." *Marc is upstairs in my room? Wife? What the heck is going on here?* "Thank you for the message, Mr. . . ."

"Bennett, Everett Bennett. If there's anything I can get you two, just ring me." Caroline quickly reached into her purse for a tip but he stopped her. "Oh, no need for that, Ms. Brown. Do you prefer to be called Brown or Pierce?"

I like Mrs. Brown best of all. She wasn't sure if she should have liked it, though, being one to always overreact. She didn't want that happening, causing Marc to run off scared with an Iisha complex. "Ms. Pierce is fine."

"Mr. Brown gave me a tip already, but thanks."

Hmm. Let me get my ass up there and see what that delicious thing is up to. The elevator couldn't reach the twelfth floor fast enough. She was dancing on one foot in anticipation of the *Mrs. Brown* thing. Finally, the elevator stopped. She stepped from the elevator and was met by a trail of rose petals leading directly to *their* room. After scooping a few into her hand, she smiled at the sentiment. "What has he gone and done?"

She quickly unlocked the door and there Marc was standing in the middle of the floor wearing nothing but a stiff cock and a smile that stretched from the Atlantic to the Pacific. He held a bouquet of fresh pink roses.

Her purse fell, the award almost fell and her mouth was

wide open at the vision before her. All she could do was shut the door quickly and walk over to him. "M—Marc! What are you doing here?"

"I wanted to surprise my baby . . . surprise!"

"I'll say." She dropped everything onto the bed and melted into his arms. His thick erection pressed hard against her upper stomach and she reached down to fondle it. "Umm, it feels so good to have you in my arms. All I've done since leaving you was daydream about making love to you."

"Now you don't have to imagine. We can do it all night and tomorrow. We can even do it on the plane going home."

She smiled into his loving face. "Then the friendly skies could definitely live up to their name, right?"

He didn't answer verbally. His response came in the order of a languid and bittersweet tongue curl. The tip of his tongue teased her lips, delicately treading around the curve of her lower lip, then her top before taking every inch of her. Her warm, willing mouth felt so good against his that his already sky-high phallus peaked at mountain range dimensions. The pressure filling his tip to exquisite hardness was on its way to erupting if something wasn't done about it soon.

As if reading his mind, Caroline's hands slid from around his shoulders, played devilishly with the muscles on his flat stomach, then moved further south to heaven on earth. Fingernails tenderly grazed his scrotum and he moaned in utter disbelief. She cupped it, massaging back and forth moments longer before placing her tight hand around the base of his shaft, pulling in slow, rhythmic strokes. Her mouth pulled away from his momentarily. "Is this good, baby?"

"Umm, better than your dad's medical journal."

"I showed that to you?"

"Yeah, once; and you don't know how close you were to having me stand up and strip for you, saying, "This is what the real thing looks like, girl!"

"You should have."

"Your dad would have killed me."

She stared into his eyes as if she were the only woman in love that night. She pulled on his joint, making it stretch across her body even further. "Take that stiff mass of glorious perfection and feed it to me inch by fucking inch."

Her lusty language shocked him into laughing. "Caroline! I didn't know you used those words."

"I do with you. I want so much of you rammed inside of me that I'll be able to taste you for the next three days."

"Just three days? I can do better than that." Backing away from her was agony. He didn't want any separation between them—that and the fact that his hard-on was so volcanic-rock-hard made moving painful. But what he had to do unfortunately took a bit of walking across the room. Not a long walk, but long enough while sporting a hard-on. He bent as best he could and retrieved something from under her pillow. "I was trying to save this for later, but I can tell we'll be extremely busy." He kept the object behind him until he was, again, face to face with his angel.

Her suspicious stare alerted him. "Don't worry. This won't hurt you."

"Good. You wouldn't, by any chance, have more of Iisha's hair behind your back, would you?"

"Iisha's . . . ! Come on, girl, get real. This is a special moment for me. Why the fuck would I bring Iisha's hair on vacation with me? The very idea of it nauseates me."

She tried peeking around him but he maneuvered. "Come on, Marc. Let me in on the secret." She had ideas, especially after the manager told her that her husband was waiting for her, but she chalked that up to wishful thinking. She knew Marc was wild about her, but marriage? She knew he didn't want that. He'd just delivered himself from the tar pits of hell being married to Iisha for eight miserable years. Why would he step into another trap, even if it was with her?

Her voice lowered to a soft, seductive enticement. "*Marrrc,* what are you holding back there?"

"Really want to see it, huh?"

"You want me to pull your chain again or do you want to hand over what's behind your back?"

"Pull the chain, baby. I like how you do that."

As she reached for his erection, he took her hand and placed a white satin box in it. She stared down at it, then back into his eyes. "Marc, is. . . is this what I think it is?"

"Let's open it and see." Without hesitation, he slipped the white bow from it and pulled back the top to reveal a sparkling sapphire and diamond studded engagement band. She gasped at the size of it; holding the box up to her face. "Marc . . . this is awesome."

"Awesome and all yours." He took the ring from the box and slipped it on her finger. "All you have to do is say yes and wear this. That's all, Caroline; no dilemmas, no questions, no nothing." He tried bending to his knee but the still stiff erection prevented it. Instead, he laid across the bed and pulled her on top. His fingers tugged at the side of her panties until he found her juicy nectar and plunged deeply into it. "Now you can't say no to me. You're trapped."

She took another look at the ring, then to Marc, feeling his fever pressing against her back, something she missed so much . . . and now it was there, and had a ring to boot. Her lips met his again briefly. "What woman in her right mind would say no to you, Marc?" She touched the delicate points on the ring again, then, with that same hand, stroked his stomach, circled his pecs and six-pack. "You know I'll marry you. I would have married you the minute I saw you in Midway. I would have married you the first time you spoke to me in literature class."

"Then I guess that's a yes!"

"It's yes millions and millions of times over." She removed her suit jacket and bent to him again. "I have always loved you. And each passing year without you, there was a void in my soul that couldn't get filled."

"You feel that way, too?"

"You just can't fathom how bad I have it for you, Marc.

Since we were kids. With each taco we ate and movie we attended, I fell harder for you. The more you came over and played videos and tapes with me, the harder I fell. The more you taught me to slow dance, the more I knew I had to have you one day if I could."

"Then have me, Caroline. Have me for the rest of our lives. Have me now, right here on this bed at the Marriott . . . have me until you split at the seams."

The damp dress still constricting her movements was soon over her head with Marc's help. Her half-slip ripped off and her stockings slowly moved down her legs and off her small feet. He wasn't satisfied until not a stitch was left on her, and to prove that, his magnificent destruction started at her neck, feeling her tender skin as he stroked it. Her hair grazed his warm hands and he moved it aside. Her shoulders felt as soft as a delicate flower in a spring rain. Hot-as-fire breasts moved slowly against his skin, rocking along with him as he moved.

The fire became lethal as his fingers moved across her stomach and hips. His touch made her hips move in rhythm to his advances, and he liked it, loved it, wanted more of it. His throat bobbed up and down at the feel of her velvety core. Eyes shut from eroticism soon opened again to watch his own fingers sliding in and out of her.

Upon impact of his icy-hot fingers, her back arched, her jaw trembled. Her hand on his made the strong strokes within her body that much more potent. Their hands rocked in unison, feeling her slick folds, darting across her G-spot, nibbling her clit until her whole body vibrated against him. After her return to earth, he slowly pulled from within her, saying in a raspy voice, "I gotta have it, girl." He tossed an assortment of condoms on the bed and sheathed himself with one.

"Then take it, make it glad it's alive."

He raised her slightly above, aligned himself directly with her opening and slid deeply into her, thrusting up and down like a madman, gyrating and rocking her hips so intently that her breasts were bouncing. He cupped them, toyed with the perfectly taut nipples, raking his flat hands up and down their surface.

Caroline was so deep in a pool of ecstasy that she could barely breathe. His effect upon her mind, body and soul went deeper than redwood roots in a giant forest. Tears streamed from her eyes as Marc wiped them. "Why are you crying, baby?"

"They're happy tears. The only man I've ever loved is loving me back."

"He's always loved you. And he'll spend the rest of his life showing you just how much."

He pumped in and out of her with ragged force, arching his back, squeezing his eyes shut and throwing his head back against the pillow as a massive stream jetted from him, liquid love.

Caroline just stared down at him as if he were the most outrageously glorious thing to grace earth. He was beautiful, out-fucking-standing and all hers. The idea of him belonging to her and her alone made her come like crazy, reaching for the sky, squirming against him, tightening her muscles around him. He, as well, stared up in wonder as she gave him all she had to give.

She wanted to simply collapse on top of him but he wasn't having it. He wasn't finished giving her everything she deserved. Their hands and fingers untangled and he moved her to her side. He bent to his knees, though his erection was still sky-high, and placed her buttocks on the edge of the bed. Staring into her swollen sexual core, and seeing nothing but a pot of gold at the end of a rainbow really set him off. Barely seconds passed before his lips and tongue were attacking her. Her screams and moans proved to be what really kicked him into gear. Upon hearing her voice, his tongue swelled in circles on every part of her—licking, sucking, tugging and helping everything along by inserting one of those fingers used to throw smokers at opposing teams.

She bucked against him so much until she delivered the goods, giving him what he craved to taste. Tasting her honey served him up a dose of rock-solid cock and he pitched all over the bedsheets again. They came at the same time and their calls were heard in sweet unison.

After eating their fill of caviar, they toasted to their life together with a few glasses of champagne. She fell asleep on his chest, staring at the glittering engagement band. Her last thought before drifting off: *Why am I the lucky one? Is God smiling down on me or something? He must be.*

Early the next morning she was still in the same position, on Marc's chest. A smile automatically crossed her face as the stunning ring cast a light glow against a sun-tinted wall. It was going to be a beautiful day in every way possible. Marc was in her life, the diamond on her finger and the sun was out. No matter what sorry thing was happening in her life, the shining sun always made her smile. Now that she had a true reason to be happy, the sun seemed so much brighter.

Marc's sleepy voice startled her. "So, have you decided when we should make this legal?"

His voice was always music to her ears. She raised up and kissed his lips. "Umm, now would be a good time."

"I'd love to but I can't. My All Star break will be over soon and the Yankees expect me on the mound to give them their ass-whipping."

"Is there a ticket for me?"

His arms tightened around her. "Sure. You'll be on the mound with me because there's no way in hell you're ever leaving my sight."

"I may very well be the reason you lose against the Bronx Bombers."

"Yeah, you're so damn gorgeous that they'll strike out just to get a gander at you."

Caroline still didn't understand what it was about her that Marc found irresistible. Nonetheless, it wasn't her job to know why. Her job was to keep him happy. "Well, let's think about this. Your season isn't over until the end of summer, right?"

"Sometimes longer if we go to the playoffs. I don't think we have a chance this year since Detroit and Cleveland are killing one another in the pennant race. We could easily do it in about a month. Is that good for you, baby?"

"I don't care when it is, Marc, I just want you . . . although, I have always wanted a summer wedding."

"That settles it. Late summer it is." He kissed her hand. "Let's get dressed and go for breakfast by the pool. Also, while I'm thinking about it, I really don't have to be at the ballpark for another two days. Why don't we just stay here, explore the city, find some beaches to go to, unless you have to be back at work now that you've won awards and all. Hell, I may not be able to keep up with you."

"Oh, I'll make sure we keep up with each other. I really don't have to be in the office until Tuesday but again we have a ticket issue. I'm booked to return this afternoon."

"Not a problem, we'll change it like we did before. Now, is that a plan or what?"

"No, this is a plan." She leaned him against the pillow and they made love for another hour. The only thing that stopped them was hungry stomachs. Last night's caviar could only last so long.

After showering together they went to the hotel's dress shop and bought her a few things to wear since she'd only packed business attire. Caroline liked a white, off-the-shoulder floral sundress and disappeared behind the curtains to try it on. She stepped out two minutes later and treated Marc to a look at the wonderful, skimpy dress. His eyes danced as hints of her perky breasts edged above the slightly low neckline. He smiled and ran his hand across the crepe material. "I love it, but—" He grabbed a red dress from the chair and handed it to her. "I think you'll look better in this one. Try it on."

"I don't look good in red." She remembered the red flames she thought Iisha should have worn at their wedding and looked at the red dress again. "Well, if you think I'll look good in it, I'll try it on."

It felt like she was wearing a cloud. The soft, clingy material draped across every curve. She smiled into the mirror. *Marc should really like this*. She stepped out and did a half turn before him. "What do you think?"

His eyes alighted upon an African queen decked out in red sequins. "I think it's boner time again. Look at my pants."

Not being able to help herself, she looked at it and it was massive. "Hmm, maybe we should go back to the room and finish what we started this morning."

"Yeah, let's do that."

He took her hand but she retracted. "Marc, don't we have to pay for these things first?"

"Forgot about that."

"Which one do you like?"

"I like them both so let's get them. You'll also need more thongs for me to rip off of you."

"What good would the outfits and panties be without perfume?"

"If you want some but you're sweet smelling enough for me—for any man."

They relaxed by the poolside for lunch and ordered crab and lobster, favorites of both of them. As the plate arrived, Marc remembered the time Caroline's father gave them spending money and told them to get something good to eat after the show. He'd taken her to Captain Jim O'Brady's for the all you can eat buffet. They ran out of money and had to have Mr. Pierce rescue them, but in the process, he'd loved watching Caroline get her fill of shrimp. He could never have fun like that with Iisha. She always had to have some of the hoochies with them but kicked them out before she and Marc had sex in the back of his father's station wagon. That was the difference between Iisha and Caroline; with Iisha it always was sex, but with Caroline, it was love.

Watching Caroline dive into her fried crab special brought back so many wonderful memories, memories he planned on remembering for as long as he lived . . . and making more.

Caroline remembered the same things, like her father having to leave his football game and give two stupid kids more money. She knew her father hadn't expected Marc to take her to a place that expensive. The thing about Marc, he always spent money on her, even if it wasn't his money. Now was different. Stood to reason why his home had four bathrooms. It proved that beating up on Pirates, Dodgers and Red Sox definitely had its advantages.

They decided to take the long drive to upper California and stopped at a roadside café for dinner on the outskirts of Big Sur. They'd explored the coastal towns along the way and found California quite beautiful. It was full of palm trees, little fruit stands here and there, which they stopped at and enjoyed watermelon, strawberries, cherries; and even took in a festival in Pacifica. He bought her a diamond pendant in the shape of a heart. He kissed it, kissed her and placed it on the gold chain around her neck. That sealed their love because all their heat and desire was captured within that little heart. She wore it over her own.

The café was a quaint little place that gave them the luxury of being secluded in the back. They ate their salads and sandwiches but concentrated more on holding hands, kissing and getting in sneak attacks on one another. That night they took a midnight swim in the hotel pool, made love in the shower and made more love in bed until three that morning. The entire time, Caroline was either staring down that rock on her finger, or staring into Marc's loving eyes as he lay upon her.

*   *   *

The wake-up call from the main desk startled them both. Realizing they had to be on a plane and back in Chicago by one that afternoon, they hurried around practically in the dark getting dressed. A half hour later, with bags in his arms, he leaned over, kissed Caroline and thanked her for another wild and wicked evening, though they were still very sleepy.

They had exactly a half hour to grab something to eat in the hotel restaurant. They were given a private table since the entire hotel knew who he was, and were escorted to the deck overlooking a small lake. Marc sat across from her, eating eggs and ham while she settled for an English muffin loaded with sour cream and fruit on the side. It was like they were sitting in their own breakfast nook at Marc's house. There was a breeze, trees were gently swaying in the wind and the water rippled, making a babbling brook sound.

Caroline couldn't help but smile because everything was perfect.

He saw the glee on her face. "Still thinking about last night?"

"That was wild, wasn't it?"

"The best damn thing I've ever had, but it's going to get a lot better, Caroline. I promise you a life full of every thinkable thing you can imagine, but most of all, I promise you a life so full of love that you'll beg me to leave you alone for a microsecond."

"I'll never want you to leave me alone. I've found paradise again. Who'd want to leave paradise?"

"A nut, like Iisha. I gave her everything. I gave her a son and she hardly spends time with him. Most of the time he's in school or at some camp. I hardly have time to spend with him other than the off season."

"Do you see him a lot then?"

"He practically spends the winters with me. I hope that's okay with you? If not, I'll work something out."

"Marc, he's your son. Of course I don't mind. I'd think you were a terrible father if you didn't want Winston with you. Besides, I love kids and I'd love to meet him."

"You will. In fact, before I go back to work, I'd like to stop by Iisha's and pick him up, let him spend a day or so with us. I want him to know my new wife and I know he'll love the ground you walk on. . . . like his father does."

"I'd love that. Then he'll know that his father finally found someone who loves him back. And I promise you, I will never want to date your ATM card."

"My ATM—girl, you are so crazy!"

"Yeah, crazy in love."

"The only way to be crazy."

Caroline kind of danced around her next question, not exactly knowing how to ask it. "Will . . . will Iisha be there when we pick Winston up?"

"Either there or at the beauty parlor fixing things up. Why?"

"Just wondering."

He wrapped his warm hand around hers. "Don't be afraid of Iisha. She has matured some and I won't let anything happen to you. Have I ever let anyone hurt you while in my presence?"

"No! It's not that I'm scared of her. It's more like I'll remember all the sick shit she used to do to me. I won't be rude to her, but I can't help but think."

"You have every right to feel the way you do, but don't worry about her. She has other things to do besides making someone else do her Shakespeare homework."

"You knew about that?"

"I've known about that for years. Your brother, Casey told me."

"Who didn't that damn Casey tell? That boy's mouth was so big that all of Peoria could fit into it. He's always been that way."

"And I'm glad. You never told me what those chumps did to you."

"I didn't want to look like a fool to you."

"That was never an issue, Caroline." He looked at his watch. "We'd better get a cab over here. Girl, talking to you can make a guy late to his own funeral."

"We have about seventy years before that happens." She kissed his juice-flavored lips and they retreated to the front desk to order a cab.

Caroline was glad they didn't have a four-hour delay, though she did have something to occupy her mind. Their flight was quick and smooth; everything associated with Marc was smooth, including his lovemaking. That, he was an expert at. Iisha had to have been some kind of a damn fool to let him go.

When he was given permission for cell phone usage aboard, he called his son. Caroline listened briefly as the proud father made arrangements to pick him up. "Hey, little dude! You want to spend a few days with your old man before he has to hunt down the Anaheim Angels? . . . Yes, I know you can't wait . . . yes, we can go to the beach. Doesn't your mother take you there sometimes? . . . I know, she doesn't want to get her hair wet . . . yep! Be ready by noon tomorrow, and there's someone I want you to meet. . . . no, not A-Rod, some-one prettier than him. No, I'm not telling you. I want this to be a surprise."

Caroline continued to listen in glee as he spoke so fondly of her. She couldn't wait to start her life with him; a life that should have started years ago, if not for Iisha. She'd fooled Marc back then, but he was no longer a boy, in more ways than one.

Marc slipped the cell phone into his pocket and turned to his soon-to-be new Mrs. "I can't wait to show you off to my family. Winston thought you were A-Rod or Derek Jeter."

"I have a few more curves."

"Damn right you do, and I'd love to see them in midair."

"What? What are you talking about?"

He lowered his voice so no one could possibly hear. "Just what I said."

"Marc, we'd get arrested for indecent exposure."

"Not if we're in the bathroom. I know how you like tight *little spots*. I have two tight spots for you, me and that cramped little bathroom; it's just small enough to force everything together."

"But . . . there's no shower in that one."

"I'm quite certain that won't ruin us, Caroline. Know what I'm saying?"

"You really want to do that in midair?"

"Any time I can get higher and higher with you, I'm all for it. What better place to skyrocket than in a plane?"

"Where did you learn to get so damn freaky?"

"Is that a bad thing?"

"Nothing is bad with you, Marc, but I'm not sure about this. Someone might need the bathroom while we're in the middle of things. Know what I mean?"

"Are you scared to do it in there?"

"A little."

"Then I've got a better idea. Hand me the *New York Times*."

"What are you going to do with that?"

"You'll see."

He spread it across her lap and slid his hand underneath, stroking her velvety-soft thighs. His voice lowered. "I just have to touch you."

She gave in, letting Marc massage her inner thighs, stroking them in soft circular motions and stopping at the brink of her sex. Her body wanted him to delve deeper, but her mind was hoping he'd play it safe. The more he strummed her flesh, the tighter his pants bunched up in front and she loved the sight of it. She almost took what was left of the paper and put it across his lap, but decided not to. She'd never be able to stop once any part of Marc was in her hands.

Moments later, he gave her a luscious kiss, pulled her skirt back down and tried to watch the flight movie. For the rest of the trip, he had to be content with resting his head upon her shoulder and imagining what he'd do to her in bed that night.

That evening, Caroline lay awake in bed next to Marc. He was sleeping the sleep of the undead due to jet lag and getting nailed by her only hours before. As she looked at the high ceiling, she felt at home, safe; she felt that was the only place she was ever really supposed to be. She'd made her own way in life as a successful modeling agency owner, had just won an award and a grant and got her share of congrats from many an executive, but her proudest moment was seeing Marc in Midway a few days ago. Within a span of three days, she'd become engaged, and told she'd be the stepmother to an awesome child she truly hoped didn't look too much like Iisha. From Winston's picture, taken five years ago, he looked like a mixture, but time changes people. She only hoped life remained kind to Winston and gave him an ounce more of Marc.

She couldn't help a shiver at the thought of actually seeing Iisha the following afternoon. Iisha always had a way of deflating the highest of egos and people didn't change *that* much. Caroline told herself not to worry too much. She knew Marc would jack Iisha at the very indication of rudeness.

The following afternoon after fixing Marc a wonderful breakfast with appliances she could only dream of, they sat on his patio and stared at Lake Michigan. It was calming, peaceful, and just being with Marc like this was all Caroline ever wanted out of life. However, when he mentioned fetching Winston, her demeanor changed. Marc noticed and took her hand. "Are you afraid of Winston not liking you?"

"No, I get along really well with children."

"Then what is it? You look so lost all of a sudden."

"Really, I'm fine. I'm just eager to settle into my new life."

"Come on, I know it's something. I've known you over twelve years, Caroline. Is it that I have to leave after my games here and be away from you for a few days?"

She smiled. "Well, that doesn't exactly make me happy, but that is the life of a baseball wife."

"That's the very word, baby—*wife*! I'm coming back. And I really don't think we're going to the playoffs this year unless things turn around for the team, so I'll be here for you."

She moved into him, kissing his neck. "I know that, baby. That is your job, but that's not the problem. I'd wait months to be with you if I had to."

He stared into her desperate eyes. "Darling, what's wrong? You can tell me. Is it the house, the—"

"It's . . . it's Iisha."

"Iisha! You said you didn't give a damn about her."

"I lied. Marc, she and others made me feel so bad, and in ways I never told you."

"Don't let her get in the way. You'll have to see her on occasions and I can't help that." He held her close to his chest. "I promise; I will never let her say a damn thing out of the way to you. If she does, you have my permission to deck her. Hell, you won't need my permission, just do it. Believe me, I know you're strong, Caroline. You wrestle me in bed and wear me out. You can do anything you want, baby, and I'll always back you."

"You will?"

"Forever. You keep forgetting that I just figured out how much I have always loved you. It's a revelation. Nothing. . . . nothing you can do will ever change that." He cupped her chin. "So, you coming with me to get Winston or are you going to never get the chance to deck Iisha?"

That made her smile, gave her confidence. "Let's go and get that kid."

"That's my girl."

They pulled up to a well-manicured house, pretty flowers in neat borders, a bicycle on the porch and a blue Mercedes in the driveway. Caroline eyed the house suspiciously. "Iisha lives here?"

"Yeah, why?"

"Well, not to be funny, but I assumed she'd live in a place with a barbeque grill on the front porch, brown grass and neighbors' kids running all over the place. I just didn't expect her to have a nice house, since she never took care of anything else."

"You got that right. You must be psychic, Caroline. When the mansion was ours, she never took care of it, always had her friends and liquor bottles all over the damn place. She kept it a mess while I was gone. After the divorce, I bought this place for her and one of the stipulations was that if she didn't provide a nice home for Winston, I'd fight her in court for him. Don't get me wrong, she loves our son, but she simply adores the child support checks every month. That's how she got that Benz. She told me she needed a decent car to tote him around to Little League."

"Marc, a decent car is a Pontiac, Honda, Ford, something like that. A Benz is not decent, it's downright luxurious."

"Right, but I went along with it to get her out of my hair." He kissed her hand. "Let's get Winston and jet to Northern Lakes Sea Food. I know that's your favorite place."

"Anywhere you are is my favorite place."

He kissed her lips, walked around to the other side and helped her from the car. Arm and arm, they walked the short distance to Iisha's front door and he whispered, "Don't worry, things will be fine. I'll make them fine."

Every vision of Iisha that clouded her mind as they waited on that porch was one of sincere ugliness. But to her surprise when she finally looked in Iisha's face, all she saw was . . . beauty. Iisha actually looked like she knew how to take care of herself.

But Caroline continued to stay close to Marc in case her rival proved to be her same old trash-talking self.

Iisha smiled and opened the door while blowing a puff of smoke from the burning cigarette in her hand. "Hey, Marc. A little early, aren't you?"

"Not really. I did call. Can we come in?"

"We?"

Realizing she hadn't recognized Caroline, he smiled a wicked smile as if glad to introduce the new and improved model. He pulled the wary Caroline closer to him. "Hey, don't you know who I'm with?"

Iisha squinted through the smoke. "Not really. Why don't you two come in?"

As they stepped into the house, Marc tried telling her but Iisha cut him off. "Winston is at the store buying my Kools. I ran out. He'll be back soon."

That made Marc temporarily forget introductions. "What the hell is Winston doing buying cigarettes, Iisha?"

"They know him down at the store. We go there all the time."

Feeling himself sliding into a heated rage, he calmed his voice. "I don't want my child buying cigarettes, Iisha."

"He's my child, too."

"Then why would you—" He stopped before he made a fool out of himself in front of the one woman he loved. Besides, arguing with Iisha was a non-happening event in his life. He was done with the drama. He wrapped his arm around Caroline's waist. "I'm sure you'll remember who this is after hearing her name."

Iisha smiled at Caroline. "Sorry for the diss. You are. . . ?"

Caroline automatically reached for Iisha's hand. "I'm Caroline Pierce. I remember you."

Iisha's shocked expression would have made a bear shit bullets. "What? You're Caroline? That little skinny—"

Not in the mood to hear bullshit, Caroline stopped her dead in her tracks. "Yes, one and the same."

Iisha moved closer to her. "Well, I'll be damned."

"You may very well be."

Ignoring Marc's comment, a smile suddenly graced Iisha's face. It was a smile of sincere joy and sincere shock. "Look at you, girlfriend. You're absolutely gorgeous! What happened to you to cause this transformation?"

Marc cut in. "She was always gorgeous, Iisha. You just never bothered to look."

Caroline held up a hand. "It's okay, Marc, I know I wasn't much back then."

Iisha blew a puff of smoke casually in Marc's direction. "You always did love her, didn't you?" She returned to Caroline. "I knew that all along and I guess I was just jealous." She sat down and crumpled the butt of the cigarette into an ashtray. "Have a seat, both of you. Winston will be in soon. By the way, Caroline, I always wanted to apologize about how rude I was to you, once I grew up some."

That took Caroline by surprise. She never expected to hear the infamous Iisha Burns say she was sorry for any damn thing. She actually felt sorry for Iisha, seeing the look on her face, the look of a woman who still loved a man who didn't love her. Iisha didn't know how to handle a man like Marc, but Caroline sure did—and she planned to for the rest of her life. Though as not to add insult to injury, she softened the blow. "You were a kid like me, Iisha. We all grow up, and you of course, you are still as beautiful as the day I met you." Okay, so it was a lie but Caroline was never one to hurt someone's feelings.

Marc's eyes rolled at that comment but he never said a word as the two women continued talking.

"I appreciate that, Caroline. I really am sorry about how I was back then. I can't imagine how you felt. I wouldn't want someone like me going to school with Winston."

"We all change, Iisha, but thanks for the kind words."

Marc, getting tired of waiting for a child to return from buying cigarettes, immediately interjected with words less frilly, but words that nonetheless needed to be spoken. "Caroline and I are getting married in a month."

Judging by the look on her face, that wasn't exactly what Iisha wanted to hear. And as usual, a callous reply could be counted on. "Really now. I thought you were done with the marriage game."

"Apparently I'm not."

"I guess I wasn't enough for you, right?"

"That was the problem, Iisha, you *were* enough. The last straw, actually."

Before Iisha could reply, Winston came in, slamming the screen door behind him. "Mom, here's your cancer sticks."

Yes, the remark was rude, but he cared about his mother. At that point, Caroline knew he was someone she'd like immensely. The child, who did look a little like Iisha, though cuter, entered the room and Caroline stood to meet him. "This has got to be your son, Marc. He's long and lean like you."

Marc hugged his son, then immediately introduced him to his soon-to-be legal soul mate. "Winston, this is Caroline Pierce."

The boy looked at her and smiled. "I know that name. She's the one you said you liked a lot in school."

At that, Iisha blew a larger puff of smoke into the air, one that everyone, including Winston, chose to ignore.

"She's the one."

Winston remembered his manners and extended his hand to Caroline. "Pleased to meet you."

Caroline politely took the little hand he stretched out. His eyes were so intelligent, his words so adult. She couldn't help but want to pinch his dimpled cheeks. "You are a very handsome young man and I'm pleased to meet you myself."

Marc approached the two and wrapped his arm around Caroline; looking Winston in the face. "How would you feel about me getting married again?"

"Well. . ." He looked quickly to his mother, who proceeded to shrug her shoulders, then returned to his father and

Caroline. "I think it would be cool. Does she make you happy?"

Marc smiled down at Caroline. "Very." They shared a brief kiss as Iisha coughed over the last drag of her coffin nail.

Winston's voice brought everyone back to reality. "I like it when dad is happy."

Caroline reassured him. "I like it when your dad is happy, too. Let's both see to that." They high-fived one another.

"Get your bags, Winston. Caroline and I are taking you to the beach."

"Coolllllll." Winston disappeared into a back bedroom.

Iisha lit another cigarette. Between puffs she uttered, "Make sure you have him back by Sunday morning. Asia is taking him to see our new establishment before the grand opening."

"How is Asia doing these days?"

"She's okay, Caroline. She and I are opening up a new beauty parlor, Ms. Nadine's on the Boulevard. We named it after her daughter since she takes care of the business aspect of it. Have you heard of it?"

"I sure have, Marc told me about it. It should be a nice shop once together."

Minutes later, Winston was raring to go and the three walked from Iisha's house. Winston immediately took hold of Caroline's hand and smiled up at her.

One month later . . .

"I just can't believe I'm finally going to Hawaii and with Mr. Marc Brown on my arm." Caroline reclined her first-class seat and took her headphones off.

"That's only part of the deal."

"What? What else have you planned other than a seaside wedding and flying both families out to it?"

He leaned in closer. "Well, you know how I love flying high."

"What are you getting at?"

"I haven't forgotten the tight little place you refused to enter with me." He pointed in the general direction of the restrooms. "The facilities in 747's are much bigger. I mean, it's cramped but there's a little more leeway. Come on, indulge me."

"I don't know about that. Someone might really need it."

"Everybody on board is sleeping, that movie is so boring. Come on, girl, this'll get me harder than anything has yet, other than you."

She smiled in surprise. "You really want to join the Mile-High Club?"

"Yeah!"

"Well. . ."

"I'll go in first and you come in, in about five minutes."

"If this is what you really want."

"It is. Five minutes—remember. Knock two times, then two more."

Caroline watched him walk the long aisle and duck into the bathroom. She loosened the tie on her bright red halter top and adjusted her sandals. *I can't believe I'm doing this.* On the very dot, she slid into the aisleway and trekked into Marc's private fantasy. She tapped on the door then quickly got inside, folding the awkward door. Marc was sitting on the corner of the sink with his jeans unzipped. He was sporting a massive one already. The sight of it forced her into his arms to feel what surely awaited her.

He moved into her, kissed her like mad, then reached under her swing skirt for panties, which practically fell apart in his strong hands. "If these got any skimpier, they'd barely stay on you."

Her lips briefly moved from his warm neck. "Don't talk, just rip 'em."

Their mouths met and matched as they lusted after one another in a wickedly wild frenzy. Marc's fingers slid into her softness and rocked her with virile power. Caroline, at the same time, reached into his open pants and grabbed a throbbing erection that was ready for action.

Without further hesitation, Marc lifted her and with one slick, yet forceful stroke, he was inside her love stuff, pumping her, rocking her slowly up and down his impatient shaft. The intensity was so great that he had to kiss her again to stop them both from screaming. Their lips matched the sensual rhythm of their sex, eating everything they saw. He pulled the string of her halter and her erect nipples faced him, ready for him, ready to be devoured.

The friction of his hands and his hard-on doing double duty made her see fireworks behind her eyes. She could barely see straight due to the incredible sensations he was giving her in such tight quarters.

Turbulence forced him deeper into her, making them both feel the need to release. He looked into Caroline's face, her cheeks were flushed, her lips trembling, eyes pleading. "You want to come, don't you?"

"More than I want to breathe."

"Do it, then! Let's dream the same dream."

She released onto him and he released into her, and once the last drop was delivered, they stared at one another. For minutes nothing else in the world mattered, nothing existed but them and the love they felt for each other.

A bump brought them back to the real world. At any moment, someone was liable to need a release from their miniature mai-tais. Between clothes being fixed in a rush, he stopped and took her hand. "We'll be in Hawaii soon. Ready?"

"For the rest of my life? I was born ready for you."

atten-tion!

I get all kinds of creeps in here despite the fact that this establishment is just on the outskirts of a military base. These aren't your usual creeps, though, mostly PFCs corporals, regular Army personnel in other words, but some of them have tastes that are really out there, and that's what I like!

Besides the regular Army Joes, there are some big boys scampering around here, and their needs are exactly what I'm looking to satisfy. Base Commander David Alan Carrington is one of those big boys.

You see, I work about five minutes from Fort Benning Army Base. We have access to everything related to the Army, by the end of the soldiers' day, they have equal access to us, and they crawl in here for their weekly massage. Yes, I run the best massage parlor this side of the Mississippi, so I get 'em all and see it all. Working out the kinks from all those hot and bothered gentlemen sworn in to protect and serve our country does wonders for a girl's morale.

I love my job, and all the sexy-ass men come in and tell me I'm the best. Damn right I am. If a sergeant tells me I've got the hook-up, then I know I'm straight up on my game. Far cry from the little skinny black girl who barely graduated high school in Detroit, Michigan, wouldn't you say? There are other things that skinny black child did; we can talk later about that, however. Today, our assignment is discovering how I really got mine.

Everything was going wonderful for me. My exotic little establishment made a mint and I was as happy as a shark in a pool of blood. I'd finally had an idea that made a ton of the mean green and in the meantime got to work out a few frustrations of my own. When I say "work out," I really mean it. I'd single-handedly concocted a plan that kept cash in the Coach purse and my libido happily satisfied without being called a hooker.

I had a closed-circuit television in my parlor, so when Sheila, my receptionist, was out, I could still see who walked in to get theirs. If any Army personnel walked in and they didn't have an appointment, we made it a point to squeeze them in. I mean that literally as well.

Sheila had the day off and the rest of us were on double duty, protecting that front door much the same way a Doberman Pinscher protects his one and only steak. My hands were full of hulking red-hot meat from some deliciously overworked GI when I saw the hunk of the century insert his passkey into the front door and let himself in. I thought I recognized him. He waited in the reception area for that lucky-ass Jasmine, my top operator, to lead him to paradise and sex him completely out. From the looks of him, I knew she'd do exactly that!

As he waited, I got a good look at him; prettiest damn thing I'd ever set my eyes on. It was a black and white monitor, but I could see what that man was sporting. His dark wavy hair was cut into the most delicious crew imaginable. Staring at that dude, I almost left poor PFC Malone with his khakis around his bootstraps. When your eyes narrow in on delicious prey, you lose control of everything, including your self-respect. The way that man looked tapping his passkey against his pants leg while awaiting Jasmine, well . . . it almost brought me to tears—tears of sexual gratification.

Damn! The man hadn't even laid an eye on me and I was losing it in a major way. Goodness, what I would have done to have his passkey sliding in and out of my lock! The possibilities were endless, and so was my imagination.

Realizing I was getting way too carried away with a client who wasn't even mine, I returned to PFC Malone and turned his ass out. Funny thing, I'd never wailed on him before, but after seeing Jasmine's client, I couldn't think of anything else but to get into mode and wax someone.

We were done twenty minutes later. PFC Malone was a good feel but still too quick for me and was ready to go back to work. I helped him clean up, and he took my face into his hands. "You laid it on thick today. Why was that?"

"Did you enjoy it?"

"Hell yes!"

"Then my mission is complete." I sure the hell couldn't tell him the sight of another client put me in overdrive and landed me directly in climax heaven. I didn't have to pass Go or collect $200.00 dollars, either. My Monopoly was building continuously, and the cause was David Alan Carrington.

My delicious little PFC kissed my cheek, paid his bill then walked out. That left me with time to kill until Lieutenant Bergman appeared—another fine ass, but not as cute as Jasmine's client, who was getting his rocks off. I sat up front and covered the front desk in Sheila's absence. It was pure murder sitting up there because Jasmine's room was directly behind me. I could hear everything she was doing to that pretty man. There were wails, shrieks, screams and all of them were coming from her. I thought *she* was the one supposed to be giving the massages, not getting one. Yeah, right. Who was I to tell her not to scream so loud when my own heat could have set off the water sprinklers? Now, that's an idea. Being wet in every possible way is always a good idea. I'll have to add that to my regimen! Nonetheless, it was hard listening to Jasmine getting hers and wishing it were me getting mine . . . again.

Finally, I had the distinct pleasure of hearing his voice, a throaty voice, deep and sexy beyond human reasoning. He was the kind who spoke while getting nailed. He said things so outrageously enticing that my panties were getting wet, and not from the sprinkler idea. I heard him screaming to Jasmine. "Do it! Do it, girl. Take it hard and deep. Make me spray bullets. . . . kill me with it!"

Damn, I was losing my ever-loving mind over his words alone. Yes indeed, he looked like he could jam, and I hated Jasmine because she was getting everything I wanted. There was freaky things going on in there, but hey, as long as the client was satisfied, that was our mission. The good thing was that the cops looked the other way. If they didn't, I'd be dead out on the street; so would Jasmine and my other girls. All those poor captains, generals and commanders would have to take their frustrations out on the newcomers in basic training. If Jasmine's client were to conduct basic training, I'd sure the fuck join up and be stationed on the front line!

I had to calm down because, again, I was getting in too deep over a man I had seen once. I'd never gotten into a jam fixating over a client, and wasn't about to start. Having to return to Detroit because I screwed up here wasn't a cheery thought. This state and this place was my life, and nothing else would suffice.

Jasmine's door opened thirty minutes later, and I swiveled my chair back around, pretending I hadn't heard a thing. How could I pretend that I hadn't heard delicious screams and shouts from a man that had set my loins on fire? Impossible, but I put on an act. I picked up my nail file and waited for them to approach the desk. Normally Jasmine comes out and makes the next appointment herself, but she stayed in the room this time. I guess she had to clean up from getting severely screwed by pretty boy. I kept my head down so my red cheeks wouldn't be seen, but from the top of my glasses I could see the familiar khakis and smelled a strong hint of sex and Cool Water aftershave. Let me tell you, it smelled great!

Being forced to lift my head and make his next appointment was drudgery. I knew the man was a darker shade of fine, but for some reason it was hard to look at him after he'd practically broken Jasmine in half. I was also embarrassed over the fact that a man's voice had made me come so hard that I'd practically ruined Sheila's chair.

I took that step to ecstasy and looked up. My eyes slowly moved up from the khaki pants with the still-stiff erection practically in my face. I narrowed in on his broad shoulders, muscled light brown arms, and row after row of military bars across his shirt. Hell, I kept going on from there—no way was I *not* going to get a close-up gander at him. I knew he was my best girl's client, but damn! Eye candy is a heck of a thing to avoid.

My eyes finally met his, and he was staring at me like he was still hungry. Maybe he was, and I'd have been too glad to breastfeed that baby. He stared down into my cinnamon shoulder-length hair; his stare was so powerful that I thought he'd tan my brown skin another shade darker. I could just imagine how his eyes would burn into mine, turning my hazel eyes into embers.

My God, was he ever beautiful. That closed-circuit television did him no justice. His complexion was like bronzed honey—smooth and sweet. That jet-black hair sent shivers up and down my spine; his pencil-thin mustache made me ache for what his body could do for mine. A microsecond later, it hit me. He was the man I had followed into the PX one day. Just a look at his profile, and the way his tight ass filled out those khakis had controlled me. I lost track of him that day as he disappeared into the power-tools aisle, but there he was standing before me, turning me into a puddle of quivering jelly.

My panties were sopping wet by that time. Sheila's desk

chair was trashed. A trip to Office Surplus was on the horizon for later, or Sheila would wonder what the fuck was going on while she was away.

I didn't know if I'd been staring uncontrollably, but all I could imagine doing was tasting that delicious mustache with the tip of my seductive tongue and eating him out from there on. Being the professional that I am, though, I pleasantly smiled up at him and asked, "May I schedule your next appointment for you?"

He didn't comment on that, but kept staring at me and said, "What's your name, darlin'?"

His southern accent made me tremble; it was so erotic sounding. Being in Georgia, I was used to hearing southern drawls but this man's was straight-up naughty! I don't know if it was the sexiness of the accent itself, or the fact that he was actually talking to me. "My name's Marliss Tanner. I'm the owner."

His eyes lit up like a Fourth of July birthday celebration. "Really? The owner, huh? So, you're the one."

"The one?"

"That's right, darlin'. You were the one making those wickedly fantastic screams when I came in. I asked who that was, and Jasmine told me who you were."

I covered my face. "Remind me to kill her later! Was I that loud? I'm so sorry."

"Don't you dare apologize. Hell, those sexy screams made me cut loose. I just hope Ms. Jasmine can recover, and whoever else that was in the room with you."

"He'll recover. It's an act. He likes it when I scream, and I give him a good show for his money."

"There are some men in this world who could make those screams really meaningful."

No doubt!

He moved in closer, producing a Cheshire cat smile that made me want to drop to my knees. "I'm truly pleased to finally meet the mastermind of this fine establishment. I'm the new base commander."

"Then you're the one who replaced Dennis Rogers?"

"Yes, ma'am. Was he a client here?"

"A major one."

"Yours personally?"

"Yes, actually."

"Then I'm sorry to say I haven't completely replaced him. That could change, though."

"I, um—"

"I know I'm embarrassing you, Ms. Marliss, and I'm sorry." He extended his hand. "I'm David Alan Carrington, but you can call me . . . anything you like." He slowly licked his lower lip, and my thong, which was already wet, was now sticking to my skin and Sheila's chair. All I wanted to do was peel it off and hand it to him with a pretty red cherry on top. I took his hand, feeling the softest, warmest hands that a commander could possibly have. His fingers were long and well manicured. That was a good sign. In my experience, a man with long fingers could twist and turn them inside of a woman so expertly that she could faint from the mere thought of it. I was truly enticed. He had a hell of a grip, too, one that didn't want to let go.

It was my mission to pull my hand away before embarrassing myself. "I'm glad to finally meet you. I often wondered who had replaced Commander Rogers."

"Now you know." He sat on the corner of my desk, barely inches away from me. His eyes had a direct view to my V-neck sweater. The smile on his face indicated total satisfaction with his new seat. "I plan on making this place a habit."

"Indeed. I'm glad you like my establishment well enough to come back."

He reached across me for the sign-out sheet, and his aroma captivated me more than any other man's ever had. He was a good mixture of everything seductive, and it was all natural.

He looked like raw, natural sex; the type of man who looked good in any situation. *In any position!* Heavens, my mind was running on adrenaline.

His voice brought me back to the real. "I'll definitely be back, Ms. Marliss."

"I'll look forward to that, Commander Carrington. Maybe I'll see you in the PX again sometime."

"You've seen me in there?"

"Only a glimpse from behind. Every woman worth her pantyliners would watch you walking around base. She'd be a complete idiot if she didn't go out of her way to watch you walking. I just never knew you were the new commander." I couldn't believe I'd just said that to him. Normally I'm rather shy, but I guess he brought out the bonafide freak in me.

His fingers traced the side of my cheek. "I'll have to check out the pantyliners for myself someday, sugah." His thumb grazed my lips, leaving a pink lipstick smear on his skin that he proceeded to lick off. I almost slid from the chair I already had to replace. He winked. "I'll be back next Tuesday. Pencil in a spot for me; I could use a little double duty."

I could barely talk, but made sure to sound a little professional no matter what tempting devil was beckoning me. "I'm sorry, sir, but we have a strict policy: one operator per customer."

"That's really too bad; I've seen your room before. There'd be plenty of room for two. However, a little one-on-one with the owner of this fine establishment seems like a much better idea."

At that, he planted the slightest erotic kiss on my lower jaw. My composure was pretty much out of the window after feeling his thin mustache tickling my skin. I couldn't help but wonder how expertly he could tickle everything else. By that time, I was ready to give in and hand it to him right there on the computer table. Who the hell would arrest me for indecent exposure? I'm the owner of the damn place, and was in the company of the sexiest base commander in the history of the Army. He looked like a hell of a fighter, too.

Though I desperately wanted to, I didn't spread out the honey even though his dark almond eyes scanned me religiously. I cleared my throat. "I'm sorry, Commander. Once I assign a client to one of my girls, I don't take him away from her."

He leaned in again, whispering in the most erotic voice a girl could stand without melting like she was the Wicked Witch of the West or something. "Certainly you could make an exception, beautiful Ms. Marliss."

"Are you not satisfied with Jasmine? If not, I can discuss—"

"Jasmine's delicious, but I see another entrée that's more appetizing. Ummm, and it smells so damn good. Coco Chanel, right?"

"You certainly know your fragrances."

"I know yours, but further exploration will be needed. I tried getting Jasmine to tell me more about you, but she refused, wanting me all for herself."

"That is the point, Commander Carrington."

"No, the point is that I want you, now that I've seen you. Don't forget that I heard what you can give a man. That's something not to be forgotten, and I . . . just want my share of it. Surely you can understand that!"

I decided to bait-and-switch him. "Certainly changing operators is the client's decision; it's also something Jasmine and I should discuss, seeing as she is the other party. For now, however, shall I schedule you with Jasmine for Tuesday, sir?"

His shoulders relaxed. "Sure, but definitely have that talk with her. Now that I've had a taste . . . I want the rest of it. I'm the kind of man that, when he sees what he wants, he is relentless in getting it. I will be back"

His words made my face blush and my mouth open, saying things I never thought I'd say. "Please do come back any time you like, sir. It's always open to you."

He looked down at my high-riding skirt. "I sure hope it is open to me, any time I want it."

"What I mean is—"

"I know what you mean, and I know what I mean as well."

Was he direct or what? I couldn't believe the conversation I was having with him. He wanted me, and I don't mean the way the billboard for the US Army says that they want people. No, he wasn't wearing a red, white, and blue top hat and pointing a big finger at me enticing me to join up. He wanted me to join, all right; join him in an orgy of two. Inviting? Hell, yeah! I would certainly have gone for it if he hadn't been Jasmine's Tuesday man. I couldn't take him from her. She'd quit, and I wouldn't blame her. Besides, dating a client was against policy.

I thought that over and decided I hate policies; they cramp my style.

Commander Carrington was the type of man you'd want to go for no matter which of your friends was waxing him royally. I'd never seen a man like that before and I'd been at this establishment almost three years. The men in Detroit were fine as hell, but nothing that could compare to David Carrington. I didn't think anything in the world could compare to him, and I didn't care. My eyes were too busy with him to consider thinking about another man, especially my other clients.

David kissed my hand again and walked to the door. At the last minute, I stopped him. "Commander? Hold on a second."

He slowly approached my desk, wearing the most luscious smile a man could have, and leaned over the desk. "Changed your mind about teaming up with Jasmine and me?"

"Not exactly, but you did say something that triggered a thought."

"Such as?"

"You said you'd like to be in my room. How do you know which one is mine?"

"There's a perfectly good explanation. I walked into the wrong room one day. Jasmine told me to go in and take off my clothes. When I walked in, I saw everything I wanted to see, everything a delicious woman would have in her room when she's taking care of Army personnel."

"That could be any of our rooms. Jennifer has a room, Toya has hers, Cheryl has—"

"It was yours. I'll admit something to you. I've seen you walking around the base a couple of times myself. I'd see you walk in here but assumed you were one of the operators. I hoped to see you in here, maybe have you be the one to set my world on fire, but it never happened until today. I just never knew you were the brains of the operation."

"That doesn't explain why you thought that room was mine."

"Simple, darlin'. A room that has that many sex toys had to belong to someone as sexy as you. Anyway, I tinkered with the toys before Jasmine pulled me out. You have everything in there a man could scream over." He cupped my chin. "However, the only thing in there that could truly make a man like me scream . . . is you. You're the perfect toy for me, small and slim."

What the hell could I say? He laid it on the line for a sister, and it was damn hard making that appointment for Jasmine instead of for me. I wanted that man, and now that I'd had a close-up view, I had to find a way to get to him without causing strife between me and one of my best operators. I knew Jasmine liked him. Who wouldn't? I'd noticed her reaction when I'd asked who was coming in today. She smiled as though she'd landed in a chocolate swimming pool, saying, "Commander Carrington, among others." She could barely walk away without her knees giving in. Yeah, she thought she could fool me by playing it cool. After seeing him, I knew why her body was an inferno. I thought I should take him anyway so her damn knees could straighten up.

Commander Carrington left, and I pretty much lost it just by watching his tight butt in those khakis. I wanted to say "yes" so bad to that pretty thing that my sex ached for him. It was sopping wet and ready to fly wide open for him. No man's ever had that effect on me before, and believe me, I've had some hell-ifying meat in my day. I soon realized that I was thinking like a sex-crazed barbarian. Yes, David Carrington was the sexiest man ever created, but if I let myself go that stark raving mad over one cute man, Lord knows I'd be screwing every man on base, and the civilians, too. I couldn't let that happen again. I had run from Detroit because of my libido. There wasn't a man in the city that I wasn't scoping out to get down with. My grades lagged because of it, along with a few relationships. No way was that going to happen again.

Jasmine came out time enough to see me wipe the drool from my bottom lip. She was fixing the belt to her gown. Yeah, like I wouldn't have known she was nude under there from her slam session with Mr. Base Commander. She sashayed over to me. "I see you met David."

"How can you tell?"

"Maybe it's that sex-me-down expression on your face."

"Is it that obvious?"

"Sure the hell is, sistah. Don't sweat it, I know how you feel. The first time I saw David I could barely breathe."

"Or walk. I saw you this morning trying to regroup after a mere mention of his name."

"Some men bring out the ho in you. David is one of those men."

"How lucky can you get, Jasmine? He's the prettiest man I've ever seen."

A look of euphoria clouded her face. "He is a sweet, juicy thing all right. The thing about David, though, he just wants it straight. You know the type, by the books, do or die. The erection is fabulous, though, and it taste so sweet, like rock candy, just as hard!

"No doubt, but if it's so straight, why do you yell so much when you're with him? I know those screams aren't an act, Jasmine."

That euphoric smile happened again. "It isn't. I scream like that because he goes *so* deep. If I didn't know any better I'd swear I can feel him penetrating my heart."

"That deep, huh?"

"Yes, ma'am."

I stared at that glow she was sporting. It rather concerned me, because we're not supposed to get too attached to the clients. I, myself, had to fight like hell to keep David's memory away. "Jasmine, I know that look; I've had it many times. You're falling for him."

"Really, I'm not. He's just a client to me."

"Get real. You have it bad for David Carrington. Don't do that, Jasmine. Don't fall for these clowns."

"He's not a clown, Marliss. He's a sweet man: kind, sensitive, erotic. True, it could be easy to fall for a man like him, but I haven't."

"Then why are you defending him so adamantly?"

"I didn't know that I was."

I looked into Jasmine's beautiful, dark face, the face of an angel, an angel that was falling from glory and into the devil's arms. I felt sorry for her, knew her plight . . . knew it all too well. One look at David made me falter the way Jasmine had, but I was better at controlling myself. I leaned back in my chair. "Sorry for coming down on you so hard. I just don't want you to get hurt."

"David would never hurt me."

"I know, but dating clients is the number one rule not to break around here."

She tightened her belt. "You have nothing to worry about, Marliss. I love my job, and I love you. I would never do that to you. I know how hard you've worked to get this place off the ground. Remember, I've been here with you practically since you've opened the place."

"Yes, you have, and you're my best girl and my best friend." I had to ease off or she'd discover the real reason I didn't want her getting too attached to him. I brightened my smile and switched topics to something I knew she'd still get a bang out of; more David, but in different ways. "How new is he to the base? I've only seen him once or twice, but never in here."

"He was stationed in Mississippi, and put in for a transfer here. He's only been here two months. That's all I know about him, other than the fact that he eats me out sooo good."

"Worth the money, in other words."

"That and more. Hell, I'd pay him if you wouldn't kill me for dishing out the money."

"Is his family here with him?"

"All alone, Marliss, so your rule of no married men still stands intact."

"Good." *In more ways than one.* "How the hell did I get around not seeing him in here before? Certainly I would have remembered. When did he start?"

Jasmine took a seat next to me. "Well, since I'm second in command here, he walked in one day with all kinds of recommendations from other personnel and told me he wanted to see if the legend of this place was correct. He found out the good way just how correct it was."

"Where was I?"

"In Detroit, attending your cousin Debra's wedding."

"Right! I remember now. I see you managed to give him the grand tour."

"What do you mean?"

I took a much-needed sip from my Coke, then placed it back on my desk. "David was in my room. He told me he was."

"True. On his first day, Jennifer escorted him to the wrong room. When I finally found him, he was completely nude and playing with your ball busters. Those seem to be his thing. He sure likes it when I bust his."

"That had to be a hell of a sight, walking in on him raw as the day he was born. He looks like he's stacked."

"If you only knew, girl. David will take your damn breath away. Toya had to nudge me to breathe when I first saw him. She started to pencil him in for herself, but I snatched him up for my own party."

"I know you did; can't say that I blame you."

Jasmine watched as I narrowed in on my next question. "What are you thinking about now, Marliss? I know David has affected you way more than you're letting on."

I finished the Coke and tossed it into recycling can. "David told me something else today, Jasmine."

"Like what?"

A smile brightened my face. "You told David that was me screaming my bloody head off."

"How could I not? You were wailing so damn good on that poor PFC that we were both tempted to join you. What was PFC Malone doing so big time that he hadn't done to you before?"

I wasn't going to admit a damn word of truth to her. I was so tempted to go back on my word and take her Tuesday man away from her, but I couldn't do it. I was a woman of my word. I only hoped that I could stay that way. I countered with the best lie I could concoct. "Tony Malone has finally learned my lessons, how to please a girl righteously. He's still quick with it, though. In-and-out missions are what he does best."

Jasmine stretched her long, lean arms over her head while yawning. "I guess. So long as he learned something. Sounded like you learned something, too." She checked her watch. "Captain January will be in shortly, and I'd better get ready. Are you done for the day?"

"No, I've got Sergeant Bergman coming in, in about forty minutes."

"I see. It's dominatrix night, is it?"

"I don't know if I'm really in the mood for it. Being everything to a man, even for an hour, is hard work. He likes the whips, chains, butt plugs, everything."

"Don't sweat it. It could be fun, maybe exactly what you need. Working with spikes and chains can take you away. Besides, you need a little fantasy in your life, and Sergeant Bergman is just the man to lay it out. His ass is fine, girlfriend. I've seen those muscles and pecs. I've also seen that juicy rod of his."

That definitely took me aback. "How in the hell have you seen him? He's always been my customer."

"Yes, but one time when you went to refill the lavender bottle, he had a question and buzzed the front desk. I picked up and went to him. He had the highest erection, and he was just laying there uncovered, letting it all hang out. Anyone would have noticed that thick, juicy steak. It was slammin', sister. You're a lucky dame to be able to get your rocks off with him tonight."

"Is David Carrington just as hot?"

There it was again, that euphoric look. Had I not known it was physically impossible, I'd have sworn she was about to take flight and soar. "Well, Commander Carrington has more length; it's thicker, meatier." She shook herself, then tapped my desk. "Tonight is yours. You'll enjoy Bergman like you always do. Show out for his ass, and make him beg. Draw out the fantasy."

Little did she know that David Alan Carrington was all the fantasy I needed, but even that was unwelcome at that point in my life.

"Did you schedule David for next Tuesday?"

I lifted my eyes. "Yes, I scheduled Commander Carrington for May 12th at 2:20 as usual, darling." She walked off with a giddy look on her face, a look that can only be brought on by a ferocious erection. Lucky heifer!

Before she left, she turned back to me. "Are we still on for our Friday-night drink?"

"Sure."

"You need one. You've been working too hard. I can see it on your face."

What she saw on my face was not overwork, but a brain working on overdrive figuring out ways to stay away from David. I knew he'd track me down to get what he wanted. I'm known to do the same thing, though I was suppressing it. I also knew Jasmine liked him more than a little, and it would kill her to know that I was the one he wanted his next appointment with. I relaxed in my chair, lit a cigarette, and thought over my predicament.

While sudsing myself down in preparation for Sergeant Bergman, my mind drifted back to David Carrington. I remembered how he looked at me, sizing me up like I was his next meal. If ever an entrée *wanted* to be eaten, it surely would be me. Those seductive eyes had scanned me so damn well, and all I wanted was to be taken in any way, shape, or form by him.

The warm water felt great trickling down my bronze body, and the body sponge tickled me in places I wanted only David to touch me. My mind's eye saw David in that shower with me, feeling me with wet, soapy hands, caressing and stroking me in every thinkable way. I could imagine David's taut erection pressing into me while he kissed my neck, my breasts, trailing down to my stomach . . . oh, God! "What was I doing?" I heard my own voice screaming in response to him and it was driving me crazy! I couldn't be a hypocrite, telling Jasmine one thing, and doing the other. From that point on, David was a no-no in my life; no thoughts of him allowed in my brain.

To make sure there were no more thoughts of him, at least that night, I stepped from the soothing shower and prepared for Sergeant Bergman. Yes, he'd take my mind from Carrington country and deliver me to his own wetlands. That was the ticket, and my salvation for the night. I hoped!

Sergeant Bergman was on time as usual, and I was the perfect angel that he looked forward to seeing every Tuesday evening. My hair was dolled up in the Victorian style that he adored, with ringlet curls dancing free around my neck. My lacy black crotchless bodysuit with metal rings attached fit me to the max. It hugged all the right curves. What truly kicked the suit into full gear was the matching satin gloves that stretched to my elbows, with corresponding black patent leather thigh-high boots. One look at me, and Courtney Bergman was ready to burn the joint up! Even I had to admit that I looked like Helen Blazes, though I felt as vulnerable as a battered lamb chop ready for the frying pan.

It was actually a relief to see him. Courtney was enough man for any woman to want to concentrate on. He was sexy, tall, thick hued, but he wasn't black; far from it, but I liked every inch of him. The only thing, he still wasn't Carrington material. I hadn't been able to release myself from his mind games since our encounter at Sheila's desk. David was continuing to be a predatory animal, and I was his prey.

I stripped Courtney from his embroidered shirt and licked his tight abs and pecs, but saw the tanned, smooth brown skin of David Carrington instead. Shaking that thought off was immediate because the last thing I needed was calling out the wrong name. My mission continued, and I stripped Sergeant Bergman from his pants. His erection felt like fire blazing through his underwear. I stroked it, feeling that delicious hard muscle throbbing against my hot hand. "I see you're nice and ready for your spanking." That was the only thing about Courtney, he liked abuse, and I was good at delivering it. That night I had to rid myself of some added frustration anyway; why not take it out on him and kill two birds with one stone?

After Courtney lay across my table, I greased my hands down with a baby oil–sage mix and got ready. He knew what was coming because he paid royally for it. My felt and velour whip rested at the foot of the table, and he watched me grab it. "Can I really have it tonight, Marliss?"

"Depends. How bad have you been?"

"Horrible. I made some new trainees cry today."

"You *are* an evil man, Courtney, but that's not bad enough. What else have you done to deserve this ass whipping?"

I could see his muscles flexing, the veins on the side of his head moving. His voice cracked. "Marliss please, just give it to me!"

"No way, tell me what I need to hear."

"I need this like you wouldn't believe."

I leaned over him, letting the feathery whip dangle across his muscular back. "What about my needs, huh? What do I deserve tonight?"

"Whatever you need."

"What I need is to hear the abuse. Tell me, what naughty things have you been doing lately?"

"I trashed the latrine on purpose and made the new recruits clean it up because their beds weren't made correctly."

"I want more grit, Sergeant Bergman! Get down and dirty with me or the whip goes away."

"Okay! Okay! I pulled your picture out last night and jacked off while looking at it. Is that dirty enough?"

"Filthy; just what I need, baby."

"Do I get it?"

Whack! The sash of the whip lashed across his back; he screamed out in pleasurable pain. I did it again and again, leaving barely-there lashes across his back and behind. I screamed at him, "Are you going to be bad like that again?"

"Yes, yes, damn it. I can't help it with you."

"I am displeased, Courtney." My terrible little whip pounced on him once more. "You are *soo* in for it." I placed the loose cuffs around his wrists and ankles and sat on top of him. My knuckles dug into his back, working out the kinks of the day. The more I massaged him, the louder he screamed.

Courtney was absolutely beautiful, and I'd been doing so well thinking of him only; then it happened! The minute my hands started caressing is lower back and buttocks, my mind jumped to David. Suddenly the skin was darker, the muscles were tighter, and that southern drawl made its way to my mind. I lost it. There was no holding back now. I flipped Sergeant Bergman on his back, still cuffed, and lost my ever-loving mind.

The madness started at his forehead, pretending I was stroking *David's* hair. My wicked behavior continued as I sucked his juicy lips; drippy, wet kisses adorned him like crazy. I kissed a mustache that really wasn't there, but I felt it because, remember, David was laying on my table, not Courtney.

My God, it became worse as I got into it. Courtney was begging for the coochie, sweating for it. His erection pressed stiffly against my buttocks. I could feel the tremendous pressure practically ready to pour from it, and I liked it; I liked *David's* erection pulsating against me.

Rough, ragged tongue licks dampened his chest and stomach, circling his nipples, nibbling them as though they were rich, dark chocolate drops. Yes, I was on fire, and all it took to get me there was the thought of one man.

Those greasy, active fingers of mine pawed him. The look on his face alerted me to his acceptance of my craziness. The only thing, he didn't know he was another man.

Sergeant Bergman howled, trying to get loose from those cuffs to devour me, but I kept the torture flowing. The restraints were beginning to frustrate him; he wanted freedom to juice me because my antics were new, something he hadn't expected. He'd always liked the dominatrix role I portrayed, but I really turned on the jets, and lowered to that outrageous cock!

David was all over my mind, occupying every single crevice. He was the driving force, and Courtney was the thankful recipient. Courtney's tip oozed with come, yet he tried his absolute best to contain it, save it for the grand slam! What wasn't helping his cause was my lips tackling that nice, tight tip. Though my throat was hungry for him, I took it rather slow, tasting that dripping tip with long strokes. He bucked and pleaded for me to release him, but no, I wanted more, more David, because that was who I saw. My tempo picked up, taking more of his shaft into my waiting mouth, then I milked him with long, stiff strokes. My tongue was like a snake, coiling around him and hugging him tight. Never in my wildest dreams had I figured on doing one man while seeing another. That was how potent David Carrington was, and I liked the medicine he dished out to me.

The more Courtney begged me to punish him, the more insane my desire became. I lowered to his shins and sat, leaning forward, until his stiff joint was between my breasts, and I rode him. The friction was magnificent, either that or the thought of who I wanted him to be drove me. Either way, I got my kicks because the sounds coming from my own mouth astounded me. I could have sworn it was another woman in that room with us, but it was me, all me, fantasizing about a man I surely had no business even thinking about.

I quickly sat up, peeled the body suit off, and reached for the bottle of oil, letting it drizzle down my body and on to his. The places I put the rest of the oil should have been enough evidence to drive me out of Georgia, but there was a new marshal in town, and I wasn't leaving. My cupped hand held the drops of oil, and lathered my core with it. I was slick, hot, and ready to be impaled with the stiffest knife in the drawer, but it didn't belong to the right carver. However, I made it work because I was ready to erupt!

Courtney's voice beckoned me. "Come on, Marliss, give me what I ache for each week."

"You want it, baby?"

"I want it now. Lower that sopping wet sugar onto me."

Why did he have to say that? "Sugah" was what "pretty thing" called me. "Okay, boy, you've got it." I reached for my nut restraints and wrapped them around him. The thick rubber device gave him the erection from hell, and I was his personal demon for the time being. Everything in me pressed onto that lovely cock, and I screamed bloody murder! My lips trembled, my body shook . . . and again I almost made the ultimate mistake, calling him David. As excited as I was, though, I managed to remember my place and called out the right name. I might have been hot and bothered, but I was still smart about my business.

Courtney shook me like I was a rag doll and climaxed all over the damn place. We lay together briefly. The only noise in the place came from him. "Marliss, you're so damn beautiful. I think I may really have something for you."

"Don't fall for me, Courtney . . . regulations prevent it."

"Break them."

"No!" No more words. I released him and helped him dress.

Before leaving, he cupped my chin and said, "Damn! That was incredible."

"You liked it?"

"I can't zip my pants, Marliss."

"Then I performed well tonight." I tugged at that heated zipper until I managed to close it. He expected his usual evening kiss, and I gave it to him, but not in my usual way. I wanted to give him something else to remember the evening by, and since I wasn't about to go overboard kissing "Dr. Sugah," I figured giving it to him was almost as good. I took Courtney into my arms, wrapped my fingers around his light brown curls, and drained him. Our lips danced in glory, tasting, caressing, capturing one another for a good five minutes . . . then I released him. He stood back and stared at me. "Wow! I must have been extra bad to get that."

"You were." *So was I.*

He was the last client for the night, and I walked him to the door. After locking it, I sat back in Sheila's chair. I was done in, but not physically. In actuality, I hated my performance that night because my mind wasn't on the man I was with. I didn't want to run my business that way. That was why my ass was in a sling in Detroit, and I wasn't about to revisit that part of my life.

Until ten that evening, all I did was sit in the dark listening to the soundtrack of *Mo' Better Blues* and John Lucien on the CD player while I smoked one of my Salem Slims. Both CDs had a way of putting me in a mellow, calmer mood. The mixture of John's seductive South American flavor and Spike Lee's forties-style choices took all my pain away, at least until the tracks ended. Then it was time to go home and face more music, the lonely kind. Going home was the hard part. Sure, I could put on more music and play with Donut, my loving terrier mix, but David would still be in the back of my mind. If I hadn't known any better, I'd have sworn he was the Holy One; either that or he was the Antichrist! Either way, I was screwed.

Friday wasn't turning out to be my best day. My inkjet printer broke, and as I tried fixing the damn thing, it squirted ink all over my tan blazer. Sheila's damn chair was still jacked because of my mind antics with David three days ago, and I had to bust a move over to the PX to buy another one before meeting Jasmine at The Americana Bar and Grill. The day was specifically created in hell, but little did I know, it was about to get terrifyingly worse.

Since Wednesday, I'd taken on more clients, clients who'd been on a waiting list since February. I should have been content to leave them there another month until some spots were available, but I like self-torture for some reason. I needed to stay busy and keep my mind on track because if I didn't, David Carrington would set up camp in my soul and play his devilish little harp until I succumbed to him.

Normally, I didn't overload my girls with client after client. They deserved a breather between hunks, and I'd stuck to that. The two new men were mine, and from the Tuesday I met

David until late Thursday evening, I was busy. I wouldn't have been surprised if there was a hole in my table burned in by hot, seething come from my now fifteen personal clients. I wanted to be too tired to think of David, but I knew that was a crock of shit! When a specific man dances around in your head, jumping from a twenty-story building won't alleviate the pressure.

Life must go on, right? I went to the PX, bought a new copier and ink, and an expensive-ass chair that no one had better fuck up, not even me. I didn't care what horrific commander, lieutenant, corporal or whatever marched around, this new chair was leather, and it couldn't get jacked! Besides that, I had boxes of paper to load into my compact BMW-Z class, so my hands and mind were on overload. Good! There was a lot to carry out, and it was all heavy. Wouldn't you know, there was no one to carry this crap out for me? So, I made two trips, saving the chair for last since it was heavy. Sheila had better appreciate that chair and guard it with her life. After all, there were people like me around who were notorious for waxing chairs.

Once everything else was in the backseat, I returned for the chair. I had to drag the damn thing out because the carts at the PX were either broken or stolen. Imagine the gall of someone to steal something from an Army base. Maybe it was the intelligence personnel; they're slick with everything around here.

The car seemed like such a long way off, only across the street in actuality. I managed to get to the car and leaned the chair against the door while popping the trunk. Unfortunately, the box the chair was packed in fell, landing on my middle toe. I screamed like crazy while slamming my purse down and echoing a few choice words for anyone who would listen. What made the moment truly special was that when I tried regrouping, I stumbled and fell into the arms of, you guessed it, David Carrington.

Life just ain't right sometimes.

The last thing I needed was feeling him against my chest. If anything, I needed to get something off my chest, and I didn't mean thick, hot tongues belonging to Army personnel. I moved back, trying to act as cool and calm as possible, knowing all along it was Miller Time, and I needed a stiff one really, really bad. Instead, I smiled into his perfect face. "David, what are you doing here?"

"I called The Sensation Station, and Sheila told me you were at the PX buying chairs."

"You didn't speak to Jasmine?"

"No, sugah, my business was with you, only."

Thank God he didn't ask for her. My goose would have been marinated!

I leaned against the car because my foot was killing me, but tried pretending everything was copacetic. "So, what is it that you wanted with me?"

Instead of answering me, he bent down on his knees. "I know that toe hurts, Ms. Marliss. I saw the box fall but couldn't stop it." He started massaging my foot. "What the hell was a little girl like you doing moving around big ole boxes?"

"David, please don't do that. People are staring at us."

"Let them stare. Does it hurt a lot?"

The minute he touched it, the pain left, leaving nothing but a pleasurable, soothing massage from the one man who could easily drain everything from inside of me. "Yes, it does hurt, but people are still looking."

"I don't care. I want the pain to go away. Here, lean back into the car and let me work my magic." He massaged in circular motions around my throbbing toe. Only the toe was now throbbing due to what he was doing. Those magic fingers worked up and down, around, between, and he did it so expertly. I thought I was the massage therapist. The boy put my tactics to shame, and I loved it. I could feel my body slowly losing control, my nipples perking against my soft silk blouse. My feminine core oozed from want of his thick mass.

If his penis was as good as those damn fingers, I'd soon be on the horizon of killing Jasmine to get to him, but that was not what I needed. In fact, David Carrington was the last thing I needed, but the first thing I wanted.

The loud noises of the streets brought me back to reality, and I moved my foot. "It's all better now, and I need to run." I slipped my stiletto back on and looked him in the face. "Thanks for your concern."

"But I'm not finished."

"*We are* finished."

He gave me that seductive little smile that made me want to crash right to his feet. "Ms. Marliss, I haven't told you why I came down here to talk to you. I don't have your cell number or your e-mail, so I had to come in person."

Another thing I didn't need was to be cyberconnected to him. Getting agitated, I delivered a small huff. "Okay, why are you trying to track me down?"

"I want you to do something for me."

"Do something for you? Like?"

"Have a drink with me."

"I can't do that."

"Sure you can. Anyone brave enough to lift heavy boxes and put them into their trunk can do any damn thing they want to."

"It was only a chair. I can handle that."

"Apparently not today. Don't ever lift anything that heavy. If I hear of this again, I'll be forced to spank you for not following directions."

Everything the man said, he uttered with a hint of sexual wildness in it. And for him to just appear out of nowhere, sheesh! I couldn't catch a break. I leaned against the car, staring up at him. "A spanking, huh? I haven't had one of those since I was eleven years old. That's when everyone stopped caring." What the hell did I say that for? The last thing I wanted was David Carrington knowing my life. "What I mean is—"

"Darlin', I don't know what kind of people were in your life, but I *do* care. You could take your back out." His hand grazed my blushing cheek. "How can I expect to have that well-needed twosome if you're in traction?"

"David, I—"

"No, don't talk, just follow me to Laskey's and have a drink with me. I promise it will only be a drink, so long as you don't let me have too many. I'm fool enough around a beautiful woman while sober. Who's to say what animal I'll turn into with the likes of lovely Ms. Marliss at my side?"

How could I not smile at that sentiment? He was the sweetest, sexiest damn thing that ever graced my life, but he was a target I couldn't aim for. He practically belonged to Jasmine, the way she was salivating over him. "David, really, I can't go with you."

"Why not? You own the town. Since meeting you and becoming a client in your establishment, I've heard all kinds of wonderful things about you. Hell, you could run this base on respect alone. These men worship you and your girls, so who would complain if the satin doll of the base took liberties with a certain young commander?"

"Really, I can't. First, I'm almost late for a prior commitment. Second, I can't date a client."

"Who said date? It's a drink, darlin'."

His arms trapped me on either side, forcing me within his clutches. He smelled so fucking good, and his skin looked so clear and flawless, sexy enough to lick every inch of him. The heat from his enormously stiff erection made me sizzle from want of it, and reaching for it in broad daylight normally wouldn't have been a problem, had I not been a different person from that silly chick years ago. The fact remained, I was trapped like a mouse with cheese dangling from its little mouth. There was nowhere to go, and it made me nervous. Here a man was that I was having orgasms over morning, noon, and night, and I wasn't allowing myself the privilege of discovering how one of his real orgasms felt. Any other dame would have jumped right in his game. I had a conscience suddenly, and I imagined that Jasmine would smell him all over my body.

I got away from his incredible restraints. "I can't do this. It's my policy to keep things professional."

"One rum and Coke, I promise. No one will think anything."

My body began to do things that it hadn't in a long time, tensing. My hand clutched the handle of my purse, my breathing began to quicken. What was this man doing to me? What was I allowing him to do? This had to stop before all those passersby saw me have a nervous breakdown. It felt as if my eyes were pleading to his, when in actuality it was my voice. "David, please. Please don't do this to me. I like you, and you know that, but it's difficult for me."

The tear in the corner of my eye dissolved into his fingertip. His other hand stroked my hair, relishing the soft cinnamon brown strands; his voice softened with concern. "Hey, hey, Marliss, don't get upset. Just calm down, beautiful." His hankie dabbed at a tear in the corner of my other eye. "I didn't mean to scare you. I'm really sorry if I said or did anything you didn't want me to."

Was I scared? Yes, for the first time in years. I wasn't scared of him physically, but his body scared me, what that body could turn mine into. He felt good in my arms, like I was his home that he was homesick for. "No, no, David, it's me, not you. You're wonderful with everything you do."

"Then it's just a bad day, right?"

"You could say that, and with that box falling, well, it was the straw that broke the camel's back."

"All the more reason to have a drink, Marliss. We can just talk if you want to. We can go anywhere, do anything, as long as you're with me."

"That's so sweet, but I . . . I can't. Really, there is somewhere I have to be." I looked down at my watch again, realizing I had fifteen minutes to get across town to Jasmine. "I need to go."

I tried peeling myself from his grasp but he held on, giving me a hug. His tender voice soothed me, his sexy mustache tickled me, and I smiled.

"You feel better, Ms. Marliss?"

"Actually, yes. You always make me feel good, for some reason."

"Not as good as I'd like to."

"Let's not go there."

"You're right, and I'm sorry. Are you okay now?"

"Yes." I could see he wasn't convinced. "Really, I'm fine."

"You sure as fuck are! Sorry again about my word choice, but you bring out the arrogant criminal in me."

"I've heard worse." He saw remnants of pain still on my face.

"Maybe I should trail you, just in case that toe acts up."

"I'm a big girl, Commander."

"I know you are. Only big girls are as together as you are."

"I practically cried in your arms. How together is that?"

"You can cry on me any time you like, but I'd rather you laugh, hopefully moan . . . one day."

"I don't know, maybe."

"I'll keep asking until you say yes. I told you that the other day."

At that, we parted. I could feel him watching me until my little dark blue BMW disappeared from sight. There were voices in my head telling me what to do, how to feel, but the only one I paid attention to was the voice saying, *Marliss, come and get me, I'm waiting. Why do you make me wait so long for you?* That was Jack Daniel's talking to me, telling me he was ready, willing, and able to be poured into any drink of my choice. I was ready for his ass, too, and ready to down him as soon as my hot hands wrapped around the glass.

I looked in my rearview again, but David was too far away for me to see. My nerves really took over then, and they were laced with sexual longing.

By the time I made it to The Americana, I was a mess; my mascara was running, and my blush was smeared across my face. My lipstick was gone, and my hair, I'm sure, was a total bird's nest. My only hope was that Jasmine wasn't there yet so I could fix myself in the ladies' room and appear normal, even though I didn't feel like I was. As I toured the parking lot, I noticed Jasmine's red Saab was nowhere to be seen, and I was glad. In fact, maybe I needed a stiff drink before facing her. I felt like such a backstabber even though nothing had happened between David and me.

Why was I like this? There'd been plenty of men in my life before now, but none could take control of my thought processes the way he had. I stared at my face in the rearview mirror, feeling like the clown I knew I looked like, but there was nothing that could be done about that until I could get to a real mirror. Maybe the face that would stare back at me would be a kinder face, a face that was forgiving, realizing that she was only human. I hoped I'd see that person instead of the one I felt was living within my heart.

Inside the ladies' room I found that mirror, and the brown face looking back at me was the one I'd hoped for: the human and compassionate one; the one who saw a scared little girl who really did care what others thought of her. I fixed my hair, took a few deep breaths, and straightened my skirt. From that point on, I was ready to face Jasmine, ready to have a wonderful girl's night out . . . and have as many stiff drinks as legally allowed.

My first drink was a Long Island iced tea. Some starter, huh? I planned on not feeling a damn thing in about an hour or two. Halfway through the drink, I saw Jasmine waving and running in my direction. I wasn't up to putting on a happy face, but knew I'd have to keep my real feelings from her.

Jasmine bounced into the chair with her usual giddy personality. I'd never seen someone so enthusiastic after a long day at the office. One thing I could say, she loved her job. Who wouldn't? You can get screwed all day long.

The minute Jasmine looked into my face, though, her jaw dropped, and that whiny little voice of hers spoke up. "Ohh, darling, what's wrong?"

I thought I looked okay. The tears were gone, my hair fixed nicely. I thought all evidence of a bad day was gone. Then again, it always took my eyes a while to rid themselves of the puffiness. There was no way I telling her that Mr. Base Commander was sweating me. I didn't want to talk about him at all, but I knew she'd persist until she got something workable from me. I sipped my drink again for a little extra nerve, then said, "I'm just tired from the week, but things are fine." It wasn't really that I had to convince her, it was more convincing myself.

"Then why did you take on those new clients? We really have enough for the next few months. They never seem to leave, just build in numbers, but everyone has their limit, Marliss. You overwork yourself way too much!"

"These men expect to get satisfied, Jasmine, and it's really not the job that's got me so tired. It's other things."

"Such as?"

I waited for the waitress to take her order before getting into it. Jasmine ordered a Black Russian with a side order of chicken wings, curly fries, coleslaw, and fried mushrooms. Side order? Get real! I knew she could throw down on some food like a bonafide starving wild boar, but damn! I looked at her as if she'd stolen the Hope Diamond after she placed that order. "A little hungry, are you?"

"You want some of it?"

"I assumed that amount *was* for both of us."

"Fine, eat up. But as I was saying, you look so tired, girl. What's going on in your life, other than the clients, that's got you stressed?"

"Everything; things you wouldn't begin to believe."

The mushrooms arrived, and she immediately popped the fattest, juiciest one into her mouth, then licked her fingers as she spoke. "You know what you need?"

I could see the grease oozing from the corner of her mouth from the food, and had Jack Daniel's not given me a strong stomach, I'd have puked. "No, Jasmine, but I'm sure you'll be happy to tell me what I need so my boat can row, row, row merrily down the stream."

"You're right. I didn't get my degree in counseling for nothing."

Hmm! A degree in counseling, yet she's making a mint screwing the armed forces. That makes sense! I leaned back, sipping what was left of my drink, content to listen to the reasons why a dick in my house would solve all of my problems. Hmm, maybe it would.

"Marliss, what you need is a trip!"

A trip? That one caught me way off guard. I thought it was going to be the man conversation. "Jasmine, if I took a vacation now, what would happen to my clients? Many of those men are new, and they've seen only me. How can I just up and leave—"

"Simple! Men are men, and as long as testosterone is pumping, they don't care what honey well they're dipping into. Really, when you think about it, that's all a man cares about."

"Not all men are like that."

"No, not all, but the majority are. Commander Carrington isn't like that."

I knew that man would slide his delicious tight ass into this conversation. I had to set her straight; that, or I was trying to get her not to like him so much. But why, what would it gain me? I didn't *even* want to hear his name, let alone sit and listen to her mouth-off about how good he waxes her every Tuesday. The only thing I wanted was for those chicken wings to hurry up so her mouth could be occupied at least for five minutes. "Jasmine, what do you really know about Commander Carrington, other than the fact that he's sexually worth every dollar he slams down? After all, you don't know him. His personal life could be filled with things that would scare the hell out of you."

"If he were that bad, the Army would have found out by now, and he'd be court-martialed. No, Commander Carrington talks to me before we get started. He talks to me about his two daughters who live in Mississippi with his ex. He talks to me about how their marriage failed because she didn't like being an Army wife. I know what he likes, what he does on his time off, everything."

"Really? What does he like to do?" *Yeah, knowing this would really help my cause. Sheesh!*

"He loves his daughters and sends for them on his off-time. They go to the ocean, eat out at the oceanfront restaurants, spend time together. They're very small children, only four and six. Hell, David himself is only thirty-three years old, pretty young to be a base commander. I think he said he's the third youngest in the armed forces."

"He tells you that much, huh?"

"Yeah. He's a really nice dude, Marliss."

"You don't have to tell me that. I did read his report the night I first saw him."

"The night you stayed late with Sergeant Bergman?"

"Yeah. I had paperwork to finish, and I ran across it. Seems like a cool dude."

"He is."

"But, Jasmine, like I said before, don't get wrapped around this guy. It sounds like you're already trying to become a stepmother to his girls."

"It's not like that."

"I sure hope not, because I don't want you to get hurt. Men are still men, even those who cherish their daughters. I remember how Douglas hurt you, and it killed me to see you like that. All those evenings I'd sit with you because I was afraid to leave you alone. That killed me, Jasmine. You're my best and only friend here. Besides, you know how I feel about the client-relationship thing."

"Yes, and you don't have to worry. Besides, I think David has someone he likes. I only wish it were me."

Damn! Please don't let it be me.

Jasmine kept talking about David; David this, David that. I was tired of it, and wished like hell that damn chicken was ready because the mushrooms were gone, so was her drink, and she had nothing else to do with her mouth. Then she said the ultimate, thing: "That's what you need, Marliss. You need a man in your life."

My God! The madness would never end. I finished the Long Island iced tea, slid the glass across the table, and looked at her. "I don't need a man, Jasmine. Actually, that's the last thing I need."

"Every woman wants a man, whether she admits it or not."

"And you know this because you're the voice of Georgia, right?"

"I know this because I know women. I grew up around them, having three older sisters, and I've worked around them. Women talk about men."

"That doesn't mean I want one."

"Come on, Marliss. Look at you, you're gorgeous. I hate walking around the PX next to you because you get all the stares. You can't know how many times I've wanted to bitch-slap you while we're somewhere together. Even other women turn clear around to look at you."

"Really? I haven't noticed that before."

"You haven't had to. The thing is, you're outstanding." Jasmine leaned in closer to me. "Does the rest of your family look like you?"

"I guess. Why?"

"Because if they do, I will never step my ass into Detroit.

All I'd need is a whole city of men and women looking at everyone but me."

I couldn't help but laugh at her. "You are bananas, Jasmine. I do have a younger sister who looks like me, but we've never been close."

"On another topic, I remember you telling me about having to spend some time in foster homes, but you never really told me why."

"I don't want to get into it tonight, Jasmine. It's a long, horrid story."

She saw the look on my face and decided to let sleeping dogs lie, other than one last comment. "You'll tell me one day. Anyway, to get back to what I was saying before, I'd give anything to have your creamy brown complexion and big dark eyes. You're lovely, and you know it."

"So are you, but as far as men, I'm just not interested right now." A bloody lie and a half, but it had to suffice.

The chicken finally came, and Jasmine couldn't wait to get more grease all over her hands, of course while talking to me. "You don't hate men, do you?" She handed me a fatty wing.

"I love men. There's nothing I adore more than a wonderful man."

"Then what's the deal?"

I peeled the gobs of fat from the chicken, took a bite, then decided the only way Jasmine was going to get off my damn back was to tell her the real deal. The greasy chicken slid down my throat, and I followed it up with the glass of water before me. The Americana wasn't known for their food, despite how Jasmine raved about it. For me, it was their liquor, and I needed more of it before exposing parts of my life. I quickly ordered another drink with Mr. Jack in it, and got Jasmine whatever she wanted. I knew she needed another drink, if for nothing else than to wash down that barely cooked chicken. Yuck! If the GIs ate in that place, they wouldn't have to worry about being killed on the front lines.

She offered me another piece, which I quickly refused, and settled for a salad. The Americana couldn't be so hopeless as to mess up a salad. I ordered it with the drinks and settled back to let my girlfriend in on some information that, until that time, was hidden from the public. Just thinking about how I was in school made me want to wither away. But until Jasmine got some workable answers as to why I was off men, she would be relentless. "In school, I was a high-riding bitch. Every boy I wanted, I got. Not to toot my own horn, but I was a looker back then, with long reddish hair, this skin tone, and curves. I was too developed for my age, and all the girls hated me because of it."

"High school?"

"This was eighth grade, Jasmine. I hadn't even made it to high school yet. I wasn't a good student, either. My grades were mostly C's and D's because I didn't try. I was smart enough to get A's and B's, but I didn't care about that. What concerned me was kissing boys and going out on dates."

"You weren't sexually active in eighth grade, were you?"

"No, but I was headed up that hill. I didn't have any friends because I took their boyfriends from them. I would fight with everyone and get kicked out of school, and everything I did was because I was rebellious."

"Why? That's what I can't understand, Marliss."

"I don't know how to talk about that right now, Jasmine. I will one day, but it's still hard to look at that part of my life. I can talk about being a hell-raiser in school because that doesn't hurt as much, though it had its consequences; and those consequences are the reason I can live without a man." *At least I think I can.*

My salad finally came. Before getting into the real guts of the conversation, I looked at the salad to make sure nothing was moving in it. All I needed was to be dying from some type of salmonella poisoning. Once I inspected it and it met my specifications, I dug in and tasted. Surprisingly it was good, and delicious food has always had a way of making me seem more confident. Don't ask why, I think it's some child-hood thing.

My gaze met back with Jasmine, who was eying me as if to say, *Don't leave me hanging on a limb here.* "Let me guess. You want to know why I don't have to have a man."

"Damn right, because I know you're not gay."

"Right, but there are other reasons for not wanting a man."

"Is that what you want, Marliss, to be alone?"

"Frankly, I don't know what I want, but until I find out, I'd just as soon stay the way I am." I watched as Jasmine ate another piece of that chicken. The funny thing about it, she really thought that shit was great tasting. Instead of dogging her out about it, I ate more of my salad and prayed it wouldn't turn on me from some root that they'd cut up in it. I swallowed my fill, then looked at Jasmine. "Actually, what I told you a little while ago was not true. The hell-raiser part was, but I lied about not having friends. I had a girlfriend in eleventh grade, Angela. She was just like me: rebellious, pretty, a man-getter, and we did everything together. By that time I was eighteen and having sex like crazy. I was held back a year because of my grades, and so was she."

"Are you two still close?"

"No! As bad as Angela was, I was still worse. I did something to her that couldn't be repaired. I took her man from her."

"You were young, Marliss. Girls that age do stupid things like that."

"The thing is, I knew Jarred was the only real thing she ever cared about, yet I still took him, and he gladly went. I really thought I was something. I thought I could still have my friend and her man at the same time. It really cost me something that could have lasted, a friend."

"That was years ago, Marliss. It's sad that happened, but you've grown since then. Besides, you have another friend." She smiled another giddy smile with grease all over her lips.

That brightened my night because Jasmine was someone I really wanted in my life. That was all the more reason for me to stay away from David. I didn't want another Angela experience. We'd ended up fighting over that damn boy, who was terrible in bed anyway. I'd won the fight that day, but I lost everything else, including my self-respect. Moving to Georgia years later helped a lot, but trouble always seemed to find me.

That night at home, I stared into my mirror, still seeing that girl who'd made a terrible mistake at Henry Ford High School. Not even Jack Daniel's could hide who I really saw in that mirror, someone lonely and sad. All I had was a girlfriend to eat chicken and salad with. I fell asleep with Donut cuddled next to me. For some reason, males seem to like my bed; they seem to never want to leave it, and yes, that would include Donut. He's not the only dog to have graced my bed within the last few years, although the relationship with him has been much better than with the others.

After our parking-lot extravaganza two weeks ago, David was on me like bees on honey. Every Tuesday before his *massage*, and I use the term loosely, he would come in early. You see, David was a smart, calculating guy, knowing exactly when Jasmine would finish with the customer before him. That's when he'd do everything in his power to put his hands on me. Subconsciously I loved the way he'd stroke my jaw, coming close enough to kiss me, but regrouping before Jasmine opened the door with a mile-wide smile, escorting him into her kingdom of love. What she didn't know was that I was the one who mixed his love potion, and felt less like the backstabbing bitch I thought I was turning into. I was acting human for the first time in years, wanting the love and attention every woman needed. With me, however, it had always come from the wrong man.

The following Tuesday, I was at the front desk booking my next appointment with Lieutenant Alvarez, when David walked in, naturally at his earliest convenience. Every day at one, Sheila would take her lunch and one of us covered for her. The more I did that, the more I liked doing it because I knew David would be in soon. Besides, the girls were booked solid due to the influx of new customers. Our rule was *Tease 'em and please 'em*. No man was left with his joint waving in the air, even if we had to do double duty to see to that! That was fine for me because that meant more money for the honeys.

David walked in as usual, looked at his watch, reassuring himself that he had time to flirt, then sat on the corner of my desk. That delicious southern flair brightened my senses. His mysterious eyes stared into mine; his tantalizing smile made me weak for what I wanted but still thought I had no right to.

"Ms. Marliss, the queen of the base. How are you today?"

I smiled into that angelic face of his. "I'm fine, Commander Carrington."

"Why the formalities?"

"Because everyone in here calls you that. Why should I be any different?"

"Because you are." His tender caress against my cheek infiltrated me, lit me up and burned me down all at the same time. He saw the reaction on my face and relished in it. "I could make that feeling last if you'd let me."

"I know you could *if* I'd let you, which I won't."

"We'll have to work on changing that, darlin'."

Before I could reject anymore of his advances, I felt his finger graze down my raw silk blouse and stop where the V peeked into my cleavage. The pad of his finger played there, stroking me in delicate circular motions. "You feel good, Marliss; good enough to really eat up, and I have an enormous appetite."

I quickly removed that wicked finger, though I loved how it felt. "Commander, you really should learn to like a woman for attributes besides her body."

"I do! We clicked a few weeks ago, and you know it. All I want is to learn more about Ms. Marliss, discover how she thinks, what she thinks about," his eyes lowered to my cleavage again, "and how many times she thinks about it. Is that too much to ask?"

"For the time being, it is."

"You are relentless in your efforts, aren't you?"

"Well, I do work on an Army base commander, where relentless endeavors are a must. I learn well and quickly."

"Indeed."

He looked at his watch again and retreated to the row of leather seats across from me. However, David Alan Carrington was not finished with me. He pointed to Sheila's desk chair. "Where's the new one?"

"At home, still in the box. I haven't had time or the patience to put it together."

Jasmine opened her door right at one-thirty, smiling at everyone as if the sun shined only in her window. "Commander, good timing as usual. Come on in, sweetheart, and I'll get you fixed up. Oh, by the way, Marliss, Jennifer will be late returning from lunch. She called while you were with PFC Jamison. She was in a fender bender with a Mercedes."

"God! Is she okay?"

"Sure, but she has to make a police report."

"A Mercedes slammed into her?"

"No, she slammed into the Mercedes. Well, if you're going to be in a wreck, might as well be with something worth your while. Give her another half hour." At that, she smiled into that pretty commander's face. "Come on, baby. I've got good stuff for you today."

As David passed my chair, he slipped me a look that meant only one damn thing: *Your ass will be mine by hook or by crook!* And I knew that. It was matter of time before David wore me down to the nub, sucking what marrow I had left. Damn him, and damn me for liking the idea of it! There was one thing that put me at ease: the fact that Jasmine remained clueless to the vibes David and I tossed about the room like a Frisbee.

Fridays were usually easy and laid-back around the office. All the commanders, generals, PFCs and the like were finishing their missions for the week, and that allowed me to close shop early. For me, early meant around three o' clock. I really needed the break. After spending a week attending to everyone else's needs, it was time to cater to my own. I slipped into my favorite loose-fitting jeans and oversized top that still looked sexy and put on dinner. While waiting for my rice to cook, I looked through my front door. The sun was still shining, making the end of the day still look crystal clear. What got my attention was my neighbor's four-year-old twin daughters playing too close to the street, with no one attending them. I kept my eye on them in case I had to run out and push them out of harm's way from the many speeding vehicles that used this block as a racetrack.

Finally, my neighbor, Juanita, yelled at the girls and made them get back on the porch. Thank God! I stayed at the door taking in more sunshine while listening to Incognito in the background, feeling free, relaxed, and so ready to do nothing but veg out over my dinner, a glass of Chardonnay, and my CD player. I'd actually entertained the idea of grilling but didn't feel like the hassle. It was an afternoon to enjoy with as little responsibility as possible.

As I stared at the lovely trees swinging against a gentle wind, a mint-green Jaguar pulled in a few houses down. Naturally I stared; I always stared like a child looking in the window of a candy store when anything more expensive than my BMW pulled up. I kept watching, waiting for whoever it was to get out and make an appearance. For all intent and purposes, it could have been the Queen of England. All I wanted was the car.

The door opened, and out stepped this man holding a case, some flowers, and something in a brown bag. The vehicle made a chirping sound, alarming itself, while the man kept walking. I couldn't see his face at first due to the distance, but he looked fly. One of my female neighbors was in for something really good, I assumed. Whoever he was, he looked good in those dark slacks and tan shirt. Upon further inspection, I realized who he was. David. God! I hadn't recognized him because he wasn't wearing Army attire.

What the hell is he doing here? I could barely speak, see, or breathe. What first occurred to me was to close the door and not answer the bell, but, too late, David smiled at me as he ascended my walkway. My feet were glue anyway, not being able to move from watching him walk. It was something about that damn sexy-ass walk that mesmerized me.

David stood directly in front of my door, smiling. "Darlin', do I get invited in, or do I fix Sheila's chair on your porch?"

"Oh, sorry!" Quickly I unlocked the screen door and held it open for him. I could smell his cologne and it was making me crazy. It was something dark and sensual, like him. It melted into his skin, mixing with his DNA, trapping me like an animal.

His first words to me were, "Something smells awfully good, Ms. Marliss. Is that dinner?"

"I . . . I just cooked up a pot of salmon and rice. My mother is from the south, and when she cooked, it was usually that."

"I sure hope I'm invited to stay and sample that home cooking. I brought a bottle of wine, something sweet that lingers on your tongue, like how you linger on my mind."

What could I say to him other than, "Certainly you can stay." I didn't want to say it, but it was fitting for the occasion, and he looked so damn good in those tight slacks. I set the wine on the kitchen table, then returned to him. "David, why are you here? I mean . . . How do you even know where I live?"

"Simple. I followed you home one evening."

"Why?"

"Because I wanted to know where you lived, for future reference."

"For future ref . . . You're a rat for doing that."

"A rat that wants to get trapped. Besides, doesn't Sheila's chair have to get fixed?"

"I can do that."

"But you didn't, not yet anyway." He saw the bewildered look on my face, a face that was trying to think of any sane reason for him to leave. There wasn't one, so his torture of my senses began. "Tell me I can stay, Marliss. I *did* buy you flowers."

"I didn't ask you to."

"You didn't have to. All sexy women need flowers."

He handed them to me, and my natural response was to sniff the fragrant bouquet. "No roses?"

"Roses are typical, Marliss. The last thing you are is typical. Sure, roses are lovely, but I thought you'd enjoy gardenias. They're so fragrant and delicate, but strong, able to withstand any turbulent weather."

"Thank you. I love gardenias. These are gorgeous, but the way I look today, dandelions would be too good for me. I look like a bum in these worn jeans and oversized top."

"Nonsense! You look like a queen." He moved into me. "And you smell so regal. What are you wearing?"

"I'm not wearing anything."

"I wish! Seriously, what scent is that?"

"Really, I haven't put on anything."

"I figured that. Only someone as beautiful as you are would smell naturally seductive."

Not knowing how to combat that, I looked away. "I should put these in water and finish making dinner. I take it you're staying."

"Nothing could drag me out of here. Besides, I'm anxious to taste your cooking. If it tastes the way *you* look, it should taste incredible!"

"Let's not go there. You'd better taste it first, Commander."

"David. Remember that. By the way, where's the chair? I can put it together in nothing flat."

"The food is almost ready. Why not eat first? In fact, you can set the table."

"Yes! That's one of many things I've wanted to hear you say to me."

With David working in there side by side with me, it felt so natural, like he was meant to be with me. He was such a gentleman, pulling out the chair for me, pouring me more wine, everything I wanted in a man. What excited me most about him was how he ate. David devoured the meal in nothing flat! The way he chewed excited me, the way he quickly licked his fingers, even the way he buttered his roll made me wonder what he'd do to my body if he got the chance. Would he devour me? He sure looked like he could, and would, marinate my soul as well as my body in his wonderful sauce.

I couldn't help but continue to stare at him as he finished the meal because he was miraculous, his conversation was stimulating, and even the way he smiled at me made me feel truly at home with him. I could imagine cooking for him every day, and staring across from him the rest of my life. I wanted him, and Jasmine, in that moment in time, wasn't even a thought.

Once our meal was completed, he even helped with the dishes, despite me telling him not to. I wanted him to sit at the table and have his dessert. He told me he had his dessert, and that he was staring at it. That made my sex drench for him. Not only did I like the way he looked, I also liked the man he was. I wasn't sure if it was simply a ploy to get me into the sack, but it was working, and I really thought he was sincere in his desire to capture *all* of me, not just my body.

As I loaded the dishwasher, he moved in behind me. I could feel that intense pressure in his pants forcing itself against my back, and his hands gently wrapping around my waist. I wanted those long fingers to embrace my nipples, pull on them, stroke them, make them harder than they already were. Had he touched them, surely their harder-than-diamonds state would have cut his skin. I had plenty of Band-Aids in the medicine cabinet, in case he wanted to take that chance.

I thought David would whisper sweet nothings into my ear, because I knew he wasn't there solely to fix a damn chair and have dinner with me. He wanted dinner, all right, but I was to be the entrée. But the sweet nothings he whispered turned out to be, "Where's the chair?"

"The chair? Oh, that." I pointed to the corner. "That box still has my blood stains on it from the toe incident."

"Did it hurt you that badly?"

"I'm joking, David."

"Too bad. I was hoping for a reason to deliver another foot massage."

"I, uh . . . Would you like something to drink while I finish here in the kitchen?"

"More wine. I operate better when I'm mellow." His eyes slowly scanned my frame as I stood before him. "I could also stand some company while fixing it."

"Sure, just let me get the wine and wash my hands."

I helped David with the chair and I liked how we worked together. He was fun, entertaining, and so incredible to look at. He looked sexy with his sleeves rolled up, tussling on the floor with the difficult parts of the chair. Each time David flexed, my clit did flip-flops from utter want. His skin was so perfectly tanned with a natural hue, his muscle tone was awesome, and how his thighs filled out his pants was amazing. What really caught my attention was the tightness in his crotch. Was I wishing a boner on him, or was he really sporting one? I didn't know, but I wanted to.

Once the chair was finished, he stood it up and sat on it. "I need to test it to see if can withstand pressure." He pulled me onto his lap, holding me around my waist so I wouldn't hop away. "If this chair can withstand our pressure, it's a good chair, and Sheila will be pleased."

I was completely helpless, not being able to move away from him, not really wanting to because he felt fantastic. The heat from his lap ignited me, and that damn wonderful erection was higher than ever before. It was hot and fiery, burning through fabric as it pressed against my buttocks. I could feel his hot tip moving, pressing, squirming for freedom, filling with delicious white cream.

I tried moving, but he held me, whispering in my ear. "Lean against me, and let's test the back."

"David, I—"

"Just a second." As we leaned back, I felt his erection practically span the length of my back; his tip throbbed against me with pure velocity, his thighs flexed, tensing to the pleasure of my hands stroking them. His hips rocked slowly, allowing me to feel every rigid inch of him as he glided against my buttocks. It made me uncomfortable, but at the same time, the friction of our restrained bodies burned within me. His hands inched up to my breasts, breasts already perky from the idea of me on his lap. My nipples practically reached out to him, begging him to manipulate them to his utter satisfaction.

The heat from David's hands surrounded my breasts though he wasn't touching them; he was teasing me instead, leaving me teetering on the edge of eroticism from the idea of what he could do to those taut nipples.

Again, I tried to gain release from him, but he held on. "No, not just yet. I know you're uncomfortable here with me practically forcing myself on you, and I promise to let you go, but let me just feel you a minute longer. I want you to know just how potent you make me."

"David, please."

He said nothing, but slowly got to his feet, standing me with him. That beautiful, massive cock continued to press into my back. Tiny nibbles assaulted my neck and jawline as his hands tightened around my waist. I didn't know how to feel about his advances, but I knew he was something my body desperately needed.

My hands tightened around his wrists. "David! David, please!"

"Don't tell me to stop, Marliss. Please don't tell me that." He swung me around to face him. He was so beautiful, soft yet hard in all the right places. I watched as his delicious mouth tried forming words, but what I truly wanted was for him to just go for the gusto, take me, nail me against the wall, and slide deeply into me. But David was way more subtle than that. He wanted this to be more than a sexual encounter. He wanted this to mean something to me as well as to himself, and for that, I admired him.

My hands brushed against his lips, feeling words trembling from them. "Marliss, please don't tell me not to do this. I . . . I can't hear those words tonight." His hands slowly moved up and down my spine, reaching inside my big shirt to unsnap my bra. The moment it popped free, my worries vanished, my world of shame and hidden desire evaporated, and what was left was a woman ready to give into a man, the only man she'd wanted in years. "David, you know I can't promise you anything beyond this night."

His soft, sultry lips gently kissed my chin before leveling eye to eye with me. "I plan to take my time with you. This is not a quick lesson in intercourse, Marliss. What I want is you, and for whatever amount of time you'll give me. There are no rules here, just desire."

Our lips finally touched, brushing against one another at first, and then fiery heat exploded. Our tongues swirled and tangled and my only thought was, *David, David, yes, God yes!* He felt natural in my arms. My hands uncontrollably ravaged his hair, his back, and his muscled arms, as though they had no final destination. I could feel that incredible pressure in his pants gnawing at me, enticing me to set it free. Lord! I had no idea a man could feel the way David felt with me. It had been such a long time since I'd let a man into my heart, and I just didn't know what to do other than to let him finish me.

David tugged at the hem of my shirt and lifted it over my head. His eyes widened to the treasures he'd uncovered, as my hands crossed my chest to hide them.

"No. Don't you dare cover yourself. I've imagined seeing you like this since the day we met." He removed my hands and reached for what was his. Delicately he touched my hardened dark nipples, delivering feathery touches upon them. He smiled at their feel, then smiled at me. "I knew they were like this: plump, voluptuous, and made for my lips."

"Then take them."

"I will, but slowly. I have other treasures to uncover. So do you."

His fingers trickled down my chest and onto my belly, circling my navel, darting his fingertip in and out of it before unzipping my pants. The idea of someone I've lusted after but restrained myself from made me tremble within his clutches. There was no going back now; I had to have him. Fuck Jasmine, fuck the no-dating-clients rule, fuck the world, the man was mine from that point on, and I didn't have time to consider any feelings about my actions. My mission was to let him conquer me, and to do some conquering of my own.

My jeans slid down my legs, his feathery touch curved around my calves and ankles, and I kicked off my sandals. I stood before him wearing nothing but lacy pink panties that were soaking wet from anticipation. He liked that. His eyes toured my unclothed frame before concentrating on the only stitch I had left. David slid the panties to my ankles and stroked the dark brown curls of my mound. Once I was ripe enough for the plucking, he slid two very excited fingers inside and rocked in and out, gently at first, then enhancing his rhythm. Our eyes met as he spoke. "Do you like this, honey?"

I was barely rational, but I managed the response he awaited. "Words can't explain. Just slice and dice me."

"Not just yet. I love what I'm doing to you right now. Your flavor is so luscious, so thick, and all I want to do is wallow within you. I just can't believe you're letting me do this to you."

Me not stopping him was his clue to continue. His fingers inched further and further into me, stroking my clit with a feverish tempo, pulling me into him. My arms wrapped around him again, fingers playing with his ears, sideburns, his neck, loosening the first two buttons on his shirt. Our lips met again in ragged form for seconds before we pulled away again. He bent to his knees, widened my thighs even more, then tipped his head. His tongue massacred me, nibbled my labia, my clit, and everything else within his reach. My arms reached to the sky, much the same way Linda Blair's shadow did in *The Exorcist*. I clawed at air the more he clawed at me. His tongue and fingers exposed me in long, wicked strokes as my knees buckled, but he stood me erect to finish his job. As I climaxed in fitful spasms, I cried out to him, "David, please!"

"Right away, darlin', I swear."

He faced me with a wild, hungry look in those sex-tainted eyes. His chest heaved as he spoke. "It's your turn. Take it all off of me, and don't you dare leave one strip. I want to leave here with fingernail scratches up and down my back, Marliss."

I could barely wait to take his shirt off. The days and hours I'd imagined ripping that Army uniform from his chest and licking him down to the band of his underwear practically untamed me. With him, I didn't want to be tamed; I wanted to be as rough and primal as humanly possible. David brought out that side of me.

I moved into his arms again, and we kissed as if we'd been lovers for years. My nervous hands then separated each button, and as I did that, I could see hints of honey-brown skin aching for exposure. Once the last button was undone, I spread the shirt to see what I craved. He was perfect; pecs taut and hard, dotted with unimaginably erect nipples. His stomach was smooth and rippled with tight muscles narrowing down to his navel. His velvety touch sent shivers up and down my spine, and when I kissed his nipples, my mouth watered, saliva trickled down his chest and dripped onto that sexy extended navel, and I massaged it in.

The descent was on. My kisses and licks stopped temporarily at the band of his Jockeys; his engorged clothed penis pressed against my chin. I could feel flames coming from that oozing tip. His hips rocked a bit, forcing that rigid, intense member closer to my face as his voice beckoned me. "Take it, Marliss, it's yours. Take it all night, and well into tomorrow, because I belong to you."

I stared up at him, wanting so badly to just do what he said. But as much as I wanted it, reality crept into my mind, telling me in a terribly sorry voice, *He is your client, and you know how much your girl likes him. Why are you doing this?* The last thing I needed was my ego telling me what to do. No, the only voice I wanted to hear was from that awful, wicked, disgusting id; the one that told me to go on and have a good time with the prettiest man I'd ever seen. Indeed, that was my voice of reason for that night, and David confirmed everything by running his fingers through my long tangles, saying, "It's yours, baby; claim what's yours."

His zipper busted free within my hands and David's erection squirmed from his shorts. A perfectly stiff erection faced me, his tip dripping with liquid fire, trembling from pent-up power. What was natural for me was taking him whole, nonstop, until that powerful tool hid behind my lips. I heard his pants drop to the ground with a thud and soft jazz playing in the background, but beyond that, I heard nothing and became lost in him.

My pace quickened as he rocked his hips. He groaned from absolute pleasure, knowing that the one woman he'd wanted to claim, wanted to claim him as well. With that in mind, his taut loins continued to accost the back of my throat. Within minutes of what his wonderful Marliss started doing to him, he pulled away, leaving me wondering, but he quickly reassured me. "It's time, darlin'. It's time to let me feel what it's like to really be your client."

I had a clear shot of him, as all six feet three inches of him stood completely nude in the middle of my living room. A man that stacked should have been arrested the minute he reached maturity, because he was too wicked to look at without having multiple orgasms. There he was, however, giving me fits of passion with that nine-inch assault rifle of his.

He laid me on the plush carpeting and reached for the condom that had fallen out of his pocket when his pants came off. Both of us slid it on him. David looked down upon me and smiled the most satisfied smile he could have produced. The idea of looking down at me made him crazy, it seemed. All he could see was a queen with rich, plump breasts awaiting him. He took one thick, perky nipple into his mouth and sucked with a gentle, pulling motion. His other hand massaged my other nipple, kneading it between his strong fingers, and my back arched in insane pleasure.

Seconds later, he could barely contain the pressure. I could feel the stiffness of his erection gliding across my thigh, inching toward my valley, but before he entered me, I stopped him. "David, the bedroom."

"I can barely stand, let alone carry you into the bedroom. The only way you should enter a bedroom is with a strong man carrying you. I'm not strong right now, Marliss. You wouldn't believe how weak and easy I am to you right now."

Ohhh, I loved the sound of that! I needed him to be weak and easy for me because I liked having that kind of power, especially with Army personnel.

David kissed me once again, and my legs desperately wrapped around his hips, ready for my ride from hell to heaven. The minute David's throbbing tip entered me, the pages of my life started turning swiftly. I could see that fast little girl who took everyone's boyfriend; I could see the first time I had sex with anyone. I could see myself in the middle of my living room making exquisite love to a juicy brown king, and my body lit up. The further David's length invaded my walls, the more I wanted him to thrust more into me. I knew I wouldn't be satisfied until I could feel him pumping next to my beating heart. And as I screamed for more of him, I could hear him, thrusting, panting, his scrotum slamming against my body. He was twisting me like a wire under his pressure, and release was but minutes away. But I wanted it to last. I didn't want my house, or his, crashing down until it was truly time. It would never be time because I knew I wanted this man for the rest of my life.

I looked into David's face as he made love to me. It was the sweetest face, the most sincere expression, as if all he'd ever wanted to do in life was please me, and he did. The back of my hand smoothed across his sweaty cheek before I took a hold of his shoulders and back, giving him what he wanted to leave my house with, scratches and marks.

Seconds before our moment came, I could hear Harold Melvin and the Blue Notes singing "If You Don't Know Me by Now." How fitting. I didn't know much about this wonderful man who was taking my body to heaven and my mind south, but what I did know was that he aimed to please. But with David it was beyond that. Something clicked with us, though I tried denying it. He wanted me, and I felt it way beyond anything we did in my living room that night.

As promised, David shook within me, spilling his wonderful seeds into my basket, by way of a condom, and took me to the stars along with him, screaming and panting. My body quivered around his, pulled tightly on his shaft and rode him practically across my plush carpeting. When we finished, our eyes met, we smiled, and we kissed again, over and over. Our moisture mixed in potent ways, and we held one another for the rest of the evening.

Later on, we retired to my bed and did it all again. When we finished and David was soundly asleep next to me. I rolled over, laid my head upon his heaving chest, and let my mind wander. I didn't know how to feel about what we'd done, but I knew I needed it in my life, needed him in my life.

Hours later, we showered together. The feel of his wet hands sudsing my private places made me climb all over him again, and we did it to a slow pace as warm water drenched us. Like a good little lover, I made him a big breakfast with coffee, packed him a shrimp salad sandwich with Coke and chips, and sent him on his way. He had a weekend tour to do with new trainees, and I wouldn't be able to see him until Tuesday evening. I knew I'd miss him terribly, and was actually okay with the fact that I needed him. My defenses were broken, that little girl in school had grown up and faced the fact that she was human. While missing David, I rented any movie that wouldn't remind me of him, every horror film I could get my hands on.

Tuesday evening came, and I closed shop prepared to meet up with him. We'd planned a midnight rendezvous that started with a drink at Camden's Pub and ended in my bed. Before we left for Camden's, he met me at the Sensation Station at nine, and the minute he entered, I fell into his arms, kissing him as though I were a ravaged girl lost in the woods. Letting go of David was hard, but I did it, smiling into his face. "I missed you so much."

He pinched my behind. "Really? I've always wanted to hear you say that."

"Have you missed me?"

"Humm, let me think! Hell yeah, girl!"

"Really?"

"More than I've ever missed any woman."

"Why do you like me? You hardly know me; you don't even know about my past."

"But I want to. I want to know everything about Marliss

Tanner. What I do know, I like. You're terribly gorgeous. The minute I laid eyes on you, my heart fluttered. I love your hair, your scent, the way you talk to me."

"That's all?"

He took my face into his hands. "Marliss, that's just the beginning. The way you use your head lets me know there's brains in that sexy head. What woman other than you can run this place the way you do? You run this place, Marliss. There's men in the tri-state area that knows of you and your girls. You're *soo* smart, yet you have this little-girl charm about you." He stood straight, staring into my overwhelmed face. "That's what I love about you, and I know there's so much more to learn . . . if you'll let me."

The only muscle I could move were the smile muscles on my face. He was such a glorious wonder to me, and the only response to his query was, "Yes; yes, I'll let you, Mr. Base Commander."

I locked up and we left together, hand in hand, heart in heart.

Wednesday morning was a real busy one for Sensation Station, and my top girl was late: Jasmine. It wasn't like her to be late and not call in, so I got worried. It was still early, however, and my other girls were already at work with the hunks because today was theme day; only PFCs were scheduled. We were booked solid, and I needed Jasmine's ass in there. Sheila wasn't due in for another twenty minutes, I had a client in forty minutes, and PFC Stockton was diligently awaiting Jasmine.

Ten minutes later, I saw Jasmine's car pull up, and my mind was at ease. However, the look on her face made that ease diminish. *What the hell is wrong with her? Is she ill or something?*

Jasmine stormed through the double doors, stopped in front of me, and tossed a folded piece of paper at me. Before

I picked it up I asked, "Jasmine, are you okay? What's the deal?"

She continued to stand there, arms folded, tapping one foot on the floor. "No, I am not okay, Marliss."

My concern was growing faster that a fire in a straw field. "Then what's wrong?"

"I quit! That damn piece of paper on Sheila's desk explains it all."

I didn't know what to think. My best friend and operator had just stormed in and laid devastating news on me. "You quit! Why?" I walked over to her and tried facing her, but she kept moving away from me. Finally, I made her stop. "Jasmine! You rushed in here and tossed a good-riddance note at me and refused to tell me anything. I deserve an explanation as to why you're mad enough to quit. Did a client do something—"

"No, Marliss! A *client* didn't do a thing to me. It would be better if a client had done something. This is something a friend did."

"Just sit down and tell me what happened."

"You happened, Marliss. It was you!"

By that time, I was really becoming unglued with her vagueness and needed her to get to the point. "What the fuck are you talking about, Jasmine? I haven't done anything to you other than be a good friend."

A cockiness tainted her voice. "Oh, that's right! You really are a good friend to me. Why else would you sleep with a man that you *knew* I wanted?"

"What?"

"Yeah, sistah, I showed up here last night to pick up my schedule for next week because I had made a mistake and left it here. What did I see when I pulled up? You kissing Commander Carrington. You backstabbing bitch! I should have known you'd do something like this. Do I look like Angela to you?"

I stood barely inches from her, and I was about to show

her exactly how much of a bitch I could be. "You wait one fucking minute! Don't you dare bring my past up. I'm sure you have one just as chalky somewhere in the sticks of southernmost Georgia. How else would you be so good at fucking around? I, at least, admit to my sordid past. This isn't really about us, though. You haven't any claim to David. I don't see any damn wedding ring on your finger, so don't you dare stand in my face and accuse me of taking him."

"You knew I cared for him."

"That's your problem. I told you not to get attached to these men."

"Yet you turned around and did!"

That caught me. I didn't quite know what to say in retaliation to that. By that time, other girls had come out and Sheila had walked in hearing the commotion. Everyone stood around, asking what the problem was, but I couldn't explain things to them. I had to get with Jasmine and protect myself. "Let me tell you this, I did not pursue him. He kept on me until I felt no choice but to give in. True, I told you not to like him while I was doing the opposite, but I didn't *take* him from you. He was never yours."

"So, that makes it okay, huh?"

"No! That makes it life!" I looked around at the other girls who were trying to console us. "Go on back to work. Those GIs don't pay us to stand around listening to arguments." They quickly disappeared into their respective rooms, and Sheila went to make copies of our newsletter. I again faced Jasmine. Both our expressions were furious. Jasmine started in again. "I guess old habits never die, do they?"

"I never meant for any of this to happen, Jasmine. I didn't want to like David, but I do, and I can't change that. Come on, can't we just talk this out after you finish with your client, who's waiting by the way."

"No. We can't talk this out because I'm done here. I can't work with a boss who backstabs her employees."

"I didn't do that, Jasmine."

"Screw you, Marliss."

"You know, I was trying to be sincere about this and maybe talk things out the way women should, but I see I can't do that with you. And since you think I'm such a bitch, here's something really bitchy for you. I can do whatever the fuck I want in here because, though you seem to have forgotten, this is *my* establishment. I don't like saying things like that to people I think of as friends, but that's really the bottom line when you think about it. I'm the boss here, not you."

She straightened her dress and stared at me. "The real bottom line is that I refuse to work for a bitch!"

"Fine. Leave. Instead of coming in here and causing a scene, why didn't you just quit by fax? Better yet, why didn't you quit by e-mail?"

"You would have liked something impersonal like that, wouldn't you?"

"Just go, Jasmine."

My glass front doors slammed in my face, and tears rolled down my cheeks as I watched my only friend walk away from me. However, I really couldn't concentrate on that at the time, since PFC Stockton needed his massage. Since I didn't have a client for a little while yet, I wiped my face, dabbed on more blush, and attended to his needs myself.

By the end of the day, all my girls had stopped into my room to see about me. I pretended I was okay, but inside I was dying. I'd lost yet another friend because of a man. Though Jasmine took way too many liberties by liking a man she wasn't supposed to, like I did as well, I still missed her. She'd said terrible things to me, maybe even things I thought I should have heard, but after thinking about it some more, I stopped beating myself up over it. I was secure in the fact that this time, I *didn't* take him; he was free and came on his own accord. No married woman or fiancée was hurt in the process . . . just two stupid girls.

*   *   *

It was Tuesday at two in the afternoon, David's scheduled appointment day. The weekend after Jasmine had left me, David and I spent together. He knew there was something different about me, something sad, but I refused to let on about what happened. Concentrating on Jasmine was the last thing I wanted to do while in David's company. I needed fun, a loving man, someone to smile at me, and lots to drink.

Naturally, his scheduled appointment time was right after Sheila went to lunch, so that left me with front-door duty. My other girls were already overstacked with work since Jasmine was gone. My being at the front door allowed me to watch him come up my walkway. It was something about how the sun cascaded against that jet-black hair that did my ass in. He was worth the turmoil Jasmine put me through—almost.

When he came in, I dared not tell him his darling massage therapist wasn't around any longer. I wanted to shock his ass to death by seeing me buck naked and dripping for him in Jasmine's place.

David approached me, snuck in a delicious kiss, and retreated before getting caught. Little did he know that he didn't have to sneak and attack, that everything was already mapped out for him. I kissed him back a little harder that day, getting the juices ready for him, and had him wait in her room. I got myself ready for my very own slam session with him because I could never really get enough of him. Yes, I was about to get some hellifying penetration again, and that certainly would take my mind off of Jasmine.

Believe it or not, I was actually nervous, and hesitated before walking in the room. I wanted David that day more than any other. I needed his touch, the gentle way he caressed me, the potent way he filled my throbbing core with such a hot, stiff cock! That was what I needed, and I was about to get it even if I had to push my own mother out of the way to do it; good idea actually, knowing my mother. I opened the door and saw him lying on the table with nothing on but a thin silk sheet. His back was to me so I spied on him. The silk sheet was clinging to his butt, making it look even sexier, if that was possible. His legs were apart and I could see just a hint of juicy nuts, just waiting to get licked and stroked. That was when I imagined his mouth on mine, my mouth on his . . . Christ, I was going bananas from the idea of him. My imagination continued roaming, seeing myself twisting his hair around my fingers, and making a trail all the way down to his crotch. True, I'd done all of that to him before, but it was something about him lying on that table that excited me. Maybe it was that we were about to play the role-playing game of a lifetime. I'd be his subtle, meek servant, and he'd be the big, strong Army man waiting to protect and guard. I liked that game a lot.

His muscles were taut and flexing a bit with every move he made. Then he called to me once hearing the door gently close. "I'll take it straight today, Jasmine."

I steadily walked toward him, collecting myself, and then I said, "I will not give it to you straight, and I'm not Jasmine."

He quickly turned over, "What the . . . ?" The sheet almost fell from his nude body. After realizing it was me, he smiled and lay back. "Hot damn! It's my girl. You're the only one I'll allow to take Jasmine's place. In fact, I prefer it. Where is she, anyway?"

"Just gone for the day."

"Just gone for the day, huh? My word, where do you plan to take me today? Adventures with you always take me away, Ms. Marliss." He tried to restrain his devilish grin, but it wasn't working.

I approached him, rubbing my hands together. "Your real journey is about to begin, Commander Carrington."

"Cool, but let me do this first." He turned over and brought my face to his. "I can't stand being in a room with you and not kissing you."

"Then go for it; it's all yours."

He kissed me slowly, taking my lip into his mouth and sucking it over and over. Every time he did that, my sex would quake. David slowly wrapped his tongue around mine. Damn, his kiss was so delicious that I started to drool, forgetting I was in there for a massage (yeah, right). His fingers reached within the kimono and rubbed each tight nipple to the point where it was ready to explode. I moaned like crazy to his touch while reaching for that thick staff of his. It glided across my hot fingers, its tip aching to be squeezed and sucked until the very life drained from it. I was ready to do all of that, but I refrained, barely separating from his perfect lips. "No. No, let's do this right. You are here for a massage, right?"

"I can't hold back with you in here, Marliss."

"You'll have to, but only for a few minutes, I promise."

He stood up, and the sheet dropped to the floor. I saw an erection that was already hot, throbbing, and waiting to get inside of something juicy and warm. I licked my lips and dropped my kimono in a crumpled-up heap on the floor. I didn't need it anymore because all I wanted touching me was every inch of him.

The smile on his face let me know that he approved of the moves I was about to make on him. Also, the fact that his rod was the size of the entire state of Georgia let me know he was ready for action. I walked across the room to retrieve more scented sage and turned as he met me halfway. I swear, watching a man walk with a juicy hard-on is the sexiest thing on the planet. It looks to be a chore to sport around while walking, but damn! It looks appetizing in the process.

He moved into me, pressing his hard-on against my stomach, making me want it like I'd never wanted anything before. His raw, husky voice took me. "The truth, Marliss. Before meeting you, I'd walk behind you in town just watching that incredible behind of yours in those tight skirts. I'd get the biggest damn hard-on and wanted to know who you were."

"Why didn't you approach me?"

"Nervous. Afraid you'd never tell me who you were."

My fingernail grazed the length of his chest. "You really don't know who I am, but you're about to."

"Damn straight I am." He gently sat me on the table and told me to lay back. I didn't know what to expect, so I did what he said. After all, I couldn't disobey a commander, could I? I looked up and saw him leaning over me, his beautiful eyes peering into mine, making me wetter and wetter by the microsecond. Almost instantaneously, his lips covered my left breast and sucked gently. My back arched, increasing the tempo of his movements. After he finished sucking each tender nipple, his tongue trailed past my stomach and circled the delicate hair surrounding my core. I wanted nothing more than for him to go deep with his tongue and lips, sucking me out until I died. He must have realized that from the expression on my face because that was exactly what he did. He probed two fingers into me. My legs parted so wide for him that I thought I'd break in half. As long as some part of him was inside me, I didn't care about being pulled apart.

When I became nice and loose, with nectar spilling all over me, he slowly started licking my folds. He went deeper, forcing his lips and teeth into me, tasting every square inch of it. "This is so good. I could eat you out for the rest of my life." *What a plan!*

It felt so good that my back lifted from the table, and I started screaming his name. Before I realized it I was almost at the edge of the table and about to fall off, but he grabbed my thighs and forced me back to his waiting lips. I thought I was losing my mind because nothing had ever felt that incredible to me before besides him another night. I'd had some of the best Army personnel on the base, but David took the cake . . . and ate it, too!

He stopped and looked up at me, saying, "You taste like peaches and cream, and this stiff rod of mine is ready to lap it all up, baby. I've been on fire from you since day one."

I was barely able to speak, let alone think rationally, but I managed a reply, "Then why didn't you come to me sooner? Was it the nerve thing again?"

"I picked the right time. It's always better when you save up for something this good. Well worth the wait. I found that out the other night." He dove back in and flipped his tongue all around my G-spot. I totally lost it then. I grazed my fingernails across his scalp and said, "Go in deeper and put out the flames."

His fingers and tongue proceeded to do double duty on me. I'd always imagined what it would be like to have a man sliding everything into me at the same time; it's beyond words. Good thing we were in there alone because I pitched some shattering screams. I found out firsthand why Jasmine screamed so much, and why she had fallen for him the way I had. Only I knew his mind, and she didn't.

He laid in on me until I begged him for the nightstick he owned, much like how I'd hear Jasmine. You know you've got it bad when you beg for it! I told him to stop, only so I could move from the table and return the favor to him. He lay down, and I nailed his ass! As I looked down upon that pretty man under me, the only thing I could do was smile. I reached for the massage oil, rubbed it into my hands, and smoothed them across his hard pecs. My palms slowly glided across his chocolate-brown nipples, leaving streaks of oil on him. A rush of heat filled me, causing me to come for the third time. His contours were perfect, tight and thick, with muscles hard enough for a girl to get lost in, and I did.

My finger trailed from his lower lip to his perfectly chiseled chest, then down his stomach. My hair bounced against his shoulders as I bent to taste his lips again. My aroma was left on his lips, and it made me crazier for him. Our tongues curled around one another while our moisture mixed with the heated oil. The pressure was so good that I was ready to explode. I didn't, though. I wanted it to build until I went completely wild from him. And from the way he was kissing me, my insanity was sure to surface. I was drowning in a pool of seduction, and didn't want to be saved.

We were at the point that if he hadn't been allowed to pump a ton of come, he'd burst into flames. Again, I made him wait, only long enough to let my tongue do the talking for me. It made curves on the underside of his erection and licked down to the base. I moved back up and teased his tip with my lips, sucking it gently. He bucked a bit as my teeth barely grazed across its center. He started squirming like mad and mouthing all kinds of erotic words at me. That was enticing on its own, but the idea of him inside me was really playing mind games with me, as he always did with my body.

I licked and sucked up and down frantically because there was something about him that I couldn't get enough of. I'd only had that feeling once, and that was with the wrong man, Angela's man, though he'd turned out to be an asshole. With David, this feeling was right, right for both of us, and I could see it in his eyes.

As I continued to caress him, he almost let it all hang out. Knowing the effect I was going for—giving him a mind-altering orgasm, one that would affect how he'd have sex from that day on—he held back. Despite the fact that he was depleting my resources in a way no man ever had, he was gentle with me, patient. Our first night together proved that he wasn't in this for the sex alone; no, he wanted satisfaction from both resources. That's what I've always wanted in a man, someone who was a *real* lover in every sense of the word, and I gave him my all because of that.

David could barely hang on and I knew within a matter of time, he'd wet me from head to toe. I liked the idea of it. His cream was so beautiful, thick and rich—nothing liquidly and runny came from David. That seemed to be the case with pretty men, and they all exploded in such delicious ways. They tense up, flex, and do anything else they can to get it all out. They don't have fear of looking crazy while coming because they're too fine to look any other way but outstanding.

This boy would have looked pretty with a gunnysack over his head, heaven forbid. That was what I was building up to, tangling myself within his web of semen, with no chance of release.

Just when I thought he was about wasted I heard him call out, "Attention!" He took me off guard. I thought I'd done something wrong. His throat bobbed up and down as he drilled me. "On your knees, straddling me. Now! This is it, girl!" He took the condom from the counter and handed it to me. "Slide it on."

I did it in nothing flat!

He growled out again. "Thrust down!"

I did it.

He held the base of his massive rod between his hands while staring up at me. His voice stiffened. "Grind!"

I did. Boy, did I. I slowly lowered myself onto his shaft, and felt everything inside of me burst wide open. He got into his rhythm, "Work it, girl. Work it harder. Harder!"

I was screaming and sweating because he was slamming so much into me. I took in so much that I felt like a meatgrinder in a chophouse. It was mad cool, and I liked the sudden demanding side of him. It was different from his gentle side, but no more attractive to me because I *loved* him no matter what. Yes, I said the L word, and it was high time that portion of my life kicked into gear.

He rocked me so hard and for so long that it was dark by the time he had his third orgasm. He even came hard and strong, pumping too much fluid into one single condom.

After we finished, he lifted me into his lap and kissed me again. "Was that good for you, baby?"

"Everything you do is good for me, David."

"Then why is that faraway look still in those haunted dark eyes?"

"The truth?"

"Sure. I wanna know what's wrong with my girl. Did I scare you with that freaky shit I did a minute ago?"

"I liked that part. We should play commander all the time."

"I'll definitely make that a mental note, since it pleases you. But you didn't answer my question. What's wrong tonight?"

I slid from his lap and stood between his legs, still feeling his massive hard-on pressing against my stomach. My arms wrapped tightly around him as I delivered soft kisses to his neck between talking. "Well . . . there is a definite reason why Jasmine wasn't here for you."

"You told me already."

"I told you a lie."

He moved back from me, staring questioningly. "What would make you lie to me?"

I felt as though I'd let him down by doing that because since dating, we'd been upfront about everything. I lowered my head. "I really had a good reason for doing so, so don't think badly of me."

He lifted my face back to his. "I know it had to be a good reason, and don't ever think I'd think badly of you about anything."

"You'd better hold that thought until hear what I have to say."

He slid from the table, taking me back into his arms. "Okay, what's going on?"

"Jasmine was not here for you because she quit."

"Quit? Why?"

"We fell out over you, David."

He stared into my eyes for what seemed to be hours before speaking. "What?"

"She fell for you the way I have."

"But I didn't do anything to make her—"

"I know, baby, I know you didn't do anything. You were nice to her, kind, talked to her, treated her like a woman when you were with her. Only a true man would do that. What woman wouldn't fall for you, David? She was vulnerable like I was the minute I laid eyes on you. You were sweet, different from anyone I'd ever met, and the fact that you were fucking mind-blowing gorgeous really didn't help either one of us."

"I'm so sorry, Marliss."

"Don't be. You didn't do anything wrong. You weren't responsible for either of us falling for you."

"What happened to cause this rift between you two?"

"Apparently she came back here one night after forgetting her schedule and saw us kissing. The next day she stomped in here and accused me of taking you."

"But . . . I took you. She got it all mixed up."

"David, that's not all of it. I've done some things in my past that I haven't told you about, and you may not want me after I tell you."

"Did you kill anyone?"

"No . . . not physically."

"Marliss, what are you getting at? I'll be crazy about you no matter what you may or may not have done in the past, and that's the word, *past*. This is now, and I love you." He cupped my chin in his strong hand. "I love you, Marliss. I think I've loved you since the day I saw you. What you have to tell me can't, won't change that. Talk to me."

"I had a bad childhood, David. My father left us when we were very small. I was the oldest, and after Dad left, Mom went on the nut and dated everyone she possibly could so she wouldn't have to be alone with us. Many times, I was the one taking care of my brother and sister. I wasn't much older than my sister, Maria, yet I had to do everything while mom was out spreading it thick with the men."

David held me closer, so close I could feel his heart beating for me. His voice rumbled against his chest, making me feel so at home, so wonderful for the first time in my life. "I'm so sorry you had to deal with that."

My own voice sounded so weak as I continued. "She brought one of those men home to live with us. That was the last thing she should have done with teenage girls in the house. The minute Wiley looked at me I knew I was in for it. He flirted with me, David, and I hated it. He'd pinch me all the time when Mom wasn't looking. Finally, I'd had enough of him and I fought back; he fell into a liquor cabinet that he'd depleted anyway, but he was cut up pretty bad, and my mother took his side. The courts took us from the house, and we all went separate places. By the time my mother got us back, I'd been in so many foster homes I'd lost count, but I'd gotten a reputation while I was away. No one cared about me, so I did what I wanted. I was a fast little bitch by the time I was sixteen."

David sat next to me on the leather loveseat next to the sex table and held my hand. I confessed the sordid tale of my 'Barbie dream-house' life, and so far, the Ken doll was still mine. The only thing missing was the plastic Barbie camper. One day . . . one day. "As horrible as I was, I'd never slept with anyone. All I did was take people's men, use them for what I could get, then toss them aside. Many times, I had to promise things in order to eat, and I'd gotten to be quite a pro, getting the money, then disappearing before the favor could be granted. I didn't want men crawling all over me."

He kissed my hand. "I know you didn't. Does all this center around Jasmine?"

"In a way. I told her that I had taken my best girlfriend's man from her when I was seventeen. When she saw me with you, she assumed I was up to my old tricks again, but I wasn't, David. I've really fallen for you. I'm not using you to get anything."

"You don't have to explain that to me. I know you care for me—"

"No! I love you. That's more than caring for someone."

He smiled into my too-serious face. "I almost had to wear you down to get to you. Glad I did, because it paid off. I love you, too, Ms. Marliss."

"I love it when you call me that, and I'm so glad you love me. No one's ever loved me before."

"I'm sorry that happened between you two. If I could take the pain away, you know I would." He held me tighter. "This only means one thing, Ms. Marliss."

"What?"

"You'll have to be the one to take her place in here with me on Tuesdays."

"Cool. So long as you don't mind being associated with a wayward dame. I'm sure your life was as close to peaches and cream as possible."

"No, but I did have parents who stayed together to raise us."

"Us?"

"I have two brothers, both older."

"Have mercy! There are three of you?"

"I've told you this before."

"I know, but I probably wasn't ready to listen to you then."

"Are you ready now?"

"A girl can't be any more ready, David."

"Ummm, I love the sound of that!"

I melted into his arms, and we stayed there the rest of the night, making love until we dropped. Someone finally loved me, and I was scared to let him go.

When we finally awakened, it was almost dawn. We showered together and before he left, I put his hat on his head, zipped his bulging zipper, and made his next appointment with me. Before he left, he turned to me. "I don't care about your past, Marliss. All I want is a future with you because you're the woman I have to have in my life, one way or another."

I took that morning off to get some shut-eye and returned by 1:00 that afternoon for my appointments. While in the middle of getting some paperwork done, Sheila buzzed me. "Marliss, Jasmine wants to see you. Should I tell her you're busy?"

I thought for a moment, then decided to face her again. Maybe it would be for the last time. I pressed the intercom. "No. Send her in."

Within a few moments, Jasmine poked her head through the door in a meek fashion, as though she were expecting me to throw an ashtray at her. Her voice even sounded meek, but that didn't fool me. I figured her ass was still up to something. She asked, "Can I come in?"

I spread my arms, inviting her in. She walked in and stood before me speechless, just staring at me as if she wasn't quite sure what to say, so I said it for her. "Why are you here, Jasmine? Back to finish the job? If so, you could have done that by fax as well. Remember that when you quit your next job after calling your boss a slut!"

"I'm not here to argue with you, Marliss."

"Really, then why bother? I'll say it again. Why are you here?"

"To apologize."

I slammed my hand against the desk (it hurt like hell, but I'd never tell her that). "You can't be serious! After all the shit you said to me, and the things you called me? Now you want to traipse back in here and—"

"I am serious, Marliss. The weeks I spent not being around you were miserable. I miss you, and I'm so sorry for what I did to you."

I didn't know what to think about that. I'd said some pretty awful things to her as well, like calling her a backwoods bitch, but I was mad. I walked around the desk to face her. "You said some awful things, Jasmine, and accused me of taking something I didn't take. It's not so easy to just come in here and say you're sorry and have things be peachy again."

"I . . . I know, but that's what I had to say to you. I was wrong to accuse you of that. I wanted David so bad that I'd have slapped my mother to get him, and in the process, I ended up destroying a relationship with someone I really care about—you. You deserve someone who loves you after what you've been through. It's apparent David loves the dirt road you drive on, and why shouldn't you be happy with him?"

"You really think that?"

"David is not the only person who loves you, Marliss. I just want you to be happy."

"I . . . I am happy, and I love you, too, Jasmine. I just didn't know what to think when you accused me of those things."

"I was jealous of you, jealous of what you and David have together. But I'm okay with that now."

My eyes narrowed. "You didn't talk to David, did you?"

"No. I haven't even seen him lately, sorry to say. How is he?"

"He's wonderful."

"And you two are . . ."

"We're wonderful as well." I thought about my words. "I hope that doesn't make you feel bad, Jasmine because I really love him."

"No, I'm happy for you, girl. You landed the big fish."

"And let me tell you, he's a piranha in some areas."

"Yeah, sex areas. You don't have to tell me that, but I'm sure his appointments are now with you, and free of charge."

"That's right."

Awkward moments passed before either one of us could say a thing, and then she looked around casually, as if she still wanted something. "I guess I'd better go. I just wanted to tell you how sorry I am. Still friends, Marliss?"

"I'd love that."

"Then give me a hug, hot ass, before I leave."

We embraced as though it'd been twenty years since seeing one another. We separated, but our hands were still entangled. "Are you working anywhere else?"

"No, still looking for something."

"You want your job back?"

She just stared in amazement. "Really? I can get my job back?"

"If you want it. It was always here for you, waiting for you to wise the fuck up and come back."

"Can I start today?"

"No, take the day off, and get a drink or some of that nasty chicken you tried slamming down my throat."

"Pardon me, but the Americana has great food."

"Yeah, for dogs, cats, and farm animals. Now get going; be in here tomorrow morning, and on time. David's brother Richard is in the Air Force, and he's making a special trip here to see the establishment. He's heard lots of good things about this place from David and wants to check the place out for himself." I wiggled my brows. "I understand they look alike, and maybe, just maybe, he'll want a massage. Get what I'm saying?"

"I'm on it then, sistah.'"

I stopped her before she floated from my office. "By the way, you'd have really slapped your own mother to get to David?"

"Well—"

"Don't slap your mother over a man, Jasmine. Slap mine instead. She needs it!" We hugged again, and she was off.

Jasmine is okay with the fact that David and I are engaged and will wed in four months, but I know that deep within her core she wishes she'd landed the big one the way I did. She is now the chief operator at the Sensation Station. I would trust her with my life but I still take care of the financial aspect of the business.

These days, and for the days of my life, I only sleep with one man, Mr. Base Commander. I go away with him to pick up his children and I love them to death. Both of his daughters look like him, especially the six-year-old. Maybe one day our own child will be like him, nice and gorgeous and with a heart of gold.

a note to mr. fine

A little food for thought: You *can* successfully sleep your way to the top, though it depends on what your idea of what the top is.

For college sophomore Arlene Cannon, her idea of the top was landing a gorgeous man with a ton of money willing to spend it all on her. Thus far, her mission hadn't been completed. She'd come close a few times, but the guy with the money and the badass car usually looked like the bottom of a worn-out shoe. In that case, she was all too willing to date the car and the bank book instead. Dating a man's ATM card was no sweat for the time being; there was more satisfaction that way, no rules other than not to exceed the limit. Ultimately, the nearness of a loved one was what she truly wanted, and she was always on the prowl for that wanted piece.

When her best friend and fellow classmate, Channel Jones, told her about the writing and performing arts seminars being held at Penn State the following Friday at the Omni, she was absolutely happy to go. The junior college they attended was okay, but their drama and lit department was nothing to write home about. No, they needed the real action, and Penn State had it going on. They'd heard mention of someone named Mr. Fine being the best in the field, the start of many well-known young writers. That was what

Arlene and Channel wanted. They wanted to be the next un-known to come from Nowhere, USA, and make it big. The only way to accomplish that was to be in Mr. Fine's face. That brought her back to the one thought she'd had many a day, sleeping her way to the top. If she had to do that with whoever the fuck Mr. Fine was, so be it.

There was always something about doing a college profes-sor that lit her up, anyway. Maybe it was the power; maybe the money they made. Whatever it was, she liked the idea be-cause it was risky. She liked being in tight jams with men, and seeing as though dating your professor was against many university rules, she knew she'd wanted to try it. Danger and risk taking were her aliases, and they had gotten her kicked out of many high schools throughout Pennsylvania. She was model material, with long dark hair, satin black skin, and lean legs. But her looks did have their drawbacks. Girls hated her, women in general were jealous of her, and male teachers drooled, but that was all they would do, due to their sense of ethics and their interest in keeping their jobs.

Along the way, Arlene had discovered she was quite the writer, having written many a note to get out of jams, includ-ing school jams. On the road to stardom, she had met Channel Jones, her partner in crime and sidekick in lustful ventures. Wherever there was a man in desperate need of a good lay, Channel had pointed the way and Arlene had taken care of business. When Arlene heard about Penn State's seminars, she was ready and raring to find her next victim. If Mr. Fine had the looks, he was definitely next!

Friday morning:

Arlene's phone rang and she grabbed it before it clicked into voicemail. She spoke into the receiver with a less-than-enthused voice while looking at the clock. "Who is this, so damn early in the morning?"

"Arlene?"

"We've established names already, Channel, what is it? I have to be ready in forty minutes, in case you have forgotten what today is."

"I haven't forgotten, but guess what?"

"Too early to guess about anything. What is it? Wait, let me guess; there's another cocker spaniel with an ATM card ready to date me, huh? You always set me up with canines, Channel. What's with that?"

"Shut up for a second. There's been a change in plans. My car won't start, but my father said he'll take us as far as Crosstown Boulevard since he works in Hill District. We can take a taxi from there."

"What hotel again?"

"The Omni William Penn. We'll swing by around nine-thirty because it starts at ten, so have yourself ready. I don't want to be late. Besides, the new head of the writing department will be there doing on-the-spot auditions. From what I heard, he came over from Cal State, and his name, of all things, is Mr. Fine. Doesn't that sound enticing?"

"Very. Does he have an ATM card?"

"Get serious, Arlene. I don't know what the dude really looks like or what kind of card he has. All I know is that this could be our big shot—little ole us from the hood. We could be writing commercials, or starring in them."

"Where the hell is your head, Channel? Why would someone aspire to do commercials when they could go for the gusto and slam writing careers like Stephen King, Michael Crichton, Nora Roberts, or someone like that? We could end up writing movies for Denzel and Wesley, and I know their asses have platinum ATM cards."

"What I'm saying, stupid, is that we can, at least, start small but end up big. Mr. Fine has launched many careers, from what I've heard."

"Really?"

"Sure."

"Don't worry, I'm in. There's got to be a way to get out of

the hood without dating a poodle's bank card or Visa Gold. I need the big time, *we* need the big time."

"That's the ticket, girl, and Mr. Fine is the ticket agent!"

By 9:30 both Channel and Arlene were in the back of her father's old '89 Seville as it bumped along, dropping parts like crazy. Arlene looked at her friend as if to say, "I can't believe I am in public in the backseat of this fucking nut-and-bolt-mobile."

As if Channel could hear her, she just shrugged her shoulders in a kind of apologetic mode. Then it started raining like crazy. The forecast for the day was a thunderstorm, but the girls had assumed they'd be nice and safe inside the Omni before it hit. Nothing doing. Arlene lowered her voice so Channel's father wouldn't hear the put-downs about to be inflicted upon his car. "Had you gotten the radiator in *your* car fixed, we wouldn't be in this rust bucket preparing to hail a cab."

"Back off, we'll be there before the rain hits hard. I know how you feel about getting your damn hair wet."

"You know me better than I thought." She looked through the window at the rain pellets slamming hard against the window. Then she heard her first clap of thunder. *Damn. I'll have to audition before Mr. Fine with a fucked-up hair style. Why is life so unfair?*

The car pulled to the curb, and Mr. Jones looked at the girls. "There's a doughnut shop you can wait in while you call for a cab."

Arlene's only thought was, *Great! I'll have a messed-up head, and white frosting all over my face . . . How attractive!*

The girls retreated from the car in time to run across the street to hail a waiting cab. At the same time, a young man ran from a newsstand and caught it before they did. Seeing the two girls standing in the rain with nothing protecting them but leather portfolios, he opened the door and called to them, "You want to share this cab with me?"

Had they a choice? Not in the least. Quickly, they approached the cab, but one look into the face of the man holding the door for them, and they were taken. His ass was magnificent; reddish brown skin, dark brown eyes, wavy hair, slender build, and a smile that wet boths pairs of thongs on impact.

They could hardly get out of the rain from looking at him, but his mellow, deep voice brought them back to the real. His eyes briefly scanned their frames. "As much as I'd like to see you two wet from head to toe, I'd rather not do it in the rain. This weather is drenching us."

They gave one another a quick glance, indicating they were electrified with the invitation, and slid in.

The minute he squeezed into the tight backseat with them, he could smell two different perfumes, and, if he smelled them long enough, they both would make his pants bust wide open. He had done everything he could think of not to lick his lips as they approached the cab; Lord knows what he'd do if he had to stay in it with them for a long period of time. To hide what he was thinking, he immediately asked where they were going. When they mentioned the Omni, that wasn't helping his cause, since he was going there, too. He leaned forward and alerted the driver. "The Omni on William Penn Place."

He turned to both women and stared, something he planned to do a lot of until they got to the hotel. He extended his hand. "I'm Aaron Ford, and you two are?"

Arlene, naturally the first one to speak up, reached for his hand. It was so soft and warm, with perfect fingers for sliding deeply into a very eager young woman. "I'm Arlene Cannon, and my girlfriend is—"

"I'm Channel Jones." What immediately brought a smile to Channel's face was knowing Arlene would have sold some of her body parts to sit next to him. No way in hell was she switching seats; she was there to stay until they reached the Omni. That was the only advantage she had over Arlene, seeing how she was shorter and less exotic-looking than her overzealous friend.

As for Aaron, he felt their eyes on him, but that was fine since he was scoping out the situation himself. His words were awkward, as they usually were when he was in the presence of lovely women, so he said something obvious. "There's a lot of functions going on at the hotel. You ladies attend Penn State?"

Arlene didn't want to tell him she went to lowly Butler Community College, seeing as how he looked like he was getting his master's; a master's in seduction. "We attend Butler. Are you familiar with it?"

"Sure. It's a good school, depending on what you're going for. Are you attending the Penn State seminars, the wedding, or the Blue/Green vacation seminar?" The way they were dressed, in short floral dresses that were way above their knees, much, much to the liking of his tenting dark slacks, he assumed it was the wedding. Getting these Bobbsey Twins into the honeymoon suite and waxing them to the max was a thought worth taking seriously. Having his hands saturated with their creamy honey was simply enticing, and they were cute as hell, too! His nerves were shattering, along with his zipper.

Always quick to the punch, Arlene volunteered, "Definitely the Penn State seminars. We're into the arts. In fact, we're both putting on the acting clinic of a lifetime trying not to come right here."

Channel nudged her, and she calmed down to normal mode. "And you? Are you going there for the Penn State seminars?"

Her previous words were not unnoticed; if anything, they were way more enticing than they should have been. He regrouped and stayed a gentleman. "Yes, ma'am. I'll be doing—"

A sharp clap of thunder cut his words. Everyone looked out at the rain drenching everything in sight. They could hardly see for the sheets of rain causing havoc on the streets. "We picked a hell of a day to go to a seminar, didn't we?"

As he spoke, all Arlene could do was sit there in a rain-covered cab and imagine them having to pull to the side of the road due to weather conditions, and the three of them engaging in a phat orgy. His cologne smelled so good, and his thin strip of a mustache made her thighs quiver for want of feeling him between them. His penetrating eyes made her nipples practically bust through her demi-bra. She was going for the push-up look, and she was certainly in the right cab to have it noticed.

She noticed how Aaron leaned over a little extra to check her out. Cool deal; that way she could peep at what she thought was a major fire smoldering within his pants. Arlene wanted the fire to rage out of control, then put it out with her warm, thick juices. Goodness, she was getting carried away with the idea of an erection, and wasn't even sure that he had one.

The cab pulled to the curb of the hotel. They looked out at the horrific rain, debating whether to tackle it and chance getting wet, or pay the cab to drive them around the city and start their orgy in the backseat. All three had that thought, but ultimately Aaron decided on the first and obvious plan of action: attending the seminar. "We can't sit here all day, despite how much I'd like to with you two. If we run in quickly, we can dodge some of it. How 'bout it?"

Imagining Aaron Ford with wet clothes sticking to him was such an awesome vision that Arlene blurted out, "Let's make a run for it." Anything to get at him, feeling wet, sticky clothes pressed against a six-pack and a hard-on. Yes, that would certainly be a good meal for her, a six-pack and a hard-on!

Aaron handed the driver a fifty, told him to keep the change, then opened the door. A gush of rain sprayed him as he got out. Arlene noticed how wet his shirt was getting, as well as the fifty he had given the driver. She was beginning to like Aaron a hell of a lot. She watched as he spread his newspaper out and held it over Channel's head. Once Channel was safely under the soggy paper, he extended his hand out to her. "You're next, Ms. Cannon."

"Arlene."

"Arlene it is." He winked at her and delivered his hand, feeling her fingers wrap around his and hold on. What would the rest of her feel like? Would her thighs hold on to him as he rocked and shook her into the next planet? He loved the idea of it, hoping he could make it a reality. First time he ever freaked out over a stranger. Live and learn, and she looked like a hell of a lesson to learn about.

Arlene took his now wet hand, and the three ran into the lobby of the empty hotel. They all looked around and noticed a near-empty lobby. "Doesn't look like a big seminar after all. Look at how dead this place is."

Looking at the lobby was the last thing on Arlene's mind. What fascinated her was Aaron's clinging pants and hints of a succulent chest oozing from his barely-dry dress shirt. Her own dress felt as though it weighed a ton. Stripping from it and handing it to him on a silver platter, along with her body, was way up her alley.

Aaron peeked into the ballroom where the seminar was scheduled, but nothing was going on, so he asked at the information counter, "What happened to the Penn State seminar that was supposed to be here today?"

The receptionist smiled at him. "They had to cancel it due to the weather. E-mail notices were posted about the date change as well."

"When's it rescheduled for?"

"Tomorrow morning, sir."

He scanned the beautiful lobby, wondering what his next move could be other than finding a room and bedding them both. Good idea as far as his forming erection was concerned, but not likely to happen. "Okay. Is there a restaurant in here? We can't go back out in that storm."

"Certainly, The Terrace Room is around the corner and to the left." She looked at the three of them rather sympathetically. "Would you like some rooms? There are still some available. Other participants showed up for the seminar and received rooms for the evening."

He looked over at us. "Can you stay?"

Arlene approached him, lowered her voice. "I don't have the money to stay here, but I did want to give you part of the cab fare back."

"Don't sweat it. Would you two like to stay? You can have your own room if you like."

By that time, Channel approached. "We really shouldn't. Maybe my mother can—"

"We'd love to stay. And we'll pay you back as soon as the seminar is over."

"Don't worry, everything's on me."

Those were not just idle words. Arlene meant to hold him to that one way or another. The idea of being *on him* again made her nipples press against the restraints of her bra.

"We'll take two rooms."

"We have joined rooms, or rooms on separate floors."

Arlene belted out, "The joined ones." Her eyes searched Aaron's. "If that's okay?"

The corners of his deliciously thick mouth curled in a delightful smile; it was obvious he appreciated her candor. "That's fine."

In awkward silence they waited a few moments for room assignments. Arlene couldn't believe she'd been that bold. Channel just stared at her as if to say, "What the hell is wrong with you? This is a stranger!"

However, no one's thoughts other than Aaron Ford's mattered to Arlene. It actually pleased her that he didn't take offense to her forwardness. She watched as he handed the woman a platinum Visa and knew he certainly wasn't a poodle with money. Then it dawned on her: What is a student doing with a card like that? Being bold, she took him by his wet shirtsleeve and asked, "What's a student doing with—"

"Sir, I'll need your driver's license."

That quickly took Aaron's attention away from Arlene, and he slid the card across the counter. They completed the transactions, and Aaron handed the women their room assignment and key. The lights in the hotel flickered off and on. Aaron looked at the blinking lobby chandelier. "That storm must really be picking up. Looks like twister weather. You ladies hungry? We can grab a bite, check out the rest of the hotel, then go upstairs."

That was the part both Arlene and Channel liked the most, going upstairs and into a hotel room right next to his. They'd be able to hear him do and say everything. If he made any noises out of the usual, they wanted to be the one forcing them out of him.

The barely lit, hardly occupied restaurant amazed both women. Their eyes lit up over the beautiful carpeting, gold and green walls, and incredible chandelier above their heads. They'd never been in the Omni before, and the beauty of it amazed them, temporarily; then it was back to business as usual, scoping the pretty Mr. Aaron Ford.

The group was escorted to a table in the back, and Aaron, like a true gentleman, pulled the women's chairs out and handed them menus. The only thing Arlene could say to herself was *I could really get used to this*. But could he be hers? After all, neither she nor Channel knew anything about him. He could be married, with four children at home. She hoped not, because she liked him beyond what he looked like he could do for her in bed.

Being alone in the secluded restaurant allowed them time to get to know one another, and naturally, Arlene started with questions. "What makes a man so adamant about saving the necks of two girls stranded in the rain?"

"Any man would have done that. I looked over and saw you two running for my cab, and I had to share it. Another thing, what man wouldn't have wanted to share a cab with beautiful women? And those dresses . . . Well, let's just say that I had to share with you."

It was a good thing the hotel bar and restaurant served everything all the time, even though it was morning, because no one wanted scrambled eggs and orange juice. The waitress came over and took drink orders. Channel had her usual, nonalcoholic pina colada; yeah, she really lived on the edge. Arlene snuffed her with a debilitating look. "You are twenty-two years old, Channel. Liquor is not illegal for you." She, in turn, ordered her usual, a RemyRed with cherry juice, and Aaron a whiskey, neat.

Aaron liked Arlene's sense of humor and the way she faced life boldly, not being afraid of a damn thing, even flirting with him. He also noticed that Arlene immediately grabbed the chair next to his, leaving Channel high and dry like Channel had done with Arlene in the cab.

Aaron could feel himself wanting to get in a little too deep, and he didn't want that, despite what his pants were telling him to do. He was just out of a relationship with a woman he thought was "the one," but she had been more interested in her law career than in having a relationship. He had given her the freedom she desired, and had gotten his . . . until he hailed that cab. Women were trouble, but he liked imagining the trouble he could get into with his two new friends. The only thing was, he didn't want to date a student, though they weren't students . . . not his, at least. However, it was his literature department that offered the class they were trying out for. He'd work it out, but not that day. What was on the menu for the moment was living. "Ladies, order whatever you want. It's on me."

There that sentence was again and Arlene loved the sound of it. How cool that Aaron was cute, rich, and willing to spend money. After ordering a lobster bisque and a shrimp salad, she was determined to find out how attainable he was. "Is there a Mrs. Aaron Ford?"

Channel nudged her. "Don't get all into his business. He may not want anyone—"

"It's okay, Ms. Jones. The only way to know anything is to ask, right?"

"Exactly, and thanks for your unwanted input, Channel. It was just a question."

"And an honest one. No, there is no Mrs. Ford, not at the moment."

"You were married?"

"Engaged."

"Children?"

"That's also a negative. All alone in the world, other than my job. Believe me, that keeps me plenty busy."

"Really, what do you do?"

"I teach—"

At that point, the waitress approached with their lunch, giving Arlene her soup and sandwich, Channel her seafood spaghetti, and Aaron his pastrami on rye. Before the waitress retreated, Aaron stopped her. "I'll have another whiskey, neat. You two?"

Both he and Arlene looked over at Channel time enough to see her wrap the spaghetti strands around the fork and slurp most of the food into her mouth. The rest fell onto the napkin in her lap. Naturally Arlene could be counted on for her comic phrases. "Oh, now, that's attractive, Channel. You want something else to help you down that forkful of crab?"

"No, I'm fine, thank you."

"You don't look it."

That made Aaron laugh. He'd never seen women cap on one another and still be such good friends. "You ladies are really something. Funny." He took a small bite of his sandwich, quickly swallowed, then got into what he really wanted to do: find out more about the princesses he shared his table with. "How long have you two known one another?"

Once the sauce was completely wiped from her mouth,

Channel volunteered, "We met in the last high school Arlene was kicked out of."

His brows rose. "Kicked out of school! What for?"

Arlene nodded, acknowledging her rowdy past. "Yes, I was a hell-raiser, but Channel and I got along good. Girls don't usually like me, for some reason, but she did. I never understood why I wasn't liked. I never bothered anyone until they bothered me."

"I know why. Beautiful women usually aren't liked."

She smiled at him, a sincere smile, a thankful smile. "Thank you." His words surprised her, since she didn't expect him to be so blunt. She looked over at Channel, who rolled her eyes since she hadn't gotten a compliment as well.

Aaron noted Arlene's shy respnse and almost felt bad for being so bold, but with her, it was easy to get lost, lost in lust. The more he watched her, the more he liked her. She was not your average African-American young woman; there was a roughness about her, yet a haunting sexual appeal.

They shared a relatively uneventful meal, other than laughing at Channel fight with pasta and chunks of shrimp. Channel was a lighthearted individual who didn't mind being the brunt of jokes; she'd laughed along with them. Aaron liked her, but it was still something about Arlene that got his Jockeys in an uproar. To avoid his real thoughts, such as nailing her right there on the table and tasting everything the good Lord gave her, he took another route and asked them some questions. "What made you two come all the way from Butler College to attend this particular seminar?"

"Mr. Fine."

"What?"

"We've both heard the legend of Mr. Fine, and Channel and I want to know if the legend is true about him."

Arlene could see Aaron's eyes searching for words. Watching Aaron Ford do anything was absolutely *fine* with her because he was an absolute marvel to partake in. Thoughts of his moustache tickling her inner thighs made her squirm in her seat, and imagining his snake between her lips was making her wet. From the looks of him, he was sporting around a damn diamondback snake in those pants. She'd never liked snakes, but in that case, she was in love with them.

"There isn't anyone on staff, to my knowledge, named Mr. Fine. There's a lot of staff at Penn State and surely I don't know them all, but that name isn't familiar."

"Really? He's supposed to be here."

"Then I must be mistaken. Anyway, from our cab ride, I remember mention of you both liking the arts. What in particular?"

"We love to write."

"Really? I would think you'd be better actors. Not to impugn your writing abilities."

Channel finished the last of her drink. "That's okay, Mr. Ford. I know Arlene is a good actress. She shows me every day."

"True, but I'm better at writing. Maybe whoever this Mr. Fine is will like my writing well enough to let me in; give me a start in life, cause it's been a real rocky road lately."

"I'm sure you'll have no problems. If you two write as well as you look, then you two should be shoe-ins." He flashed a seductive smile, then downed the rest of his drink.

Arlene didn't know if that was innuendo, or if he was just a friendly guy. She hoped it was the former. Her gaze returned to Aaron, who was already staring at her. Her hand slid beneath the table and onto his left thigh. He was already so warm, his feverish pants felt as if they'd catch fire. That meant he was hot blooded and could pump a ton of thick meat into an already quivering core. Her moves were slick, massaging his muscular thigh with delicate rakes of her fingernails. His muscles tensed. Suddenly, he grabbed her hand with his strong fingers. She didn't understand his actions, but when he slowly moved her shaking hand to his bulging erection, she most certainly got the hint.

They both eyed Channel, who was still oblivious to the

scene about to unfold, then got busy. He slid her tiny hand up and down the front of his pants, making the zipper so hot that it almost burned her. Her fingers branched out and did the rest. She cupped the tightness of his scrotum, feeling it squirm and buck against the tight fabric. That wasn't enough for Arlene; she had to feel the rest, make him wet, make him purge through those pants and set her world on fire. From what she was feeling, he certainly had enough hose to dowse the entire city with delicious white cream.

Her hand massaged his length, touching veins ready to pop. His tip was so hard and thick, and she couldn't wait to take it further. Her only hope was that Channel would get up and go somewhere. That way she could feel free to unzip him and delve right into pleasure.

Aaron unzipped his pants. Without hesitation, he wrapped her hand around a joint that was so massive and thick that she had to control herself. She knew Channel wasn't the high priestess of awareness, but even she'd notice Arlene flapping around like a dead fish from having a mind-crushing orgasm. Not being one to perform live shows, she simply bit down on her lower lip and massaged that wonderfully delicious cock, fast, up and down.

Aaron enjoyed the ride she was giving him. His shoulder muscles relaxed, his chest heaved up and down, and his eyes almost rolled. Though he was getting a complete and utter waxing, he kept enough control so no one else would notice anything. Everything was so good to him that he wanted more, and he placed his hand around hers, stroking his joint to full length. He quickly placed his napkin over his lap so she could really get busy on him.

For Arlene, touching and jerking a cock she simply knew was the prettiest damn thing on earth made her come in tiny shivers. She saw him smile, but what captured her mind was her quaking body and getting a handful of rock-solid meat.

Channel looked at Arlene. "You two finished already?" She looked at Arlene's half-eaten plate, realizing she'd never seen her friend not finish a meal. "Are you okay? You're awfully quiet."

"I'm . . . I'm fine . . . just full, about to pop," and she meant that literally.

"Fine, order me a Coke while I try and get this sauce off my dress."

Fucking dream come true. Once Channel was clearly out of sight, Aaron smiled into Arlene's flushed face, then kissed her. His tongue delicately parted her lips, then moved in for the kill, swirling around every crevice of her mouth. All Aaron knew was that she was the most succulent damn thing he'd ever tasted, and he'd tasted plenty of beautiful women. His sucking motion pulled so lavishly and so tenderly on her lips, like he was making up for lost time.

Arlene let him ravage her in any way he saw fit because he was powerful, sweet, juicy. Suddenly, all thoughts of wanting a rich man went out the window. She wanted this man, whether he had a platinum card or not. He was good for her body, pertinent to her soul.

Within seconds, she moved away from him, though still clutching his hard shaft. "I can't believe anything tastes as good as you do. One look at you in the cab, and I knew you could burn me down."

"Did you come?"

"Yeah, and I want to again. Let me look at it, see it, taste it."

"Won't she be back soon?"

"There was an awful lot of sauce on her dress."

"There are still people in here, and I'd rather go upstairs where we can be totally alone, in *my* room, on *my* bed."

"What about Channel?"

"You want her to join us?"

"Not exactly what I was thinking. I can't just leave her without telling her where I am."

"Look, she knows the deal; she can see you in my eyes and vice-versa. True, I don't want her left alone, but I can hardly

GOTTA HAVE IT 169

contain myself now that you've had your hands on me. I've
gotta have it!"

"She *does* know the score, and when she returns I'll just
tell her."

"Better yet, tell her you're going upstairs. If she follows,
meet me in the hall ten minutes later."

"Ten minutes is an awfully long time not to feed your
snake."

He gave an infectious smile again. "Then feed it again
now; Channel's not back yet." He leaned his head against the
wall, clasped his hands behind his head and awaited his release.

He was still so thick and hard, and the idea of him within
her clutches beckoned her to take him and take him hard.
Her quick, jerky movements made him hum in sheer delight,
and that egded her on. The more he moaned, the more she
jerked and pulled on him, wanting to taste him, getting ultimate satisfaction in pulling him to his limits. His warm, thick
flesh squirmed within her palm, needing that release, yet still
needing the friction, the punishment. Arlene smiled over his
apparent satisfaction. Her voice lowered. "Is it good?"

"If you only knew. I can't wait to ride that elevator up to
total release . . . then ride you."

"Then let me see it, Aaron; I wanna feel it drenching my
wrists."

"Not yet, work it more, because I have so much to give
you. I want it hot and burning, enough to make you faint for
it."

Words had never enticed her before because she was more
of an action-getter, but he was so damn smooth that she almost sat in his lap, riding out the rest of the wave. She pulled
on his hard, thick muscle until losing consciousness was her
only escape. Then he took her hand, rocked it harder. She could
feel his body tighten, his eyes slightly roll and his thighs part.
His controlled voice shook. "Take it, girl cause I'm ready to
give."

Within seconds, his nectar spilled onto the napkin on his lap. It dripped down his shaft and onto her willing hands. The feel of it made her almost scream out for mercy, but control in their situation was key. Her body quivered, giving her into tiny, fitful releases. Her eyes closed tightly while still clutching him. Within a span of a few seconds, she'd made it to heaven over and over again.

When the pounding within her body stopped, her eyes opened slowly and she smiled into his moist face. "Did you like it?"

"Do I look like I liked it?"

"You look like a damn caramel candy bar with creamy, thick filling."

"I hope I taste even better." He leaned into her again, taking her mouth into his, pulling her, soaking her, toying with her damp thighs, aching to explore further. Needing it and wanting to have it!

Just tasting Aaron made her cut loose again. She couldn't believe the taste of a man could take her there. All of her experiences were slam-bam and nothing more, but with Aaron, it was mind boggling and intense, and she'd be damned if she had to leave it. But that's exactly what she had to do. Aaron barely moved from her. "Ms. Jones is making her return. Help me with this wet napkin between my legs."

As Channel approached, the napkin fell to the floor, and Arlene stooped to retrieve it. Aaron was still exposed and she saw him, every wonderful inch of him. Instinct almost made her take him, but seeing now Channel was so near, she held on to whatever sanity she had.

"What were you doing on the floor, Arlene?"

"I dropped my spoon on the floor."

"Oh. They'll give you another one."

Just as aware as ever, aren't you?

The waitress arrived with their bill, and naturally Aaron took it, slipping a gold MasterCard and a tip large enough to make both Arlene and Channel drool. Then Aaron asked,

"What's next? Touring the hotel or watching the rain drench the windows?"

Channel, being one to enjoy all the sights and sounds of new places, quickly said that she was totally up for a tour. Arlene, well, she had other plans. "I'm a little on the tired side. Maybe I'll relax in the room, read over my presentation for tomorrow, and retire." She looked into Aaron's face and smiled.

Knowing what she meant, he added to their little intrigue. "I've got papers to review. Maybe I'll do that and try to relax."

Channel went in the direction of the grand ballroom while Arlene and Aaron headed for the bank of elevators. No one was in the elevator but them, and once the doors closed, they were on. He pulled her into him, feeling her warm body flush against his. "That was some story you gave Channel about having to review a presentation. If it's anything like what you gave me, tomorrow should be a damn blast."

"Everything I said was true. However, the relaxation part was total fabrication. The only relaxing I want going on is me lying across you after I've nailed you, though I am serious about getting into Penn State and making a life for myself."

"I hope so, because I'm sure you're smart enough to make it there. Now, as far as that relaxation part, why don't you give me about an hour? You can make up an excuse for Channel if she comes back, then tap on my door, and we can *relax* together. Is that good for you?"

"No, this is." She laid in heavy on him, taking up where their previous kiss left off. He tasted so sweet, yet so rugged, like a true man: hot and smoking. Their tongues matched rhythms, circling, swooning, and then the elevator stopped, forcing them both against the wall as the lights went off. Though she was in the arms of a deliciously strong man, elevators were not her thing, and the old story of getting caught in one and making love in it didn't even do the trick for her. She was terrified. "What . . . what just happened?"

"Don't worry, it jammed for a minute. I'm here with you, and nothing will happen other than what we were doing. Relax."

"I can't relax." She looked at the still-lit row of floor buttons. "We're stuck between seven and eight. Will the lights come back on? Will anyone find us?"

So Arlene would relax, Aaron pressed the alarm. Having a female shivering in his arms due to something other than a grand-slam sex session didn't excite him.

It was taking way too long for someone to respond to the alarm, and Arlene knew she had to do something. Otherwise Aaron would see a side of her that wasn't grown up; she'd be crying like a baby. She moved back into Aaron's arms. "Hold me?"

"Gladly, but don't be scared, they'll get us."

"You don't understand. I'm scared of the dark and claustrophobic, always have been. Small spaces scare me—I feel like I'm drowning."

"The lights will come back on, and there's no water around here, baby. If there were, I'd still protect you."

"Good thing to know if I ever get in a water jam with you."

He kissed her forehead, gently rocking her in his arms. "One day we'll have to work on your fear of drowning—in a nice, hot Jacuzzi. Sound good to you?"

She hugged him closely, smelling his aftershave and letting it comfort her to a small degree. "Sounds great, but what sounds better is someone getting us out of here."

"It'll happen, but until it does, I know a way we can pass the time."

"Is it what I'm thinking?"

"Only if you're thinking about making out."

"That would be it."

"Sure you want to?"

"I wanted to all along, but when the elevator stopped, well, I just got so nervous."

"This is a perfect opportunity, Arlene. Just let me hold you, make you feel safe, because you are. It's just the storm. Okay?"

"Yeah, more darkness and water, just what I need."

"The water's not near you, and the dark can be so much fun. I'm near you, so let me comfort you."

A breathy "okay" escaped her lips.

Their mouths met again, slowly at first, then with speed. Aaron was such an expert at kissing that her fear of being stuck in an elevator soon disappeared. Ultimately, what came first was Aaron's nearness, his gentle kisses, his hands parting her thighs and stroking her creamy flesh in circles, spiraling to her dampened sex. Aaron stroked the nub of her tender folds, tickling it, petting it, dipping the tips of his fingers into it; and the way he kissed her was so outrageous. She'd never been kissed like that: so intense, fierce, primal, as though he'd been saving up for her.

Aaron moved her against the wall, pressing into her, plowing his way into her. His movements were almost out of control as he delved into her moistness with quick, rugged strokes. For him, he couldn't believe a stranger brought out the bonafide animal in him, but with Arlene, for some reason, he felt like a raving maniac that couldn't get enough of a good thing. Normally strangers did nothing for him, but her kisses; her sly, seductive ways; and her personality were irresistible. Also, that fact that she felt like a satin dream and tasted much the same had something to do with it.

The length of his erection almost floored him. It had been some time since any female took him to that point, not even the woman he had been engaged to. He could feel his stiff, thick phallus poking at her, wanting entrance, demanding it. Her hands, which had been busy ravaging his chest and hair, were trapped momentarily and forced to his crotch. His breathy voice made it to her ear. "Take it and claim it because at this point in time, it belongs to no one but you."

Absolutely mind blowing! Not one man anywhere in the

state had ever given her a line like that. She stared into his dark eyes for seconds, then kissed lips that, once again, made her hungry beyond reason. Her hot, jittery hands found that flaming zipper and snatched it down. In one movement, Arlene had him. All of him was within her clutches, and she stroked it, making it stiffer and harder with every manipulation. The last time she had anything that damn wonderful in her reach was never. Never in her twenty-two years of living had the actual feel of a man's body excited her so much. His tip was so soft, so palatable. Tiny droplets of moisture saturated it, and she knew he was ready. She moved his hands to the side of her panties. "Rip them off."

No words, just action. He slid the tiny, flowery thong down her legs, then quickly put it in his pocket as he regained his momentum. His hips rocked against hers, and his penis rubbed against her soft fur. He kissed her once again, then tilted to her ear, sucking the delicate lobe.

Everything twisted into knots as he gave her the hardest-hitting orgasm she'd ever experienced without actual penetration. Everything that man did to her was groundbreaking, feelings never experienced before. She stepped back a bit and stared at him in amazement. He was a miracle worker in her eyes, and she couldn't help but graze his cheeks, his full lips, his damp curls. "What kind of a man are you, Aaron?"

That took him by surprise. "What . . . what do you mean?"

"I've never experienced anything like you before. It could be that I want you too much, and having you is unbelievable."

"You haven't had me yet, darling."

"Do you still want to after, you know . . . what we just did in the restaurant?"

"That was just the icing. I haven't had my cake yet."

Her arms encircled his neck and shoulders, while she felt a still-stiff erection pressing into her. "Do you want that cake now?"

"Every layer of it."

"Take it. Let me feel what it's like to have you inside of me. That's what I thought about the minute I laid eyes on you. It clouded my judgment. I could barely speak when I saw you, which is a first for a mouth like mine. But it wasn't just your looks, it was how you received us, treated us."

"Aren't you used to men treating you like the queen you are?"

"Not really, and I blame myself. I give in too easily, but I can't help it with you."

His fingers delicately covered her trembling lips. "Don't talk. I love what you did for me, to me, and all I want is more. Now."

She kissed him once again. "What are you like, Aaron?"

"Hungry, relentless, and ready."

The elevator shook, the lights returned, and the elevator started to move. The jerk startled them both, shoving one into the other. Aaron held her as the smooth ride quickened. "Are you okay?"

"Yeah, first time I didn't want to leave a trapped elevator."

Aaron decided to fix his clothes in case people awaited the elevator once it opened. The last thing he wanted was to have it all hanging out, in front of anyone other than Arlene. "I guess we have to resume this later. It's probably better this way because you need to be made love to on a bed, Arlene, not an elevator."

She couldn't help but agree for the first time. She wanted it to be special with him, unlike some of her previous experiences. There was no way in hell she wanted to do it to him in the back of a car, in her backyard, or in a police station. Yes, she had actually nailed a cop on duty. No, Aaron was too classy to be treated like that, and she wanted to be classy with him.

The doors opened, and they walked the short distance to their rooms. He kissed her again, opened her door, and made a quick check of the room to be sure she was safe. Finally he said, "If you need me, call me. Get some work done on that blockbuster of a story for tomorrow, and if you still want to, come and see me later."

"I still want to. There aren't too many men in the world like Aaron Ford."

"More than you think." He closed her door and slowly walked to his room.

A warm shower relaxed his muscles, especially one really large one. That was what he needed, because he realized he'd gone way too far. After all, she was a potential student at Penn State. Nailing a student would lose him his prestigious job, but until she got admitted, it was still open season on her. Sudsing the still-stiff parts of his body was little compensation for what he could have had. She was perfect for him in every possible way: funny, smart, and so incredibly sexy. Her aroma and taste still drenched his body, his senses, and he wanted her. His hands still tingled from the velvety softness of her skin, and if he could drown in her, he'd gladly toss back the life preserver.

Arlene lay across her bed wearing nothing but a thin terry cloth robe supplied by the hotel, and Aaron's fingerprints. The last thing she had expected to happen that day was giving a man a hard-on in a restaurant and making out with him in a stuck elevator. Those were things she used to do. She wanted to break away from that type of lifestyle, no matter how she teased about dating a man's ATM card. What she really wanted was a loving relationship, something that her parents had never had and had never instilled in her. She wanted to be the one to break the chain, since her brother and sister had failed to with their divorces. Aaron Ford took her places in her mind that she didn't know existed. He was amazing, real, upper class, compared to the lowlifes she used to take on. One thing stuck in her mind, however. Could he really be serious about a woman who delivered the goods so quickly? She knew how men operated; once they got what they wanted, they were pretty much history. Was he like that? Would she ever see him again?

Aaron Ford was not about to consume all of her time despite the fact that she loved thinking about him. She just hoped he didn't simply see her as a piece of ass. To rid her mind of him, she reached for her briefcase and retrieved her story. It was a good story, too, and she was really getting into correcting minor details when the lights flickered. The TV shut off, along with the air conditioner, leaving her alone in the dark again. Once power was restored, thanks to the emergency generator, she returned to her story, but everything soon shut off again. She waited for the power to be restored, but it never was.

She was scared, and there was no Aaron Ford to wrap her in his strong arms like in the elevator. The room was pitch black, and she was barely able to see anything in front of her. She managed to make it to the window without breaking her neck, and looked out. The entire city was dark. Her emotions played havoc with her again as she remembered parts of her childhood. She recalled how, as a child, she and her siblings always seemed to be some dark room while their parents were nowhere to be found. That happened quite often until her parents were made to take parenting classes. They eventually got themselves together, but the damage had been done, and a dark room in a large hotel definitely wasn't making things better.

Something creaked on the other side of the room, but she could see nothing. It creaked again. "Is that you, Channel?" Feeling her way around in the dark, she picked up a lamp, then heard the best-sounding voice on earth—Aaron's.

"Are you okay in here, Arlene?"

"Thank God it's you. Where are you?"

He shined a small flashlight that was attached to his key chain. "Sorry I didn't call to you first."

She saw the light and rushed to him. "I was so scared."

"Let me guess, it's the dark and the elevator thing, right?"

"It's a long story."

"It's still dark, Arlene, but you're not alone. I just wanted to check on you."

"I'm okay now. Are you?"

"I'm fine."

"That, you are, but I'm concerned about Channel. What happened, anyway?"

"A citywide blackout. I heard about it on my battery-operated portable radio."

"Wow, you have everything, don't you?"

"Not exactly. I still don't have you in my arms."

"We can certainly take care of that, but I'm really concerned about Channel. She may have been on an elevator or something."

"There's nothing we can do right now. To get to her, we'd have to walk down eight flights of steps, and the entrances will be locked. What about your front door, was it locked?"

"No, I left it unlocked for Channel."

"It's locked now due to automatic security."

"I don't think I like that. I need to be able to get to her. She's the only person I'd give my life for if I had to."

"You really love her, don't you?"

"Ya gotta love someone."

"That's why I'm here. We can't help Channel right now, and both of our doors are locked, other than that joining door. Even with that, I had to pick the lock to get in."

"I'd have opened it for you."

"It was locked, Arlene. You couldn't have gotten around that unless you're a criminal like me."

"I've done a lot of things, but picking locks isn't one of them."

"I've picked a lot of locks in my day, but the last time I was caught. After that, I straightened up and traded a life of crime for a college degree."

"In what?"

"Writing."

"No wonder you're at the seminar. What do you do with your writing?"

At that moment, mechanical noises sounded around and under them, and Arlene tensed in Aaron's arms. "What's going on here?"

"It's okay, honey. That's just the emergency generator trying to start."

"Does it have to sound so damn bad?"

He pulled her into the crook of his arm. "Don't be scared. I'm here with you and won't let anything happen."

"You promise?"

"What could happen? We're safe. Here, walk me to the bed so we can at least sit down. Can we do that?"

"Sure, nothing else to do."

He lightly tapped her behind. "There are a few things we *could* do. We could finish what we started in the elevator."

"Channel might walk in on us."

"Then she could join in."

That brought a smile to Arlene's face. "Wouldn't she get a damn kick out of that?"

"Would you get a kick out of it?"

"Yes, but I'd rather have you to myself."

"That could happen."

They walked slowly through the dark room, taking their time and feeling around, but Arlene stumbled on a corner of a chair and fell. Aaron fell with her, cushioning her fall.

"Ouch!"

"Arlene? Are you okay?"

"I stubbed my toe."

Without a second thought, he took her foot in his hands. "This one?"

"Yeah, the little toe."

He slowly massaged it, making her relax as the throbbing pain diminished. She said, "That feels better. Keep doing it." As he massaged the toe, her hand covered his, feeling his strength in his hands; she trembled from want of more than a damn toe massage. She moved up his arm, feeling rugged muscles against creamy, damp skin. Her hands moved up, catching the sleeve of his T-shirt. "Did you just shower?"

"Nothing else in there to do."

"I could have showered with you."

"Hm! I see you're not concerned about Channel anymore."

"What I meant was—"

"I thought about it, too, but wasn't sure you would have wanted to."

"I want to now."

"No water pressure. However, there is another type of pressure you could relieve."

"That'll definitely keep my mind off Channel."

Aaron stood her to her feet. "Can you walk on your foot?"

"I don't wanna walk. I'd rather take your clothes off."

He pulled her body so close to his that they were practically one, and grazed a gentle finger across her soft lips. "I was hoping you'd say that. The only thing is, we won't be able to see anything, and that's half the pleasure."

She surrendered tiny kisses to the corners of his mouth. "You know how it goes, when one sense is deprived, the others kick in and take over."

"Sounds tantalizing. Which sense kicks in the most?"

Her hand smoothed the front of his tenting pants. "The sense of touch. That's my favorite one."

"Mine too." He opened the front of her robe, letting his feathery touch go from her collarbone to her pubic hair. "Is this the sense of touch you're talking about?"

"Could be, but more study is needed."

He removed the robe from her body and kissed the nape of her neck. Hands aching to discover everything found her breasts. Hardened nipples reached out to his palms as he stroked them, pulled at them, lowered his lips to them. Upon contact of his circling tongue, her back arched in delight.

Aaron's vigorous sucking made Arlene crazy for him, and she realized she needed to feel Aaron Ford plummeting through her, shattering her insides. She'd had an all-too-brief taste of him, and it certainly wasn't enough to sustain her. The more he pulled on her, moving further south on her body, the more she knew he was the only man in the world who could do anything he pleased to her. His tender nips around the soft hair of her mound made her legs weak. "Aaron, please . . . Do me."

"All in due time. Something as magnificent as you needs to be teased into a frenzy and given an explosion you'll never recover from."

"That's what I want; that's what I want for you."

"I'm getting it . . . I'm getting it."

He parted her thighs and slowly worked his middle finger into her creamy center, stroking it, plundering inside it, toying with it until her muscles vibrated. Another slid in for double pleasure, rocking her harder and harder the more she moaned. "I've got to have it, Arlene."

"Take it, you own it."

"Indeed I do." Aaron stretched out on his back while still between her thighs. "Bend to me."

Slowly her cream met his lips and he licked in strong, vigorous motions, swirling inside of her, tugging, nipping. "You like this, baby?"

"Don't . . . don't stop."

"I don't plan to, not until you saturate me with your tequila."

"So long as the snake is still in the bottle."

"That snake is real ready."

Reaching behind her and feeling his stiff mass while he dined sufficiently was the bomb! He ate and she squeezed, and when he took her to that point, she quivered in delight, practically climbing her way to heaven. "Aaron, it's your turn. Stand up, let me get you out of those clothes before I die."

"No need for that." He stood before her and pulled at the hem of his shirt, but she stopped him.

She said, "No, that's my job." In one even movement, she pulled the shirt over his head and dropped it to the floor. Without words spoken, her hands grazed up and down his rippled chest and stomach, feeling perky dark nipples, and a stomach so flat you could make pancakes on it, and definitely lick up all the syrup. Her watering mouth lavished those tight nipples, licking and feeling the coarseness of his skin against her tongue. She said, "Umm, you had to taste like this. You simply had to. A man who looks like you has to taste like raw sex."

"I like it raw, too. Is it raw with you?"

"As raw as you want it to be, Mr. Ford!"

He put her hands on his zipper. "Pull it down and live in it."

Within seconds, his pants were at his ankles, and she was stretching the underwear from around his hips. One final pull, and he popped into her hands. It was such a relief for both to have him totally exposed. For her, it was feeling that mass of perfection once again. For him, he knew release was on its way, and releasing to someone as gorgeous as she was would be amazing.

Their lips met in fusion. Rockets shot off in their minds and bodies as they melted into one another, flesh to flesh, sex to sex, power to power. Aaron felt the Jockeys slide down his legs. He kicked them aside, along with his shoes, and took her into his arms. His only words were, "The bed, now."

Her arms tightened around his taut shoulders and hung on for dear life as he laid her across the bed. The ultimate thrill was looking into the darkness she used to be so afraid of, and seeing nothing but power staring down at her. The idea of Aaron Ford, a man she'd never laid eyes on before, pressing her into that mattress, was its own orgasm, and she couldn't wait to wrap her body around him.

Positioned in just the right place for complete penetration, he entered her slowly, then picked up the pace the deeper he moved inside. Wasn't she just what he thought she'd be? A creamy delight, and he could barely control himself once he was inside of her. He felt her body surrounding him, constricting, filling him with warmth and desire. She was but a billowy cloud for his landing, and he never wanted to touch earth again. He took her, tasting everything and leaving streaks across her dark skin.

Their ride was heavy and rocky, taking them to the limits of sexual intimacy, never to return to the way they were. Not a thought or concern was given to anything in the mortal world. When they gave in to the ultimate desire, their bodies plummeted into satisfaction, melting all barriers. Everything was complete in their lives. They had what the other wanted and needed, a seemingly perfect match.

Hours later, they lay wrapped around one another, sleepy, tired, and happy. Arlene could still feel his fury within her. That's how powerful his thrusts had been. She had ridden a wave with him that she'd never experienced before. As she looked at him resting comfortably in her arms, she saw, not a stranger, but someone soon to be a permanent fixture in her life, if he so desired. She didn't know how it had come about, but she knew he was the one. Her mind craved him because he was so different from what she was accustomed to. That's what she liked, something different, something that could eventually help her see a way out of nothingness. With that in mind, she slipped into slumber, resting in the arms of a man who could be Mr. Everything to her. He made the fear go away. He made her see that all fear was something she could overcome.

The next morning, Arlene awakened slowly to a bright new day. The blackness was gone, and her body felt free and invigorated, wanting more of Aaron, but he was gone!

Wide eyes scanned the room for remnants of him, but Aaron Ford seemed to have disappeared with the storm. On her table was a single rose and a note with simple words: *I've been crowned by a queen. Hope to see you at the seminar, your majesty; your humble servant, Aaron.* Poetic? He was that, and more. She held the rose to her face and took in its fragrant bouquet. "Indeed, you will see me again."

She walked into his room, hearing much but seeing nothing. The noise came from the bathroom. Her anxious hands rapped on the door. "Aaron, are you in there? I hope your invitation for showering together is still on." Nothing. She opened the door, and behind a steaming shower was a figure moving seductively, but she couldn't make out any details. "Aaron?" her voice danced with a playful anticipation, "Aaaaaron, I want to come in." She pushed the shower doors aside, and Channel waved back to her. "I didn't want to wake you up with the running shower."

Arlene could do nothing but stare. "What are you doing here?"

"Aaron said I could wash up in his bathroom."

"Where is he?"

"Gone. I had a light breakfast with him before he left."

That set Arlene back a few hundred years. She'd slept with the man, but Channel had shared the morning with him. "Why didn't you two awaken me? I like pancakes as well as anyone else does."

"He said you were worn out and that you needed your sleep." Channel moved closer to her as if to whisper, though no one was around to hear. "I know what you two did. That's why you're tired."

"I'm not tired, Channel!"

"Admit it. He wore your ass out."

"Yeah, so? Where were you last night?"

"Trying to get up here. Once the power went out, the remaining people on the main floor were ushered into one of the ballrooms. They gave us all the food we could possibly endure. We had shrimp, crab, roast beef, chicken—"

"I'm sure that was the high moment of your life, being trapped in a room full of food."

"Not as good as the night you had. A few hours ago, I was able to call mom to bring us more clothes, and have breakfast with Aaron. My mom should be here soon. Hope you don't mind wearing one of my dresses, though it may be a little short on you—"

"Where . . . Where did Aaron say he was going?"

"He didn't say. But he did say he'd see us at the seminar."

That put a much-needed smile on her face. "Really?"

Channel turned with a pleasant smile and closed the shower door while talking. "You really like him, don't you?"

"What's not to like? He's perfect, smart, sexy—"

"But he slept with a girl he just met. How smart is that?"

"Don't go there, Channel. I did the same thing. It happens sometimes."

"It shouldn't; not these days."

"Really, Ms. Fancy Pants? Don't tell me you wouldn't have jumped between us had you been able to get up here."

All Channel could do was smile an embarrassed smile. "Fine, you got me, but it was risky, Arlene. He could have been anyone."

"But he wasn't just anyone. I hope I see him again."

"For your sake, I hope you do, too."

"Thank God my mother caught up with yours. I'd hate to be seen in a dress up to my ass."

"I'm sure you wouldn't mind Aaron seeing you like that."

"He's already seen me at my best. By the way, I wonder where the delicious thing is."

"Probably inside getting his assignments, which, by the way, we should be doing. Let's get ours. We'll probably run into him there."

When they entered the large conference room, the entire city looked like it was in attendance. There were people running around everywhere with assignments, briefcases, folders—everything needed to survive a Penn State seminar. With their stories and bios in their briefcases, both Channel and Arlene approached the sign-in table. Arlene handed over her ID. "Where are the writing seminars being held?"

The receptionist quickly checked her ID against a name roster. "Ballroom B, on the upper level. But first we want everyone seated in the Grand Ballroom by ten." She quickly checked Channel's credentials, and both were escorted to the ballroom.

The room was busy with would-be actors and writers running all over the place until a speaker walked up to the microphone. At that, the crowd hushed and found their seats. They listened to the welcoming speeches, but the entire time, Arlene was scoping the crowd for Aaron. No Aaron, just a bunch of strangers with excitement plastered across their faces. The only part of the first speech Arlene listened to were the conference assignments. "Dance rehearsals: conference room C, with Dr. E. Jones and C. Brighton. Voice rehearsals: conference room K, with Dr. P. Altman. Writing and acting: conference room B, with Drs. Crayton Turner and Aaron Ford."

"What?" Arlene looked at Channel as practically half the crowd rushed to conference room B. "Did I hear right? Dr. Aaron Ford?"

"Arlene, do you know how many people are named Aaron?"

"But not specifically Aaron Ford. Don't tell me. God, just don't tell me it's him."

"Wouldn't that be exciting, though? You could say you lived up to one of your dreams, sleeping your way to the top!"

"Stop joking, Channel. This is serious. We never got the chance to discuss what he really did for a living. I knew he was a teacher, but that's as far as we seemed to get. Something always got in the way."

"Yeah, like screwing his lights out?"

"If he's the same man, my days of being the light of his life are gone. I won't be able to date him if he's my instructor."

"*Our* instructor. Well, the only way to find out is to get the fuck over there and see if he's the one."

They looked around at the people scampering to conference room B, but Arlene could hardly move. Channel pulled her along. "Don't be scared now. The time to have been scared was when you were in bed with him."

"Stop bringing that up. What's done is done."

"Exactly, now get a move on. I plan to hand him as great a story as humanly possible; maybe get a little extra on the side, like you did. Know what I'm saying?"

"I wouldn't stake money on it. Remember, you're the girl who wears food on her dress!"

They were among the last in line to move into the large conference room. Being seated in the very back, they were not able to see the front of the room until Arlene took it upon herself to peek around a large group. *Oh my God! It is him.* There Aaron Ford was sitting, behind a large conference table, wearing a black shirt with silver tie, looking damn fantastic, more fantastic than he'd looked the day before. She returned to the back row with Channel. "Bad news, it's him."

"How bad can that be?"

"You really don't get it, do you? I may be out of the running simply by my behavior last night. I was a freakazoid!"

"I don't think he's that shallow, Arlene. Besides, that might be what gets you in."

"I wanna get in based on my abilities on paper, not in the sheets."

Aaron spoke into the loudspeaker, introducing himself, and Arlene almost slid from her chair at the sound of his exquisite voice. Letting everyone go ahead of them was Arlene's only plan. The only problem was they had to move up toward the front as the crowd narrowed. What should have been an experience watching Aaron Ford work his magic turned into watching routine auditions, many of them being bad. Other than Aaron's looks keeping them awake and his voice saying over and over again, "We'll contact you," they were bored to tears.

By a quarter to four, everyone was finished except for them. Dr. Turner left the last few auditions to his eager counterpart. Aaron moved his chair directly in front of them and sat backward on it, resting his arms and chin on the high back, and smiled. "So ladies, what do you have for me? You've waited so patiently, and so have I. Each hour that ticked past made me more and more hungry to see what was in those portfolios."

Arlene was hypnotized by him; just seeing him spread his legs on either side of the chair caught her, made her ache for more of him, but she had business to conduct despite a hungry libido. "Well, what do you want us to do, read them to you, or leave them?"

"I'd love to hear you both read. Maybe if you're convincing enough, one of you could enter the acting department. I know you're good already; you've sure kept me busy."

"I'd like Channel to go first. I think she has better stories, if that's okay with you, Mr. Ford?"

"Mr. Ford? For some reason that sounds funny coming from you, Arlene. For the time being, you can call me Aaron."

"Then is Channel first, or me?"

"Whichever is fine."

"Funny thing, that's your nickname around here."

"What?"

"Fine, Mr. Fine."

"I didn't know I'd left such an impression on people. Who gave it to me?"

"Every female that confronts you; possibly every male."

He stared into her eyes. "Does that include you two?"

"More than you know." Before she said another incriminating word, she nudged Channel. "You're on, sister!"

Aaron would pretend he was intently into whatever Channel

was dishing out, but the entire time his mind was on Arlene: what they did in the elevator, what they finished on her bed last night. It was incredible and intoxicating, and he had no idea what he'd do if he had to face her all day in class. Actually, the idea of being around her excited him because he wanted her near, but if she made it to Penn State he'd have to keep his hands off. She wasn't there yet, and he needed to have whatever fun was allowed him right away.

As Channel read, he'd glance at Arlene. Her low-cut blouse enthralled him because he knew what was inside, tasted it. Everything about her made him strong and weak at the same time. The way she sat in the chair directly facing him wasn't helping the situation because she was exposed to him. He could see tight, muscled thighs covered by sheer material, and he remembered how he'd stroked them, making her legs wrap around him so tightly.

His eyes met hers, and it was like they were dreaming the same dream. Their expressions were the same, dreamy eyed and in the clouds. For Arlene, watching Aaron Ford watch her was lethal. She felt his eyes burning into hers while trying to listen to Channel read a sitcom skit. There was nothing funny about what was happening; this was serious, all too serious because they were now in no-touch mode. Arlene watched as his hands slid up and down his thighs, wiping the sweat from his palms. He was so tense, so stiff, wanting to let loose but knowing not to, not there. As he stood to stretch his legs, she saw something else needing stretching as well. His erection pressed so tightly against his pants that he had to stand, and Arlene watched his every move, like she was mesmerized by him.

Subconsciously, Aaron's hand moved to his crotch, feeling intense pressure building with no outlet. He hadn't meant to but the urge was uncontrollable. When his eyes met hers again, her smile was so fabulous, so enticing, and he knew she wanted to do what he'd just done: touch him, if only briefly.

The idea of touching him made her eyes roll back as poor

Channel spilled her guts to people who weren't listening. Arlene needed him in her hands, in her panties, in her body, but what had to suffice was crossing her legs and moistening her dry lips.

Aaron liked that small display of sexual frustration. It meant she was just as ravaged as he was. Channel stopped, but neither Aaron nor Arlene could. They were still intoxicated with the idea of the other. When Channel laid her paper down, Aaron cleared his throat. "That was excellent, it brought me right to the edge, kept me interested, wanting more and more." What Channel didn't understand was that he was actually talking to the temptress whose turn was next. His eyes slowly meandered back to the excited Channel. "I'd like to read it for myself so leave it, and you'll have an answer in about three weeks. I actually think you'd do well in the television script area. Those classes are not taught by me, however, and you'd have to audition again in about five months. Does that sound like something you'd enjoy?"

"Writing for television? Are you kidding? I'd like that."

"We'll see how it goes, but it looks good so far."

Silence, then Arlene's voice was heard. "What about me, Aaron? Shall I read mine, or act it out?"

He loosened his tie over that. "Definitely read for me. What do you have?"

"A scene from a romance I tried my hand at writing."

"How intense?"

"Hot!"

He looked over at Channel who'd gone off on her own high after hearing about the television department. He knew Channel knew something, and he didn't want to take any more chances. "I should read it, but with you here, so I can let you know if you're to be considered."

"I'd be happy to stay for as long as you need me to." She nudged Channel. "You should go. He has a lot of papers to read through before I can leave."

"You don't mind?"

"No, I'll talk to you tonight."

"You have cab money?"

She didn't, but after seeing Aaron's head slowly move up and down, she blurted out, "Yeah, I've got it!"

Watching Aaron Ford read about sex was almost as exciting as watching him perform it. He was so serious about it, undoing the first two buttons on his shirt and smiling at her at times. As he stood with her scene in his hand, she could see that stiff erection again, needing to do what he was reading about. Her words were so smooth and real, it was like the scene was unfolding before his eyes, as it had the night before. When he finished, his shirt was wet, his mouth dry, and that still-stiff cock needed action in the worst way. Instead, he sat behind his desk and called her to him. "Can I keep this? I'll need to review it more."

"Was it good?"

"Superb."

"What about my style?"

"It was excellent; your use of syntax, word usage, vividness, it was all wonderful. One thing puzzles me, though. Why would you bring a love scene to read, possibly in front of a room full of people?"

"I brought two scenes. This one was a whim and at the last minute. I don't know why I brought it. Maybe I knew Mr. Fine was actually you."

"Really? Lucky for you I am. What's the other scene about?"

"It's a conflict between a hero and heroine. That has more of my basic style of writing. The one you read was all lust, fantasy, heat. That's why I knew it would fit the minute I knew you were the one I was reading for."

He walked around the desk and stood barely inches away from her. "It worked. Look at me, I'm a damn mess all over a bunch of verbs and adjectives."

"Is that good?"

"Yeah, it's very good. However, I want the other scene because I want something that's all-inclusive. As far as Channel, I think she should get in Robert Winston's television writing workshop for the summer. All expenses paid. The only thing, it starts in two days. I'll call her when I think she's home. Do you think she'll go for it?"

"She's as good as there. You actually listened to her?"

"The major parts of it, though I didn't look like I was listening." He smiled. "You were screwing with my mind, and you know it."

"I know, and it was a blast. Can I still screw with it? We can start with that zipper." She grazed her hand up and down his erection, but he took her hand.

"Let's not."

"Why? Didn't you enjoy it?"

"Immensely, but now I have a problem."

"What problem? Whatever it is, I can help you overcome—"

"Absolutely not! My problem is you will probably be my student in about a month when the fall session begins."

"I got in?"

"I'm not saying that yet, but your style is good, your voice is excellent, and I think you can really go places with your writing, Arlene. I know what good writing is. After reading yours and whatever you let me get from Channel, I think this university would be glad to have such talent."

"Just us out of all those people?"

"Not just you two. There are others, but I was impressed despite my actions a few minutes ago. You had me going, Ms. Cannon. That's my problem. I can't be with you sexually if you get into Penn State." He sat on the edge of his desk. "Answer this: Are you willing to go for Penn State and drop me?"

"That's a loaded-ass question, Aaron."

"Don't trash a career for a great cock, Arlene. Life is way too serious to throw talent away."

"Don't say it like that."

"I'm serious. You're smart, Arlene, and what I wouldn't do to have you in my life is beyond saying, but I can't hold you back. Maybe that's why I took what I could from you, so I could have some part of you to remember."

"Was I that attractive?"

He took her hand into his, smiling. "You don't know what it's like to be attracted to a woman to the point where you'd deliberately avoid telling her who you were."

"Is that what you did?"

He was slow in answering. "I admit it. I wanted you, but knew I probably wouldn't have you for long. It wasn't just sex, Arlene. I liked who you were because I knew you were smart. You proved that to me in so many ways, yet you opened up to me about your fears. You're real, and I like that. I don't see much of that any more in women. Many of them take what they can get for security. You're beyond that."

"True, I do want to take care of myself. I hate depending on others, but I want you, Aaron. What you just said about me is the same for you. I have dated ATM cards before, and didn't care much about the hand attached to the card, but that wasn't for security, it was to get what I could get. You, you were different, classy, sweet, and sexy as hell, and I wanted you for you and nothing more."

"Then what's it going to be if you get in?"

"I can't say. You'll know if I show up in your class one day. If I don't, you'll know it's either because I didn't get in or I'm somewhere waiting for you to make me your queen. You'll have to wait and see."

"That's some answer. I think you'll get in."

Without another word, they continued to gaze at each other, wishing, remembering what was and maybe what could be. Aaron broke the silence by reaching into his pocket and pulling out a fifty. "Here, take this and go home. Convince Channel to take that summer seminar."

"I wasn't good enough for the seminar?"

"If you get in, I want you with me, in my class, getting smarter and smarter."

She looked down at the money. "It won't take this much to get me home. Do you have a smaller bill?"

"Keep the rest. Buy more panties because I think I ripped a pair of them."

"And it felt so fucking good, Mr. Fine."

That awkward silence arose again before he broke it. "Can I kiss you again?"

He took her face into his strong hands and devoured her lips, tasting, licking, getting it all in for the last time. When he withdrew, he stared desperately into her eyes. "That's all you get. Go on, get outta Dodge before I make you stay."

"A fight I'd love to lose. It would be a first."

She walked out, but he knew she'd be back. She was too good not to be back. Besides, he picked the new students in the writing department.

Four months later:

Arlene and Channel watched every move Aaron made as he worked his wizardry in class. That was a part of him they didn't get to see while they were cooped up in a hotel together during a blackout. Sure, they'd heard the legend of Mr. Fine, aka Aaron Ford, but he was much more than a legend, he was magic, black magic, and the females on campus were under his spell.

As he worked some of that proverbial magic on the board with sentence structure, plot, and character development, Arlene and Channel were dazed; he was smart and gorgeous, but for Arlene, it was much more than that. She hadn't touched him in over three months, and she'd burned for lack of him over the summer. At first she thought it was the dreadful and quite unexpected miserable summer heat in Philadelphia. Not a chance. This heat came from within, beckoned her, tempted her, withdrew her energy way more than what the weather could do. It was Aaron Ford, and the minute she stepped into his classroom, she knew the battle would rage. What hadn't helped was Channel walking in days later after her television internship in New York.

They'd both been antsy about Aaron from day one of the semester because they now had to act differently around him. He was no longer that fly gentleman that treated them to lunch, a cab ride, and a hotel room; he was authority, some-one who could either make them or break them, and it was workin' their nerves big time!

They both continued to stare as he excited everyone about the importance of subplots, but that day, Arlene lost track of everything he could teach her. Her mind was still on Mars be-cause he was so near. Leave it to Channel to catch the vibes and pull her desperate friend back to reality. Thus the first note was passed. *"What's your mind on other than how great he looks in those tight-ass slacks?"*

"Don't start with me, Channel. You, as you already know, can get me in some real trouble with your overactive libido."

"Not worse than yours. I know you miss not being with him."

Arlene turned to her with an expression that clearly read "Give me a damn break! You must want to see me burst into tears."

"Come on! You never really told me everything about your night with him. The least a good friend can do is let her in on a great sex scene."

"Yeah, like I'd tell you any more than you already know."

"I'll continue to press. You know how much of a high-riding bitch I can be to get what I want."

"Fine, if that will make the notes stop. I'm trying to get an education from his foine ass! Okay, but you only get a little. We started in the restaurant when you left to clean your dress . . . sloppy heifer! I caressed his thigh, but that didn't satisfy him, he needed more and more of what I gave him. I

undid his pants and laid it on thick . . . and thick was the optimum word to describe him; I could hardly wrap my hand around it. Channel, he felt almost as good in my hands as he did in my body. He rocked me to the equator and back, nonstop, girl, all fucking night long. He gave me a taste in the elevator on our way up, and when it jammed, so did he."

"You were stuck in a rocking elevator with him in the middle of a blackout? Damn, girl, that's a fucking romance novel."

"It's not a romance novel yet, but I'm workin' on him; I really like him. Satisfied? That's all you will ever get, because what he did to me was special!"

She passed the note back to Channel and returned to the lecture, but as he spoke, she couldn't help but relive what they'd shared. She could feel his hands sliding up her dress and ripping off her panties. His plundering fingers felt as though they were right there with her, melting her down, dipping in and out of her, rummaging within her like a devastating tornado. Thoughts of him made that aggravating but immense feeling between her thighs return, compelling her to open them and climb the stairway to heaven just once more, if only in her mind.

Her book fell to her lap and subconsciously, her fingers found that haunting, quivering, slick place. Her imagination spiraled out of control, feeling him slide deeply inside, taking all she had, and stretching her to her very limits. Only one prisoner was taken on that trip to Fantasy Island . . . her.

Snap! Arlene's eyes opened to Aaron standing between her and Channel, holding those damn naughty notes. The expression on his face was one of discomfort, humility, and utter shame. Her jig was up, and possibly so was her career, because what was contained in those notes was incriminating. All she could do was slump in her seat and never have eye contact with him again, or anyone else for that matter.

"What's going on here?" Aaron asked.

All she could do was sit there and try to form words to satisfy him. It didn't work. No amount of rationalizing would make up for those notes, and both she and Channel knew it.

No one answered so he turned back to Arlene, the one he was most dissatisfied with, feeling she should have known better than to expose something so private, so real between two consenting adults. The minute she looked into his eyes, she read his thoughts but couldn't say anything to defend herself.

"What's with these notes, Arlene?"

"I . . . um . . . didn't mean for those to surface."

"You didn't mean for them to surface? What are you doing?" His words slowed. "What . . . are . . . you . . . doing? Are you here because you're an excellent writer who wants to become even better, or are you here to play around? Both of you!"

The period ended, and he returned to his desk to hand out the next assignment. Arlene and Channel were the last to try to leave, but he stopped them. "Don't move, either one of you."

"But I have a class across campus, Mr. Ford."

"You should have thought about that earlier, Channel, instead of trying to incriminate me. Take a seat. The three of us need to clear the air."

He placed his desk chair before them, leaned back, and stretched his legs. His eyes bored into Arlene's. "What possessed you to write about us? Does the world know now? Is my job here not secure anymore, now that I've slept with a student?"

"I . . . I wasn't a student when we were together."

"You might as well have been, seeing as though the world probably knows." He sat up in the chair, clasping his hands together in prayerlike fashion, and sat quietly for several seconds. "Look, surely it's no surprise to Ms. Jones that you and I were together. After all, she was there with us. Also I should have used more self-control. I knew you two were prospective students but I went for what I wanted, and I loved what I got, but the difference between us is I kept it to myself. Sure, I could have told my best friend or a few of my colleagues who've done the same thing and boasted about it, but I didn't. I thought it was real, and something to think back on with delight. I was wrong, apparently, because I'm humiliated, embarrassed. I thought better of you two."

Arlene saw the hurt and pain on his face and simply wanted to crumble. The last thing she'd ever wanted to do was hurt him. She could do nothing but accept his words and crawl on her belly for the rest of her life making it up to him. That would be the last time she and Channel would share wicked notes ever! Her voice cracked with a hint of tear and a lot of shame. "I don't know what to do to make this up to you, Aaron. I was wrong to engage in that type of behavior, both Channel and I were. I hope this helps, but in all actuality, I did keep this between us. No one outside of this room knows, and they never will."

She leaned forward on her desk, trying to get as close to him as possible without moving. Her body was too stiff to move due to humility over the situation. "I hate that I did this to you because you were so sweet to me, to us, and I feel I've ruined everything. Everything, Aaron, even a chance with you if I'm allowed to graduate from this place."

Aaron said nothing and reclined in the chair, clasping his hands behind his head. "I know that's sincere, Arlene, and I appreciate your candor, but I still have to do something. I hope you know that."

Her heart sank to her high-heeled ankle boots. Her humanity evaporated, her mind dissolved into mush knowing the one man that could have made her, was about to break her instead . . . and the funny thing about it, she felt she deserved it.

Aaron saw both faces break apart, but he softened the blow. "What I have to do is actually a simple thing . . . and it won't cost any careers, as you may be thinking. I have to select two up-and-coming writers from each of my classes to attend an Upper Michigan writer's retreat, and your auditions might as well start now. Channel, I know you have a class with Andy McCarthy across campus, but you are among the best in this class; so is Arlene, and I need you both to do this. It's the least you can do for me after embarrassing the hell out of me today."

Arlene gladly secured their spots. "You know we'll do anything we can for you to make up for that."

"You don't need to make it up to me, just do a good job and accompany me to Michigan. This particular retreat is for adult romance fiction. If you can write romance and make it sell or get noticed, you have what it takes to be a writer. The Grant Scholarship is the prize at the end of the semester, and take my word for it, you want that! It will get you into a lot of doors since I had the gall to push your applications past admissions anyway. I thought you two were good; now you have to prove my point."

He got us in? Arlene beamed from excitement after realizing their gooses weren't souffléd. They'd heard of the Grant Scholarship and had always dreamed of it. Now their executor was giving them a reprieve.

"My plan for you two is this. You've got fifteen minutes to create the most erotic fantasy that you can think of. If it's not erotic enough, you have to do it again. If I'm still not satisfied, your grade will drop." He looked over at Channel. "And for you that would be detrimental because you only have a 'C' average anyway, Ms. Jones. You're too smart and talented to let your grade drop the way it has. What's the deal, too many notes to write?"

Channel knew she deserved that, and said nothing in retaliation.

"Your grade will drop if it doesn't meet my expectations because I know you two can do this. Give me what I need, ladies."

He handed out pencils and paper, sat back down. "Get going. You have fifteen minutes."

As they worked, Arlene could feel his eyes searching them, wondering about what was being written. She liked being watched. Apparently so did Channel because her pencil had flames coming from it.

When the fifteen minutes were up, they laid the pencils down and waited for further instructions. Arlene was up first. Aaron said, "Read it. Read it with feeling, read it as though it's about that wicked night we shared. I mean, I want this to be good, Ms. Cannon."

She stood before him with her legs and hands shaking like leaves in a swift wind, and she knew her piece had to be good or her 'A' average would be hovering above Philadelphia's sewer department. Her tasty tidbit, entitled "Cocktails," enthralled him immediately, and he reclined further in his chair. What she gave him was not fiction, and since he figured the world already knew, she decided to give him a taste of his own medicine . . . again.

Her vivid description of what they did under the table at the Omni brought a crease to his stern brow. The vividness of her story made him sweat and remember being stroked so hard that he literally spilled all over the damn place. Remembering how great it felt releasing to her made him squirm in his chair, though he tried to keep cool and calm. It wasn't working.

The more Arlene depicted the elevator scene, the hotter she could see him getting. The story *was* hot, scorching in fact, because it was real. What she described to him made the real scene seem like child's play. The few times she stumbled on words, he'd press, became diligent in keeping the flow, needing it to continue for her sake, and his. His pants were too hot for her to stop, his erection too high to be interrupted. "Keep your stride going, Arlene. I want this to be good, flow, like a real scene. Just remember how we were in that dangling elevator. Remember how you let me touch you, dipping my fingers inside, filling, pumping you until we were almost crazy from lust. Give it to me that way. I need it, and I demand it!"

That kicked her ass straight into gear, and she let loose describing a scene that was so hot and erotic that all three faces flushed with untamed orgasms. When Arlene finished the final page, Channel's face was hidden behind a book. Aaron's newspaper covered his lap but tented out like an erupting volcano. No matter what he did, nothing could hide length like that. As for Arlene, she had no idea her words were just as potent as her body could be. Her blushing face had a type of calmness to it because she'd been able to get off with Aaron without having touched him. She asked, "Do I pass your little test?"

"What do you think?"

A quick dip into his pool of pleasure was all she could fathom. Instead, she scanned his rising flesh. "I'll be glad to accompany you to Upper Michigan, wherever the hell that is."

His only response was, "Channel, you're up."

Channel's presentation of eating ice cream from his delicious skin did nothing to help his cause. He was double-teamed and was in the thick of double duty, enjoying the hell out of it despite not wanting to.

By the time both women had finished with him, he'd almost regretted having them audition. His pants would be mile high during his next two classes, and he knew it. Beyond that, he enjoyed the feel of his deeply engorged shaft rubbing against the roughness of his underwear; it kept him hard, kept him in Arlene mode, and God, did he ever want more of her! Releasing into her just once more would light his fire from now to eternity.

The dynamic duo accomplished their mission and took him to the point of nearly agreeing to any and everything they ran by him. There was only one thing they wanted: the green light into the writers' retreat. Arlene approached him, leaning into his chair and barely inches from his moist mustache, a mustache she'd tasted so many times that it made her weak. Her breathy voice enriched his ears. "Do we pass?"

He slowly stood, remaining so close to her that she could smell the delightfully erotic scent from his pants and she ached for him. "Yeah, you both pass."

"When's the trip?"

"The first weekend in October. Before that, you'll need brief tutoring, Arlene. Everything is great, but we have to work on your grammar."

"What about me?"

His eyes barely moved from Arlene. "You're fine, Channel. I told you how good you could be if you put your mind to it. That's what I expect from you from now on. Get it?"

"Sure, Mr. Ford."

His eyes never left Arlene as he spoke. "Go to your other class, Channel."

"What about Arlene?"

"Arlene's staying for tutoring."

Both of them heard Channel utter under her breath as she walked out, "Lucky bitch!" He delivered a faint smile over the comment, then pointed to a chair. "Take a seat while I see to my pants."

"Let me see to your pants." Her hand gently moved up and down the slick, drippy fabric.

"You've done enough, thank you. Give me a few minutes."

The few weeks before going to Michigan proved to be the hardest days of Aaron's life. Arlene neglected to make things better by sitting as close to him as possible for tutoring, allowing him an avenue by which to drool over her cleavage, her floral perfume, and her smooth, satiny dark skin.

Temptation was there on many an occasion, but he'd refrain, remembering his high status at Penn State. That was the only thing that kept Aaron Ford on an even keel around the tempting Arlene Cannon, and it was damn hard work!

Working in a coal mine would have been a cakewalk compared to that.

Her last set tutoring session came the week before the trip. By that time, both were so fed up with not getting any that they could barely stand seeing one another. Arlene plopped in the chair next to him. "Is this really necessary, seeing as how it's the last week?"

"This is the test on grammar, Arlene. I want you to win the Grant. Your schooling will be paid for for the next four years."

"But I'm ready, Aaron."

"Just please me by taking the last quiz."

"I'd rather please you another way."

"No! We can't come close like we almost did other times. We have to stay professional with this."

She shrugged her shoulders. "Fine, give it to me."

"It's easy, most of it is multiple choice. Just circle the grammatically correct sentences and then write the essay and you'll be done."

She scanned the document and saw she knew the answers. Then and only then did she realize how far he'd taken her in those few weeks despite how hard it was to concentrate on anything other than his cock, and how good it would feel to be wrapped in his arms. The thing about it, she missed more than just sex with him; she missed his closeness, having quickly gotten used to it in their all-too-brief time together.

Instead of writing the essay part of the test, she wrote a note to Mr. Fine. *"Should I tell you how much I've missed you since the Omni, or would you rather me show you?"*

He scanned it briefly. "Arlene, don't do this to me. You know my position."

"Don't talk, Aaron, write a note; it's sexier that way, mysterious, erotic."

"No, finish the quiz."

She passed another note. *"I quiz easier after a kiss; just one kiss and I'll back off."*

"*Arlene—*"

Delicate fingers covered his lips as she passed the paper to him. Just the feel of those feather-soft fingers against his mustache made him soar, but he stuck to his guns and passed the note. "*Stop sweating me.*"

"*No way, Aaron, and don't tell me you don't want this as much as I do. I see you in class squirming, refusing to walk near me, copping a glance from behind your teacher's manual. Besides, if you engage me in a little lighthearted pen play, you may enjoy it. We can get awfully wicked, and no one will know a thing.*"

"*I shouldn't. You're my student.*"

"*I was your lover first. Remember that. Now tell me what you've missed. Lay it on me thick, with no rules, no mercy. I want it raw.*"

"*You want a lot.*"

"*You have a lot.*"

He couldn't help but smile at her, liking everything she scribbled on that notepad. It enticed him into something he swore he couldn't do again with her, get down and dirty and make her enjoy it beyond the stretches of the human imagination. "*The truth, you haunt me every night. Everything I see is you.*"

"*Tell me what it's like to see me, want me, but not able to take me.*"

"*It gets so stiff and hard that I can hardly breathe . . . like now.*"

"*How hard, Aaron? I need statistics. I want to be able to look at it and scream over the idea of what it can do to me.*"

"*I'll put it to you like this, I couldn't get up if my life depended on it.*"

"*Then you need to be saved. Let me have it, experience it again, wallow in delightful misery, if only for a few seconds.*"

"*My door isn't locked.*"

She quickly fixed that by running to his door and scanning the clock. They had a half hour for a quickie.

Aaron watched her traipse to the door, her thigh-high dress fluttering as she ran, exposing a tiny nude-colored thong and shadows of everything he was zealous for. Yes, he remembered how she felt: so smooth, warm, and wet, dripping wet for him, and he needed more. Arlene was the only woman in life that could make him live on the edge, taste danger, and love its tantalizing flavor. She could very well be the woman to return him to his bad-boy days and think fondly of making that trip.

Arlene hastily sat beside him and began another note. His hand quickly covered hers. "Don't do it, just take it, Arlene. I can't fight you because I'm not strong enough anymore."

"Are you sure you want to?"

"I was sure the minute I laid my eyes on you. Had it not been for Channel, I'd have taken you in that rain-drenched cab and plowed every inch of it into you. I'd have given until it hurt or until I died, whichever came first."

"Do it now." She bent closer to him, their lips barely fractions apart, and she whispered, "Do it now, Aaron. Kiss me first; everything else is nothing until I get that."

He pulled her onto his lap, letting her feel the dynamic erection pulsing against his pants. He spread her legs and planted her slowly against it, letting it throb against her thin panties, wetting them, stroking up and down on her as he held her closely. Within seconds, the idea of having her in any way possible controlled him; his mouth ravaged hers, licking, lapping, nibbling until even that wasn't sufficient. He stood with her wrapped around him and laid her on the desk, barely able to part from her damn succulent lips. At that point, he was crazy in lust and didn't care about the world around him. The only thing in existence was the girl under him taking him on a vision quest to times and lands beyond.

His weight upon her emancipated her, staring up at him delivered her, and tasting him killed her, sending her to heaven so fast that her head was spinning. She absolutely had no idea that the want of a man could govern her, but it wasn't just any man, it was *that* man, and only that man could suffice. The throbbing pressure between her thighs ruled her, needing it to dominate her more and more with every thick inch of his flesh. Her lips moved ever so briefly from his. "At least unzip it and let me imagine you're within me, Aaron. Can you do that for me?"

"I can do any damn thing I want to because I'm crazy."

"Not crazy."

"I'm insane, Arlene, and if I can't feel you, you'll have to commit me."

"Then feel me, baby."

Before raising above her, he took one last kiss, long and lavishly, then slid two fingers inside her, rocking her and dancing to her sweet, wet music. Upon impact of her moist skin, he felt that buildup, that godly force, and placed her hand over his tight crotch, both his hands and hers stroking it hard up and down. It was intolerable the way she was racking his pants, and there was only one way to alleviate his need. He landed on top of her again, stomach to stomach, and pounded away, pretending he was maneuvering inside of her, imaging he was crawling up her walls, to her ceiling, and completely through her chimney, making it crumble. The harder he stroked her, touching her, hearing her call out to him, the crazier he seemed to have gotten . . . then the release, the lava, the hot, molten lava that wet the land and everything surrounding it.

In the midst of his release, the voice of the only thing that mattered in his life beckoned him. "Aaron, it was so good." She brought his face back to hers. "How did you manage to make me lose it without even penetrating me?"

"I don't know. Maybe because I've wanted you so badly that I could hardly see."

"You think of me that much?"

"I told you, I can't sleep at night. Why else would I look so fucking tired?"

All Arlene could do was smile at him, stroke his moist

forehead, and thank everything in sight for a rainy day and a cab ride four months ago.

Aaron looked at the clock. "We've got ten minutes to get it together before my next class."

"What are you going to do about your pants?"

"I keep a spare pair in my coatroom. Help me slip into them."

Minutes later she fastened his belt, fixed his tie, then kissed him. "Good as new."

"Not quite. I need one more kiss."

"You're not still mad, are you?"

"It's safe to say that I'm not."

"I am sorry about Channel and me. It was very immature."

"One thing though, writing notes in class is fun. First time I ever felt like Channel, but don't tell her anything because we shouldn't do this here again."

"Then where?"

"Maybe at Lake Arlene."

A smile crossed her face. "What?"

"Canyon Falls in Michigan. I've nicknamed it Lake Arlene because the idea of making love to you under a stream of water lights me up. I don't know if I can, though."

"You can, Aaron, and you want to."

"I know I want to, but what we just did might have to be our last time."

"I'm gonna work on that fear of yours whether you like it or not." She kissed him one last time and made it out before his students arrived.

Aaron stood looking at the closed door. What was it about her, other that brains and beauty, that nailed him? No answer for that one.

Saturday afternoon:

Canyon Falls was everything Aaron had described to the

students on the way up: beautiful, sunny, and warm, unusual for October in Michigan. Most of them expected to be in sweaters with hiking boots but found simple halters, T-shirts, and shorts more appropriate. After getting their tent assignments and relaxing a little the first day, Arlene and Channel wanted to check out the grounds. There were a few waterfalls on or near the premises, and that's where they headed. They got as far as the second-biggest waterfall. It was outstanding, breathtaking, everything two lowly inner-city girls from Pennsylvania had never experienced. There was another one, though, and Arlene could hear it crushing against the rocks on the other side of the cliff, calling to her, but she was scared. It was big or at least it sounded big, and that brought out her last fear, the one only Aaron knew about: deep water.

There was safety where she was because the waterfall wasn't big enough to overwhelm her. Maybe that was why Aaron eventually picked Canyon Falls for the retreat, so she could shed yet another fear. My God! She showed such a hard shell to everyone but once someone dug deeply, they could see a little girl.

Arlene stood on the edge of the cliffs and stared into the waterfall, remembering what she and Aaron did in class a week ago, and wishing she were under that waterfall with him at that very moment. She'd fallen so hard for him, wanting and needing him more than imagined, and an ATM card wasn't even in the picture.

Channel cut into the larger than life daydream. "What's going on in that head, Arlene? You're awfully damn quiet."

"Nothing's going on." Arlene didn't want to admit that she'd been swept away by the mere thought of a man being kind and attracted to her. Aaron was beyond kind, though; he was gentle, understanding, sweet, things past dogs in her life had lacked miserably. She was so used to canines that her attraction to Aaron scared her. People were used to her hard side, a side that could do without the rest of the man so long as the cock stayed, if it deserved to stay. Aaron changed all that by telling her how much of a woman she was. It was so unlike any man to even fathom risking a career to be with her, and that was the main attraction above anything else. "Since you did ask, though, I was imagining darling Mr. Ford under these falls, letting it shower down on his smooth brown skin, soaking him, puckering everything on him."

"I can see me being the one under the falls with him, but nine times out of ten, if it happens, it'll be with you."

"Not really. The last time we were together was the last time. Despite what he says, he's still hung up on that teacher-student thing. He's scared."

"Not scared enough. I saw how he watched you on the plane; his eyes could barely leave you, Arlene. At any time I thought he'd drag you into that tiny-ass bathroom and screw you right through it."

"Looks are deceiving. He may want it, but the stakes are still too high." She stared into the body of water, noticing how blue it looked against an equally blue, cloudless sky, and wondered if Aaron would ever take another dip into Lake Arlene. What made him change his mind about their love affair when just last week he couldn't wait to experience that lake with her? She slowly walked away, suddenly not wanting to see that waterfall or even imagine him under it. Arlene was smitten, but maybe with the wrong man, one who couldn't make up his mind about her.

The next couple of days were tough for Arlene, having to work hard in hot weather under the command of a man she could barely look at without wanting to cry, but the Grant Scholarship was a prize she was seriously trying for. Each day Aaron would work with her, Channel, and the other students to get their creative juices flowing, and it worked for Arlene. She perfected her romantic skills on paper, writing love songs, poetry, anything else she hoped could set a spark in his mind and heart. The way she looked at him, smiled at him, pretending to need more help than she actually did hit no chord within him, other than him slyly smiling at her from a distance when he thought the coast was clear.

For her, the coast was never clear because each night she retired to an empty tent in the middle of Canyon Falls Park, the most romantic place she'd ever seen, and fell asleep on a pillow she shared with no one.

The third day of the retreat was impossible; not once did he come near her or offer her any advice or encouragement before the presentations. Despite how empty she felt, the previous two days there she had managed to write something good, something worth the Grant Scholarship, but her heart wasn't into presenting.

As Arlene presented her masterpiece to the group of twenty-five writers aspiring to be the best in their genre, she shined the most and the brightest to Aaron. Arlene was the only woman in his history to totally capture him, make him think over his actions, motives, wants, and desires. What he found eventually was that she was the woman to bring him to his knees and make him truly want to commit. To hell with Penn State, his high-profile job, his never dating a student, Arlene was an itch that he could never really scratch deeply enough; the more he dug, the more he itched, and there was no getting around it.

Her brilliance captivated him as she read two days' worth of her writing. She was so intuitive, having benefited from his brief tutoring, but he knew her natural talent would go far and beyond anything he could teach her. She was outstanding!

His eyes stayed on her the entire time, smiling uncontrollably at her, staring directly into her eyes, delivering a gentle wink on occasions when her words were extra special ... and that was often. He stayed at the back of the crowd, listening and wanting it to be over, but not truly wanting that, because when her words stopped, his life would begin again, and she would be so real, real enough to touch.

A hush fell as her words ended much too quickly for a

pleased audience, and when she sat down, he nodded his head in assurance. She'd been the last to present, and after that, her mission was complete, but Aaron's was kicking into full force again.

Arlene loved the way Aaron watched her spill her guts out in romantic poem after poem. When he stood and looked into the distance, then back to her, she knew what had to be done. She watched as he slowly walked the narrow clearing to the deepest part of the canyon, the part she feared the most, the darkest part, the most secluded part, but Aaron was on his way there, and she was bound to follow, no matter what obstacles were in her way.

She followed his boot prints in the shallow mud and shivered practically the entire way up there. *What is he doing? He knows the dark scares me, yet he pulls me into the stillness. Where is that damn Channel when I need her?*

The babbling water was heard before it was seen. Its mammoth splashes and gushes frightened her more, but as she listened, it sounded more like a relaxation CD. Besides, Aaron was somewhere in the distance, and he would never let anything capture her, seemingly not even her own fear. She knew that she had to follow the path.

The water was closer and closer, crushing so hard against rocks that surely they were breaking on impact, but overcoming that fear and reaching Aaron made her trek on. She finally reached a clearing, and there before her was a trail of Aaron's clothing. His boots lay perfectly side by side and she picked them up as if they were bread crumbs leading her to destiny. Steps away were his jeans in a crumpled heap, then his shirt, his belt, his underwear. She could smell his scent on every piece, and that alone made her pursue him to her very limits, fear or no fear.

The mist from the giant waterfall met her first, and the idea of how huge it was made goose pimples form everywhere on her body, yet she moved on, all the while wondering where Aaron was. A large rock was now the only thing between her and Aaron. She peeked around and saw the waterfall; it was massive, water drenching everything in the area, like a large waterpark ride but more grand in scale. In the middle of it stood Aaron, awaiting her. A perfect stream of midnight-black water ran through and against him, casting shadows across his nakedness, making him vivid and more real than real to her. He stretched out a hand, beckoning her, and daring her not to fear where she was. Her next step was out of fear and into his arms.

Arlene stood there speechless, watching him, and slowly shedding her clothes. Her fingers slid around the band of her panties and dropped them to her ankles. She stepped from them, letting the coolness of the lake calm her hot skin and dowse her with droplets of heaven. The air breezed around her body, forcing her his way with each step. Her poise was so controlled, as if stepping on stone after stone was second nature to her. Her fear was leaving with each step closer to him, and his loving eyes watched her the entire way. Yes, she was safe, safe and loved, despite the dark and the monstrous water that could easily eat her in one downpour.

Only water separated them now, and his hand reached through it, taking hers and pulling her to him. She gladly accepted, needing to be pulled in and set free of all inhibition that was left. The minute his hand met hers, she didn't care about what was happening in the world other than the love between one man and one woman.

Her body melted into his, feeling the cool water against the heat of his skin. No words spoken, just the gush of swift water and stillness of the night that temporarily played havoc on her nerves. His kiss melted all reason and she gave in, letting him explore her in that water, feel her, stroke her burning flesh and excite it beyond imagination.

Briefly, she pulled away from him, staring at his semi-dark reflection, while trying to form the absolute perfect words. Finally the truth surfaced. "I love you, Aaron. I've loved you since the blackout. I know you don't believe me but—"

"I believe you. That's why I brought you here. If you loved me you'd follow me. You've answered so many of my questions by being here in something that terrifies you."

"Overcoming fear with love?"

"Love has no boundaries, like you said in your poem."

"The poem was for you."

"You are for me, right here, right now."

"You're certain of this? You've been so scared of our relationship before now."

"Now you know why we're both here. I want you no matter what the stakes are, Arlene. I'll deal with them." He lifted her face back to his. "I want you now, right here in this water, this lake. You're safe."

She smiled at the words. "Safe. I've always wanted to be safe with someone. An ATM card is too hard to make love to."

"Those words, Arlene, those crazy damn words that fit you so well, simply flow from you." He kissed her cheek. "How did I get so lucky?"

Her hand latched on to his, moving them to her taut breasts, stroking the hardened nipples until she could barely stand it. The coolness of the water and Aaron's gentle touch made her remember why she met him there: for love, for closeness, for that electrifying feeling only one man could give her. She moved his hands to her stomach, sliding them against her, and anticipated his next move, to the valley of the no longer forbidden. Her eyes met his. "Go there, make the thunder return, because I'm not scared of it anymore."

"Neither am I." As they kissed, the barely existent sun ducked beneath a silver lining and darkened their world. The water gushed against their bodies, forcing them into one another, pressing them both against a slick palate of trickling water, and Arlene was now in love with where she was, because Aaron was with her. His taut body burned against her hands as she stroked his pecs. Tasting his hardened, dark nipples took her breath away, and she let her flow drip and mix with the water tainting his chest.

A dwindling sense of etiquette made her pursue his lower extremities. His quivering stomach beckoned her to kiss him there more and more, taunting him. When her wicked tongue dipped into his navel, he bucked against her, practically plowing into her, making her take more, and *more* was what her mission was about. Just below that delicious navel was a bonfire, smoking, cooking, sizzling, and reaching to her mercilessly to be put out. Aaron stared down at her, wondering if she'd take that leap. She'd never done that to him before and didn't know if it was due to lack of experience, or lack of conquering other lands at the time. Whatever the case, he wanted her to step up to the challenge.

Arlene stared up at him in glorious wonder, having wanted to take him there so many times in the past, but never really having the opportunity. But now he was reaching out to her, the opportunity was there and presenting itself in grand fashion, and she went for it. His very taste sweetened her pot, making her want to have that tantalizing cream saturate her in so many ways. She took him deep and hard, having never experienced him quite that way before. Aaron was a taste that could never be matched, and she stayed on him as though separating would make him go away. She nailed him, took him, plowed as much girth inside her willing mouth as she could stand, over and over and over.

When she removed him from her hungry lips, he was so ready, so full, so contained, like dynamite one second before exploding. His taste mixed with the water delivered a flavor beyond anything on earth and she wanted more, but in different ways, different places. Her eyes pleaded into his. "I'm ready."

One swift move, and her back was flush against the backdrop. Aaron stared into her vivid face. "Did you like it?"

"It was better than it looked, and I've looked a lot. Copping stares of you in class as you walked around the room, displaying everything in such a delicious manner, almost made me rabid, foaming at the mouth, from wanting more of what I'd only had once."

He lifted her into his arms, and her legs naturally wrapped around him, positioning herself at the ultimate place and position for total engagement. Her arms wrapped around his slick shoulders, her lips succulently draped his and took him in, in all ways.

His tip squirmed in, danced around, familiarizing itself with something it had played in oh so briefly, and inch by magnificent inch, he climbed inside and shattered her. His hips matched her rhythm, gyrating against her, pumping in so much that he felt he was tearing her apart, splitting her seams. That's what he liked, he liked it tight, warm, and throbbing against him. He dug deeper while kissing her into oblivion. His lips soon moved to her chin, her neck, and her shoulders, and he hoisted her higher to taste her impeccable raw nipples, forcing both into his dry mouth as she screamed to him, acknowledging her receipt of pleasure.

The harder the water drenched them both, the more they clung to one another. Their faces stared into nothing but love and contentment; their bodies delivered nothing but what the other needed to have. When he flushed his serum into her, their cries echoed against the rocks, fluttered against the water, and dwindled into the nothingness of Lake Superior.

Aaron slowly lowered her to the coolness of the rocks and moved the dark, damp strands from her face. What awaited him was the most radiant smile a woman could give a man. They did nothing but hug and hold on to each other until the gentle night chill blanketed them. They slowly dressed and walked hand in hand up the dark hill that was no longer a threat to Arlene, and retired to the same tent to sleep in the luxury of their love.

As Arlene rested against him, she couldn't remember the actual moment she fell in love with him, but smiled in confidence that it had happened nonetheless. The more she thought about it, it must have been in the elevator as he helped her overcome her first fear. Now that the others were gone as well, she could live her life and live it royally, knowing that she truly had Aaron and he was no longer on the run. It was something so new for her, so real and again, no bank cards or Great Danes were involved. Her canine days were over.

Aaron's labored breathing seemed to have lulled her. She'd worn his ass out and he'd done the same for her. Her only dilemma was she didn't know if she'd be able to walk for about a day or two. He'd single-handedly withdrawn her energy in such a magnificent way.

Five A.M. the next morning, Channel found her wrapped around an almost nude Aaron Ford and shook her. She beckoned Arlene to exit the Love Shack, for more tidbits of information. She stood opened mouthed as Arlene exited from the tent and then delivered her only word: "Well?"

"There is no way in hell, Channel, that I'm going to tell you anything. You almost lost me the only man I've loved and will ever love."

"Not a chance, idiot. Aaron had it bad for you the day he shared the cab with us. What would make you think he'd drop you over a stupid little note?" She kicked at the dry grass with her sandal. "Besides, I just want to know if you're okay, if it was everything you imagined. I heard you two up there."

"How long did you listen?"

"Long enough to hear him scream out your name."

"He did that a lot . . . and seriously, that's all you get. Go back to bed."

"I just have one more thing to say to you, Arlene, my classic line: lucky bitch!"

"Ain't I just?" *About damn time something worked for me.*

Arlene continued to stare at Aaron in lecture as though she were a lovesick teenager with a zest for large erections, but it was different in her heart this time. It was more than lust, it was the real thing. Aaron's erection was part of the deal, though. She hadn't won the Grant Scholarship but she'd landed the grand prize. He helped her conquer all her fears and because of that, getting stuck in elevators was no sweat, so long as she was stuck with him.

For Aaron, his fears were also mastered. He had a woman who was willing to stick with him and not make him second to her career. He could see her all the time, listening, learning, and accomplishing her goals right before his eyes. A woman like Arlene kept him on an even keel.

Four years later:

These days Arlene and Channel share different kinds of notes, more mature notes—yeah, right! They could still write a down-and-dirty note as good as any pro could, if the mood struck. As Arlene sat at her laptop creating a scene for a new NBC sitcom she had been hired to co-write, that twinkling voice mail bell rang. She clicked over and saw Channel's new name plastered all over the screen. Channel Ford!

It seemed like it took her and Aaron's cousin Arliss, decades to tie the knot, but they made it official almost a month ago. She only wondered if Channel ever got those spaghetti stains off her wedding dress. Channel was still a sloppy chickenhead, but a married one nonetheless.

She read the message. *I bought baby Aaron a snowsuit from Switzerland. Arliss and I decided to turn my network assignment into a small honeymoon. By the way, how is Mr. Fine?*

Incredible! He's conducting a workshop in New York. The baby and I would have gone with him, but I'm under pressure with these deadlines.

You're always under pressure, but now it makes you a lot of money. Are you still romancing Aaron's ATM card?

I have my own, thank you, issued by NBC, and the first purchase I made on it was some stain remover for you. Think you need it?

Always.

Don't spill any cocktails on my baby's suit. I know he's only ten months old, but I would like for him to wear it before he outgrows it. Think you can handle that?

Eat me! Gotta go, but we'll be back in plenty of time to toast you two into fifty additional years together.

Didn't know you could count that high, Channel. Take care, sistah.

Minutes later, baby Aaron cried from his crib in the back room of their brownstone. She had plenty of time to nurse him back to comfort and plan an absolutely wicked evening for herself and Mr. Fine. The sitter would be there at eight, and from there it was a mad dash to the nearest elevator to get trapped with him.

What you want . . . how you want it.
THE HARD STUFF,
supersexy contemporary erotica with action that
doesn't quit. Look for it. From Kensington . . .

1

"Who said size doesn't matter?" Stevie asked. *Must have been a little man with a little . . .*

She whistled admiringly at the package, grateful for the unexpected perk.

Grinning, she dragged her eyes for a breathless second from the high-powered telescope and looked over her shoulder. The last thing she wanted was for one of the task force guys her lieutenant insisted on saddling her with to think she was some hard-up sexpot.

She laughed out loud. Okay, maybe she was. It had been too long since she last felt the sinful pressure of a man between her legs. And it wasn't because she was a prude. Unfortunately, the most intriguing prospects were the same ones she'd sworn off for years. Cops.

She'd learned the hard way not to be the company inkwell. Too many hassles. Too many knowing grins from her fellow officers, followed by suggestive wolf whistles.

Nope, she made damn sure she wasn't the hot topic of any lineup. Besides, since her promotion to detective two years ago, she didn't have time for a relationship anyway.

She shrugged and focused back on her subject.

Mario Vincente Spoltori, aka Rocky. Not an original alias, but hell, the man was a walking hard-on. And she bet he gave granite a run for its money.

She'd been surveilling the *escort* for nearly a week, and finally after tedious hours of watching the paint dry, she got her first look at what the privileged ladies of Sacramento couldn't get enough of.

And mamma mia, there was plenty to go around.

She couldn't blame the ladies who waited months to get an hour of this notorious stud's time. No more than she could help that familiar tingle between her legs. Not for Mario. As delightful as she was sure he was in the sack, she was more straight-laced. One-nighters weren't something she actively pursued. She'd only had one in her life, and although it was the best sex she'd ever had, and she would have followed the guy to the ends of the earth, the whole experience left her feeling . . . well, tawdry.

He never called.

No use thinking about a guy she'd never see again.

Prick.

Shaking her head, Stevie gave rock-hard Rocky her full attention, and for a minute put aside the fact he was the reason she'd worked round the clock for the last three months.

She laughed and thought how ironic her current predicament was. Here she was, a perfectly healthy female, and she was considering paying for stud service. Her life was too hectic for anything less than the occasional quickie. And as picky as she was, her options were severely limited.

Strictly as a woman to his man, Stevie considered Rocky's slick muscles and generous endowment. She sighed. Too bad she wasn't into this kind of stuff.

He bent over, flexing his taut ass at her, and continued the slow slide of his underwear down his thighs before he kicked them off.

Well . . . *maybe* . . . nah. Besides, on her cop salary she'd have to give up a lot of somethings for a roll in the hay with the likes of the Italian Stallion across the way.

"Oh, you selfish bastard."

What a waste. Looked like Adonis was sneaking some of

the goodies. As big as his cock was, his hand was larger. He stood stark naked facing her in front of his exposed window and stared across the wide boulevard that separated their respective buildings.

He smirked, closed his eyes, tilted his head back, and put on a show. If she didn't know better, she'd swear he knew he had an audience.

Impossible. While his windows were transparent, the small, stuffy office she'd begun to detest had a dark film covering the window, with just a small square cut out for her ever-watchful eyes. No way could he know he was under surveillance.

Stevie dismissed that thought and instead zeroed her attention back on what God had so benevolently given the man. His long dark fingers grasped his rod and in a slow pump he manipulated it to staggering proportions. Stevie licked her dry lips.

Jesus.

His hips ground against an imaginary pussy and he bit at his bottom lip.

Faster and faster and faster he pumped. Stevie's breath held when he splayed himself up against the window, still pumping. Her skin warmed. She didn't want to get sucked in by his erotic display, but she did nonetheless.

She screamed and about jumped out of her skin when the pressure of a large hand squeezed her shoulder.

"Am I interrupting?"

Her shock caused her to lose her balance and fall backward off her chair. As she was trying to catch herself, two large, very capable hands grabbed her. The touch sent shock waves through her body. She had the undeniable inclination to rub herself up against the hard thigh that supported her back.

"Christ, what the hell?" she yelled, collecting herself and sitting up. Quickly she twisted around and pulled her piece.

She felt the blood drain from her face.

Son of a bitch.

"Jack Thornton."

"It's been a long time, Detective Cavanaugh." His grin rivaled a wide-open barn door. He seemed taller, more muscled. The faint smile lines at the corners of his deep-set hazel eyes accentuated his natural mischievous nature.

She braced herself.

Humiliation and excitement riveted through her, running neck and neck for the finish line. Her skin flushed hot and she resisted the urge to lick her dry lips.

Instead, she did what any woman scorned would do. She slapped him. Hard. White imprints of her fingers stood boldly out against the tan of his cheek. Before her hand returned home, he grabbed it. He yanked her hard against him, the connection forcing her breath from her chest. Her sensitive nipples stiffened against the hardness of his chest.

"Was that because I didn't call you or because I wouldn't let you get on top?"

Visions of their sweaty, naked bodies writhing in passion amongst the twisted sheets in her academy dorm room sprang to mind. Jack Thornton could give Rocky across the way a few lessons in pleasing a woman. Her chest tightened while other emotions she chose to ignore vied for playtime.

Stevie's breath hitched high in her throat. "That was because you're an egotistical bastard." She pushed hard against him. He released her. She holstered her Sig.

Thorn continued to grin, but the harsh glare of his eyes belied his mirth. "What's so egotistical about making love to a beautiful woman?"

Despite the warmth of the room, her nipples stood at full mast. Stevie pulled on her jacket. The last thing she wanted was to give his inquiring eyes a show.

"More like seducing a virgin."

Thorn moved in closer. "That was your choice, Stevie, not mine." He grinned like an idiot. "By the way, thanks for picking me."

After so many years, the shock of seeing the only man she'd ever had feelings for forced her off balance. The sensation left her angry, and scared.

He backed up at her fist.

"Go ahead, dickhead," she said, "keep the BS coming, I don't need more of an excuse to nail you."

"I need less of one to nail you." He stepped forward, his face a happy place. "Since we're both in agreement, what do you say, my place after we're done here?"

"Pig."

"Pride in Grace, don't I know it."

Stevie couldn't believe it. The only guy she'd dreamed about stood in front of her more than willing to go back down that seductive road with her. If her pride weren't at stake, and her heart unwilling to get squashed again, she'd have her running shoes on.

"What are you doing here?"

Casually he walked past her and looked out the tinted window. He gave the long expanse of buildings quiet contemplation. As if he'd just come back from a coffee break, he righted the tipped-over chair, then sat down and focused in across the way.

"Hmm, looks like the Italian Stallion over there needs clean up on aisle nine."

Regaining her composure, Stevie swung the lens from him, and squatting level with it, she zeroed in herself. Geez, Rocky had his chum all over the window. "I swear, you guys just love to spread that stuff around, don't you?"

Thorn pulled the lens his way and refocused. "Yeah, it's what we do. Men hunt and propagate the species, women nurture and gather. Basic."

Stevie's eyes narrowed. Neanderthal. She'd been too starry-eyed to see it in the academy seven years ago; at least *she'd* evolved since then.

She pulled the lens back her way and focused on Rocky. "That's it, clean up your mess," she said to the gigolo. Then, as if to herself, she said, "I wonder if there was some kind of statute back then about instructors fraternizing with students?"

Thorn leaned in behind her. "No." His hot breath against her ear stirred up old familiar heat. His clean, woodsy scent engulfed her. Her blood thickened in her veins and whatever hormones she had that induced sex surged through her body. She clenched her muscles before they turned to warm mush.

Stevie remembered how she couldn't wait for her defensive tactics classes. Sergeant Jack Thornton was the instructor, and she repeatedly paid with bruises to be his test dummy.

She almost laughed. She'd had such a crush on him from the get-go. Little did she know she'd end up his parting gift.

"How's the wife and kid?"

He pulled away. "You know my divorce was final before graduation." His eyes clouded. "My stepson is with his father."

Stevie inhaled a deep breath and slowly exhaled. She didn't give a rat's ass about his home life.

"What are you doing here, Thorn?"

He grinned and stood back from the telescope. Casually he pulled back his Italian-cut suit and said, "Special Agent Thornton at your service, ma'am."

She hissed in a long breath, giving him a sideways glare. So the rumors were true. He'd dumped her for Quantico. "You damned feds, why the hell can't you leave us locals alone? Go fight your own crime."

She turned away from him, settled back on the chair he'd vacated, and refocused on Studly. "Now you made me lose him. Get out of here."

"Sorry, Detective, your crime has become our crime. We're taking over from here."

"That's a crock, Thornton. Me and my men have been working this case around the clock since the first body showed up. County is coming in to help out, and I'm lead dick." She smiled tightly, keeping her eyes focused on Spoltori. "You've been misinformed."

When there was no response from him, she looked up to find him staring down at her. His eyes narrowed and a slow tic worked his right jawline. "I'm not going to get into a pissing match with you, Cavanaugh. Your chief requested we come in. We're here, I'm heading up the task force."

Stevie sprang out of the chair, throwing her shoulders back. Her antagonism mushroomed when he chuckled and said, "You've been assigned to tag along for the ride." He lowered his voice as if there were others in the room who had no business listening in on their conversation. "And, Stevie, I promise you a helluva ride."

Fury infiltrated every cell she possessed. She worked her fists open and closed. "You've got a hell of a lot of nerve coming in here, telling me you're taking over my case and then propositioning me. Do you think so damned much of yourself or so little of me?"

Thorn's wide-eyed reaction gave her a modicum of satisfaction. He quickly recovered. "I'm sorry if I've given you the impression I have no respect for you, Detective." He grinned. "I think I can say with some accuracy you're one of the best cops out there. You should be, I trained you."

"You trained me all right." The words escaped before she could call them back. He not only mentored her in the classroom and spent countless hours coaching her on the shooting range and in defensive tactics, but he taught her how to ride out an orgasm for maximum satisfaction among other sexy little tricks. She squashed the memories and the heat that accompanied them.

Never bashful, she gave her one-night stand a long discriminating look. She would never admit she liked what she saw. He was taller than her five-eight by a good half a foot. His shoulders looked like a linebacker's, built into a rock-hard chest that tapered down to a washboard belly and further to a package that never reclined. The guy had the stamina of a prize bull.

She snorted in contempt. "You taught me my biggest life lesson to date." She traced a finger down his silk tie. "Trust no one." She stepped back and added, "By the way, I don't go for carnie rides."

His full lips slid into a tantalizing smile. His long tanned fingers slid into his trouser pockets. "Anytime you change your mind, Detective, let me know."

"Don't hold your breath. You'll suffocate if you do."

She turned back to Rocky. He'd disappeared. Probably into the shower. Their guy had an unhealthy fixation with showerheads.

Thorn pulled up the only other piece of furniture in the empty office. A straight-back chair.

"Look, Stevie, I took this case on to work with you, not against you."

Her gut clenched. "You knew this was my case?"

He nodded. "I always do my homework. Tell you what, you can keep your people, but understand they'll have to get along with mine."

Her anger flashed. This was her case, damn it! She'd be damned if she'd just step aside.

"C'mon, Detective, show me yours and I'll show you mine," Thorn offered.

Stevie grunted and, knowing he wanted to trade information, she gave him something else. She pulled her Sig. "Mine's loaded."

He smiled again, his white teeth gleaming in the filtered afternoon light. "Mine's bigger." He pulled a mini assault pistol from his shoulder holster.

Stevie whistled. "Nice piece." Replacing her weapon, she reached out her hand, palm up. "Can I touch it?"

His grin turned lethal. He handed her the weapon, his fingertips brushing her palm. Stevie ignored the warm flush the contact instigated.

"Be careful, it's cocked and will discharge at the slightest provocation."

Stevie ignored him, and ran her fingers along the smooth cold steel. She wanted one.

"The magazine holds twenty-two rounds and can discharge the whole wad in less than two seconds."

Her eyes met his. A flash of heat speared her pussy. "What's the fun in that?"

He reached out his hand and slowly withdrew the pistol, the short barrel sliding against her moist palm. In a quick movement he ejected the magazine and replaced it with another one he pulled from his jacket pocket. "Lots. It's ready for firing in less time than it takes to clean up from the first barrage."

Stevie ignored the warm wetness between her thighs and the way his nostrils flared like a dog sniffing its mate's sex.

She recognized trouble when she met it. She couldn't do this. "I'll pack up and leave you and Studly to get to know each other."

She bent down to pick up her backpack, but he grabbed her arm and pulled her up and against him. The palpable tension jolted them both. "You're not going anywhere, Detective. You know this guy better than his mother. You're stuck with me."

She yanked her arm.

"Take it up with your boss if you have a problem."

A rill of frustration swept through her. The last thing she wanted was to spend her days in this stuffy office across the street from a serial killing man–whore, and watch the guy do half of Sacramento's political wives, with her ex-lover breathing down her neck. She glanced at the three photos of the lifeless victims she'd tacked up on the wall, a constant reminder of why she was there. Her gut somersaulted.

She could do this with her own people, she was a proven detective. But now? With Thorn as a constant distraction? She scowled. No way.

"Sorry to burst your bubble, but I'll quit before I'd hole up with you eight hours a day waiting to get a lead on Romeo over there."

His eyes narrowed, their gold-green irises flaring jade. "I thought you were better trained than that, Detective. Can't stand a little heat? What the hell kind of cop are you anyway?"

That did it. She went toe to toe with him. In the breath of a second she was in his face, her chin notched high, her eyelids narrowed, her back stiffened. "The kind that has some integrity and doesn't have to put up with a sex-crazed fed."

"Chicken."

"Taunting me won't get you a thing, Thorn. I don't *have* *to* work with you. I *won't* work with you. I'd rather spend the day with Lothario over there and take my chances. At least with him I won't have to play games."

He laughed deeply. "I don't play games, Detective. I play for real." He leaned into her, his face only a few inches from hers. She could see the golden flecks in his eyes and smell the minty warmth of his breath. "That guy is connected to three dead women, and I aim to nab him before he does another one. Take another look at those faces, Detective." He pointed at the wall of death.

Dead eyes stared at her, begging to be put to rest.

"I'd work with the Wicked Witch of the West if it would bring the victims justice."

Her fists clenched and unclenched. Damn him! "My responsibility is also to the victims. But how the hell am I supposed to do my job with you breathing down my neck like a dog denied?"

"Consider it an adverse condition and deal with it."

Stevie growled. As much as she didn't want to work with Thorn she wanted to nail Spoltori more. She had a responsibility to the families of the victims and to the victims themselves. No one deserved to die the way those women had. She smiled blithely. Not even Jack Thornton.

"I'll work with you, Jack. But let's get a few facts straight first. You touch me, I punch you." She grabbed a handful of her breasts. She smiled inwardly at his sharp intake of breath. "These are mine. I only share if I want to. Touch them and I'll geld you."

Thorn laughed, the sound deep and mellow. "Oh, Stevie, I wish I'd had another day to spend with you."

She stepped back, sliding her hands into her jeans pockets. How many times through her haze of anger when she discovered him gone had she wished for the same thing?

"Yeah, me too. It would have taken me no time to skin you alive."

She was spared Thorn's response when another suit walked in. She deduced before Thorn's intro he was another fed.

"Detective Cavanaugh, meet Agent Deavers. He's my communications specialist."

Stevie extended her hand to the tall, handsome agent. "I'd say I'm glad to meet you, Deavers, but under the circumstances I'm feeling a little bit cheated."

He nodded and gave Thorn a knowing look. "We get that a lot."

Stevie gave Thorn a hard look. "We're already set up in my office, what do you say we use that as HQ for our party?"

Both men nodded, and it was a small consolation.

Take a walk on the wildest side of all . . . with
WOLF TALES by Kate Douglas.
Thrilling erotica from Kensington . . .

Warmth. The most wonderful sense of warmth, of contentment. Sighing, Xandi snuggled deeper into the blankets, aware of a slight tingling in her toes and fingers, a sense of heat radiating all around her, of weight and comfort and safety.

And something very large, very long, very solid, wedged tightly between her bare buttocks, following the crease of her labia and resting hot and hard against her clit. She blinked, opened her eyes wide, saw only darkness.

Awake now, she felt soft breath tickling the back of her neck, warm arms encircling her, a hard, muscular body enfolding hers. She held herself very still, forcing her fuzzy mind into a clarity it really wasn't ready for. Okay . . . she remembered having been lost in a snowstorm, remembered thinking about building a shelter, remembered . . . nothing. Nothing beyond the sense that it was too late, she was too cold . . . then nothing.

The body behind her shifted. The huge cock—at least that much she recognized—slipped against her clit as the person holding her thrust his hips just a bit closer to hers.

Xandi cleared her throat. Whoever held her had obviously saved her life. Everyone knew more heat was given off by naked bodies, but she'd never really thought of the concept of awakening in the dark, wrapped securely together with a totally unknown naked body. No, that really hadn't entered her mind . . . at least until now.

She fought the need to giggle. Nerves. Had to be nerves. But she felt her labia softening, engorging, knew her clit was beginning to peek out from its little hood of flesh, searching for closer contact with that hot cock. The arms holding her tightened just a bit. One of the hands moved to cover her breast.

Neither one of them spoke. He knew what she looked like. She had no idea who held her. What age he was, what race, what anything.

He saved my life.

There was that. She arched her back, forcing her breast into the huge hand that palmed it. In response, thick fingers compressed the nipple. She bit back a moan. Jared hated it when she made noises during sex.

This isn't Jared, you idiot.

The fingers pinched harder, rolled the turgid flesh between them. *Screw it.* She moaned, at the same time parting her legs just a bit so that she could settle herself on the huge cock that seemed to be growing even larger. Then she tightened her thighs around it, sliding her butt back against his rock-hard belly.

She felt the thick curl of pubic hair tickling her butt, rested against the hard root of his penis where it sprung solidly from his groin and clenched her thighs once again, holding onto him. She felt the air go out of his lungs, then the lightest touch of warm lips against her ear, the soft, exploring tip of his tongue as he circled just the outside, the soft puff of his breath.

Shivers raced along her spine. She wrapped her fingers around his wrists, anchoring herself while at the same time holding both of his hands tightly against her breasts. The hair on his arms was soft, almost silky. She tried to picture her hidden lover, but before an image came to mind, he hmmm'd against her ear, then ran his tongue along the side of her throat.

She felt the sizzle all the way to her pussy, felt his lips exploring her throat, his mobile tongue teasing the wispy little hairs at the back of her neck. His hands massaged her breasts, squeezed her nipples, then rubbed away the pain. His hips pressed against her, forcing his cock to slide very slowly back and forth between her swollen labia.

She moaned again, the sound working its way up and out of her throat before she even recognized it as her own voice. The heat surrounding her intensified. Whoever he was, whoever held her . . . she sighed. He literally radiated fire and warmth and pure carnal lust. One of his big hands slipped down to her belly, cupped her mons and pressed her against him. Still gripping his forearm tightly in her left hand, she felt his finger slide down between her legs.

His fingertip paused at her swollen clit, applying the merest bit of pressure. She held perfectly still, afraid he'd stop if she moved, afraid of her own reaction to this most intimate touch by an absolute stranger. She kept a death grip on the wrist near her breast. The fingers of her right hand dug into the corded tendons on the underside of his forearm, and everything in her cried out to thrust her hips forward, to beg him to stroke her, to bury more than just his finger in the moist heat between her legs.

Instead, as her body trembled with the fierce need to move, she held her hips immobile. After a moment that might have lasted forever, he gently rubbed his fingertip around her clit, dipping inside her wet pussy for some of her moisture, then bringing it back to stroke her once more.

She bit back a scream as his roughened fingertip touched her again, the circular motion so light as to hardly register. Her trembling increased, along with her desire, her barely controllable need to tilt and force her hips against him, to make him enter her.

She didn't care if he used his cock, his tongue, his finger . . . hell, at this point, he could use his whole fucking hand and it wouldn't be enough. She choked back a whimper as he changed the direction of his massage, moving his fingertip slowly up and down over the small hooded organ. Each stroke took him closer to her pussy. Closer, but not nearly close enough.

Her breath caught in her throat when he dipped inside her, swirled his thick finger around the streaming walls of her pussy, then returned to caress her clit once more. A small part of Xandi's mind reminded her she was being beautifully fucked by a total stranger, that her fingers were clutching thick, muscular arms, that she was clasping her thighs around the biggest cock she'd ever felt in her life—and that they still hadn't exchanged a single word.

It came to her then, in an almost blinding flash of insight, a personal epiphany of pure, carnal need and unmitigated lust, that she'd never, even in her most imaginative fantasy, been this turned on in her entire life. Never felt so tightly linked— mentally, physically, sexually—to anyone. She moaned aloud as his finger once more slipped back between her legs. His thumb stroked her clit now, and that one, thick finger plunged carefully in and out of her weeping flesh.

Suddenly, the hot tip of his tongue traced the whorl of her ear, then dipped inside. Shocked, she thrust her hips forward, forcing his fingers deep. His breath tickled the top of her ear, his tongue swirled the interior, leaving it all hot and damp, filled with lush promise.

She thrust harder against his fingers, still holding one of his hands against her breast, forcing the other deep between her legs. She felt the thick rush of fluid, the hot coil of her climax building, building with each slick thrust of his cock between her thighs, each dip of his fingers, each . . .

Without warning, he rolled her to her stomach, breaking her grip on his forearms as if it were nothing. He grabbed her hips and lifted her. Xandi moaned, spreading her legs wide, welcoming him, begging with her body. Eyes wide open, she saw nothing but darkness, felt no sense of space, lost all concept of time. She quivered, hanging at the precipice of a frightening, endless fall.

His big hands clasped her hips, held her tightly. He massaged her buttocks for a moment with both his thumbs, spreading her cheeks wide. She felt her slick moisture on his fingertip, almost preternaturally aware of each tiny spot on her body where she made contact with his.

She wondered how much he could see, if his night vision were better than hers. It was as dark as the inside of a cave, wherever they were. No matter how hard she tried, she couldn't see the soft bed beneath her, couldn't see her own hands.

Couldn't see his.

Yet the link persisted, the sense of connection, of need, of desire so gut deep it was suddenly part of her existence, of her entire world. A link she knew would be forged forever when he finally entered her, filled her with heat and pulsing need.

He lifted her higher, his hands slipping down to grab her thighs, raising her up so that her knees no longer touched the mattress, so that her weight was on her forearms, her face pressed tightly to the pillow.

She expected his thick cock to fill her pussy. Wanted his cock, now. *Please, now!* Her breath caught in short, wild gasps for air, her legs quivered, and she hung there in his grasp, waiting . . . waiting. Hovering there, held aloft, the cool air drifting across her hot, needy flesh. Waiting for him to fill her.

Instead, she felt him pull away, felt the mattress dip as he shifted his weight . . . felt the fiery wet slide of his tongue between her legs.

"Ahhh . . ." Her cry ended on a whimper. He looped his arms through her thighs and lifted her even higher, his tongue finding entry into her gushing pussy, his lips grabbing at her engorged labia, suckling each fleshy lip into his hot mouth.

He nibbled and sucked, spearing her with his tongue, nipping at her with sharp teeth, then laving her with soft, warm strokes. Suddenly his lips encircled her clit, and he suckled, hard, pressing down on the sensitive little organ with his tongue.

The scream exploded out of her. She clamped her legs against the sides of his head, peripherally aware of scratchy whiskers, strong jaw. His tongue lapped and twisted, filling her streaming pussy, as she bucked against him. He was strong, stronger than any man she'd ever known, holding her aloft, eating her out like a hungry beast, his mouth all lips and tongue and hard-edged teeth.

He dragged his tongue across her clit once more, suckled her labia between his lips and brought her to another clenching, screaming climax. Once more, licking her now, long, slow sweeps from clit to anus, each stroke taking her higher, farther. His tongue snaked across her flesh, dipping inside to lap at her moist center, tickling her sensitive clit, ringing the tight sphincter in her ass. Gasping, shivering, her legs trembling, Xandi struggled for breath, reached for yet another climax.

He left her there, once more on the edge. Cool air brushed across her damp flesh, raising goose bumps across her thighs and belly.

He lowered her until her knees once more rested on the bed. She felt his hot thighs pressing against her own, his big hands clasping her hips, the broad, velvety soft tip of his cock resting at the mouth of her vagina.

Slowly, with great care and control, he pushed into her. Damn, he was huge. She shifted her legs, relaxed her spasming muscles as best she could. Still, her flesh stretched, the lubrication from her orgasms easing the way as he slowly, inexorably, seated himself within her.

She felt him press up against the mouth of her womb at the same time his balls nestled against her clit and pubic mound. He waited a moment, giving her time to adjust to his huge girth and length, then he started to move.

Slowly at first, easing his way in, then out, stretching her, filling her. Xandi fisted the pillow in her hands as she caught his rhythm. In, out, in again, his balls tickling her clit with each careful thrust. She pressed back against him, forcing him deeper, inviting him.

He groaned, then slammed into her harder. She took him, reveled in the power and strength of her mystery lover, felt another climax beginning to build, knew she would not go alone this time.

She reached back between her legs, grasping his lightly furred sac between her fingers just as he thrust hard against her cervix. His strangled cry encouraged her. Grinning, feeling empowered—feminine and so very strong—she squeezed him gently in the palm of her hand, felt his balls contract, tighten, draw up close to his body.

She slipped one finger behind his sac, pressed the sensitive area, then ran her sharp fingernail lightly back to his testicles. He slammed into her, his body rigid with a fierce power. Shouting a warrior's cry of victory, he pounded into her harder, stronger. She kept a tight but careful hold on his balls, until the hot gush of his seed filled her.

Overwhelmed, overstimulated, she screamed and thrust her hips hard against his groin. Her vaginal muscles clamped down, wrapping around his cock, trapping and holding him close. Suddenly, he filled her even more, his cock swelling to fit tightly against the clenching muscles of her pussy, locking his body close against hers.

Linking the two of them together. A binding deeper than the act itself, more powerful than anything she'd ever known.

He slumped across her back, then rolled to his side, taking Xandi with him. She felt the hot burst of his gasping breath, the rhythmic pulsing of his cock, the pounding of her own heart. Suddenly exhausted, her pussy rippling against the heat of his still amazingly engorged penis, Xandi snuggled close to his rock-hard body and allowed her eyes to drift slowly shut.

Tomorrow. She'd learn who he was tomorrow.

Elegant. Decadent. And very, very sexy.
That's THREE by Noelle Mack.
Available now from Kensington . . .

"I want to make you wait, love. Does it excite you to watch in this way?"

"Yes," Fiona whispered.

The woman in the window turned from the mirror and went back to the bed, rummaging through the drawers of the nightstand. She took out a huge penis of ivory, with attached balls made of softer stuff, round and heavy, which swayed in the air when she gave them a playful slap.

"Ah. Now for some devilish good play." Thomas's voice roughened with male lust.

Then the woman settled back on the bed and spread her legs more widely than before, touching each bottom bedpost with an elegantly arched foot. Fiona and Thomas had an excellent view, despite the flickering of the candles next to the bed.

They watched her slide the ivory rod in and out, vigorously thrusting it into her snug pussy, obviously enjoying the bounce of the stuffed leather balls against her arse cheeks. Then, without further ado, she twisted up and around, turning her bum to them and holding the false penis. The sudden screwing motion seemed to excite her even more.

The woman crouched on her knees, reaching back between her thighs to slide the thing in even deeper, but the last inch or so of the thick ivory rod, gleaming white, stuck out from her swollen nether lips.

"I would love nothing more than to see you push that dildo in for her," Thomas said into Fiona's ear.

"We must be content to watch," Fiona replied. She heard Thomas gasp when the woman began to rock on all fours, making the dangling balls swing and slap hard upon her cunny.

He could stand it no longer. He rammed his cock into Fiona, all the way. She thrust back against him, matching his strokes, employing the same rhythm as the woman they watched, to give him even more stimulation.

Then . . . they both stopped when a door opened in the room of the house across the street and a tall, well-built man entered, quite naked.

"Perhaps he was watching her as well from the closet or the next room," Thomas said softly, holding Fiona still once more but growing even larger inside her.

Fiona nodded. The woman, half-crazy with pleasure, didn't even notice that she was no longer alone. Her face, when they could glimpse it, was wet with sweat, close to the ultimate satisfaction she craved, giving herself deep, repeated thrusts of the dildo and harder slaps from the attached balls, her mouth open in a moan.

Fiona could see that the woman's eyes were closed, until she felt the man who had entered her room caress her cheek. She raised her head, eyes wide to see his enormous erection was only an inch away from her panting lips.

Thomas began to slide in and out of Fiona's pussy again, with tantalizing slowness but he speeded up when he saw the woman take the other man's cock into her mouth and begin to suck greedily, as if it were the most delicious thing on earth.

Unattended, the ivory penis fell out, pulled down by the heavy balls. The man took his cock from her mouth, withdrawing slowly as the woman tightened her full lips around him, reluctant to let him go. Her lover or master or whoever he was grabbed the ivory one to replace his, putting it in her mouth and making her taste her own juices. The woman licked the long dildo clean, looking up at the man with lascivious affection, eager to arouse him even more.

She succeeded. The man took the dildo away and stroked her tangled hair, her back, her haunches, as if soothing her . . . or preparing her for what he wanted to do next.

Then he turned around, spreading her buttocks wide open and resting his big hands upon them while Fiona and Thomas watched, transfixed. They strained to see, joined and moving in a way that made Thomas bite his lower lip to keep from ejaculating straightaway. "What next?"

"I think I know," Fiona said softly.

The woman kept her arse up but buried her face in the pillows.

"Yes," Fiona breathed. "She loves to play the wanton. And she loves extreme stimulation. He will give her what she craves, Thomas. Just you wait."

"I can not restrain myself much longer," he growled. "Do keep still!" He clasped Fiona's hips even more tightly. "But do keep talking . . . the sound of your voice is as erotic as the show . . ." He ended with a low moan.

"A man's firm hand upon her soft flesh is what she wants," Fiona went on in a whisper calculated to arouse. "A man who will discipline her but with such gentleness that her resistance melts not from fear but from opening her soul to the one who thus commands her."

As if the man in the opposite room had heard, he curved a strong arm around the waiting woman's hips and gave her a long, sensual, and very thorough spanking with his free hand while she cried out her pleasure and her gratitude for his skill. Then he got on his knees behind her, plunging his very real and thickly satisfying cock into the woman, stroking her sensitized buttocks with especial tenderness to take her to climax at last. The lovers reached the moment at the same second, rocking so closely together that they seemed to be one being, not two, and collapsed upon the bed, twined around each other, lost in erotic bliss.